A VEILED TEMPTRESS

"I saw you ride in the contest today," he said in Latin, not sure she would understand him.

She whirled around, almost colliding with his powerful body, and when she regained her composure, replied in Latin, "Much to my shame, everyone saw me ride today."

"And I saw you dance tonight."

She shook her head, backing away. "Roman, you saw too much today. I beg you to forget my disgraceful actions. I only wish I could."

In that moment she stepped back and stumbled over the rope that secured his tent. Instantly, he reached out to steady her and found her in his arms. The sweet scent that clung to her was intoxicating, and her skin was soft to the touch. Marcellus found himself pulling her closer. "Sweet little dancer, what is that mysterious fragrance you wear?"

"It is a scent extracted from the jasmine blossom," she said breathlessly.

"I think I will never forget you, although I have never seen your face."

SWORD
OF
ROME

Constance
O'Banyon

LEISURE BOOKS NEW YORK CITY

*To Jim, who keeps the home fires
burning when I am on deadline.*

A LEISURE BOOK®

November 2007

Published by

Dorchester Publishing Co., Inc.
200 Madison Avenue
New York, NY 10016

ISBN 10: 0-8439-5822-7
ISBN 13: 978-0-8439-5822-5

Printed in the United States of America.

10 9 8 7 6 5 4 3 2 1

Visit us on the web at www.dorchesterpub.com.

SWORD

OF

ROME

CHAPTER ONE 🗡

Egypt's Western Desert
47 B.C.

Scattered members of the Badari Bedouin had been gathering from all corners of Egypt, their numbers swelling as they arrived to pay tribute to their leader. In Alexandria, Lord Ramtat might be a wealthy and powerful courtier, a trusted adviser to Queen Cleopatra and the husband of her half-sister, but to his loyal tribesmen, he was Sheik El-Badari, and therefore worthy of their respect.

The Bedouin were traveling by horseback and camel, the dust clouds from their caravans stretching for miles across the desert. The arrivals would continue steadily for many weeks before all were assembled. There would be great merrymaking—banquets that would reunite old friends, wedding festivities that would strengthen new alliances, games and competitions that would allow the young men to show their skills and prowess. Then the festivities would culminate with the contest of the Golden Arrow, where the sheik himself would award the most coveted prize to the greatest warrior among the Badari.

To escape the choking dust from the new arrivals, Heikki, son of Obet, the armorer, ducked inside the tent where the sheik's horses were kept. Lowering his head, he wiped the palms of his hands across his stinging eyes. Though he was excited and wanted to mingle with the newcomers, Heikki put duty before pleasure. He snatched a bucket and filled it with grain, moving down the row of hobbled horses until each animal had been fed. He took great pride in the fact that the Badarian horses were the finest in the world, and Lord Ramtat's were the best of the breed.

He stepped to the tent opening and glanced at the hundreds of new tents that now dotted the site, some erected overnight, while many others had a more permanent appearance. A shadow fell across his face, and he turned to find his father beside him. Obet was a strong man, wide of girth. His face was creased like dark parchment, and his hands were gnarled and rough from years of hammering metal into weapons.

"My son," he said matter-of-factly, "I never have to ask if you have completed your duties—you are ever dependable. That is why our lord has put you in charge of his personal stable."

Heikki frowned, and his words came out bitterly. "Aye, I am worthy to tend his horses, but not worthy to ask for the hand of his sister in marriage," he stated angrily.

Obet was startled by his son's pronouncement. "Hush, foolish one. Is the lord's wife not sister to the queen of all Egypt? You could never be considered for such a high marriage." Obet glanced about to make certain no one could overhear their conversation. "You are a handsome young man in your eighteenth year—many worthy women have glanced your way with hope in their eyes."

"I do not care about those women."

"Are you drunk on date wine? You are like the flowers that worship the sun—knowing they can never possess it, still they turn their blossoms skyward. You may watch Lady

Adhaniá from afar, but she can never be yours. Find happiness with another, my son. Lord Ramtat's sister will marry into her own class, as will you."

Heikki unthinkingly knotted the rope in his hands, pulling it tight in frustration. "My head knows this, yet my heart does not listen."

Obet looked at his only son with pride. Heikki stood a half-head taller than most young men of the tribe. He was square-jawed and handsome, a man of honor worthy of any woman . . . except the one he wanted. "My son, join the games—enjoy the entertainment," Obet advised him, clapping him on the back. "I have seen many lovely girls arrive today. Look to one of them for solace. You only think you love Lady Adhaniá because she is the one woman you cannot have. One day you will know the difference between love and longing."

Heikki watched his father depart before he ducked back inside the tent and opened the spigot that allowed water to fill each trough. He was about to leave when he heard someone slip through the rear entrance. Spying a slight figure moving toward the animals, he assumed it must be one of the lads who cleaned up the horse dung. But Heikki became suspicious when the boy took the reins of the white mare that belonged to Lady Adhaniá.

"You there!" Heikki called out, moving forward angrily. "Step away from that horse!"

The lad, whose head was covered with a plain brown *kiffiyeh* of poor quality, ignored Heikki. Stepping forward, Heikki jerked the reins from the boy's fingers. "This horse belongs to our sheik's sister, and you will be severely punished if you don't move away."

"So, you do not know me?" came the low voice, muffled behind the thick head covering.

"You are unknown to me. But this I do know—if you

value your life, leave now, or I will be forced to take you to
Sheik El-Badari."

The youth laughed, lowering his head. "And I insist you
do know who I am."

Heikki looked him over carefully. "You wear a robe woven of goat hair, which is a common enough garment, but
your boots are made of fine sheepskin—did you steal them,
little thief?"

"I am no thief!"

"I say you are! I know whom this animal belongs to, and
it isn't you."

Impish laughter made Heikki's blood boil with anger until the lad looked up, and he saw a familiar pair of long-
lashed amber eyes. Mischief danced in those golden eyes,
and although she was in disguise, there was no mistaking the
smooth honey-gold skin or the beautiful face of the sheik's
sister. Musical laughter rang out—familiar laughter, yet he
could not credit his own eyes or ears.

Heikki shook his head in astonishment. "Adhaniá, why
are you dressed so scandalously?" he asked, almost choking
on his words.

"You see, you do know me," she remarked with humor.
"It is not a thief who takes her own horse."

Adhaniá lifted a finely tooled red leather saddle onto the
horse's back and buckled it in place before testing it with a
hard yank to make certain it was secure. She turned back to
Heikki, a satisfied smile on her lips. "You who have known
me since birth and have been my longtime companion did
not recognize me. Therefore, I am encouraged that my
brother will not guess who I am either."

Heikki frowned. "It's not seemly for you to dress in such
a way." He was still reeling from the shock of seeing her
garbed in men's clothing. They had grown up together,
shared secrets, practiced with swords and bows and had been

taught by the best warriors of their tribe. Even though Adhaniá was a female, the sheik had always indulged his only sister and allowed her to move freely within the camp. Adhaniá had been daring even as a child, and she was more so now that she had become a young woman.

"I fooled you, Heikki—admit it," she said, laughing joyously. "I knew I could do it."

He was mesmerized by the sparkle in her eyes. She was so beautiful it hurt him to look at her, and she was completely unaware of the effect she had on him. They had been like sister and brother growing up, but his feelings had changed. Heikki was not sure when he had begun to love her as a man loves a woman. It happened so gradually, he had only lately become aware of his love for her. It had hit him like a bolt of lightning the first day he noticed that her once reed-thin body had developed into the soft curves of a woman. Looking at her now, his mouth went dry, and he could not find his voice.

If beauty had a name, it would be Adhaniá.

Her hair was like silken ebony, her face perfect in every detail. Her eyes were startlingly sultry and framed by a pair of long lashes. Heikki's face reddened, and he glanced away from the tempting swell of her breasts, visible even through the heavy robe.

"Well," she said, turning around for his inspection so he could fully examine her Bedouin attire. "Admit it, Heikki— Ramtat will never recognize me in this."

"How can you be so foolish?" he answered, unwilling to encourage her in her madness. "He will know you at first glance, as I would have if you had not kept your head down."

Ignoring his tirade, she smiled and wrinkled her nose at him, debating whether or not to tell him of her plan.

"You can't let the sheik see you like this," he continued. "You will be disgraced. Is that what you want?"

For a moment she stood rigid and silent, then she frowned. "You remind me of a disgruntled old goatherder with your complaining. I am determined to join the contest of the Golden Arrow," she said mutinously. "Ramtat will be proud of me if I win."

Heikki's face drained of color, and he reached out to grip her shoulder. The sheik guarded his sister like the precious treasure she was, and he would not be pleased if she made a spectacle of herself. "You can't do it, Adhaniá."

She brushed his protests aside. "Think about this—why was I allowed to train with the sword and bow if I am denied the use of them? Why was I allowed to race with you if I am forbidden to exhibit my horsemanship?"

"Sheik El-Badari may have allowed you to train with me, but that was when we were children—he is proud of your strong sword arm, as well as your accuracy with the bow. But you are no longer a child. He will expect—no, he will *demand* that you behave with the dignity expected of a young woman of your high station."

"You drone on like a bumblebee," Adhaniá accused. "Ramtat would never stay angry with me for long. Besides, his disapproval will be worth it if I win the Golden Arrow." She frowned and rubbed the long, sleek neck of her horse. "I still need more practice. I am having trouble stringing the bow with my horse at full gallop." She turned her best smile on Heikki. "For three weeks now I have been practicing at the old ruins to the west. Come with me today and tell me what I'm doing wrong."

After a moment of silence, Heikki shook his head, determined to stop her. Then she smiled, and helplessness swamped him like a torrent of waves did a small boat. Like a drowning man, he fought the urge to give in to her. "I will *not* help you in this. Do not ask me."

Her smile widened, and she touched his hand coaxingly.

"In three more full moons the contests begin. Come with me so you can see how I have progressed in my bowmanship."

"If I assist you in this, I will be as guilty as you." His protest sounded feeble even to his own ears.

Adhaniá turned her head and looked up into his face, her grin impish. She knew just how to win him over—she always had. "I absolve you of any guilt."

His instinct was to deny her, but his heart never could. "I will go with you, but only in hope of pointing out your recklessness. I warn you, what you are doing will lead to trouble."

She laughed as she vaulted onto her horse, flashing him her most charming smile—and no one could be more charming than Adhaniá when she wanted her own way.

"You are far too squeamish. I will wait until you are mounted, and we will race to see who is first to reach the ruins."

"You have lost all your senses," he grumbled. "But no one can stop you when you have your heart set on something."

"No one knows me better than you, Heikki," she said, hoping to tease him into good humor. "Come, we are wasting the day arguing."

Adhaniá whirled her prancing horse around, her laughter dancing on the air, lifting Heikki's heart. In that moment the wind ripped the *kiffiyeh* from her head and sent it careening through the air. He watched as she started off at a gallop, her ebony hair flying out about her. He bounded onto his own horse and raced to catch her.

Though he knew he should stop her, he could deny her nothing.

CHAPTER TWO ✦

The Roman Countryside

The sun was at its zenith when six mounted soldiers arrived at the work site. The commander, Tribune Marcellus Valerius, who rode in the lead, wore a plumed helmet, while the other soldiers' helmets were ornamented with stiff horsehair. As the tribune dismounted, he bade his men to seek shade against the oppressive heat. As he moved forward, the midday sun reflected off his bronze armor, momentarily blinding Haridas, the stonemason who approached him.

"Greetings, Tribune," Haridas said as he bowed low. "I've been expecting you since your personal servant arrived this morning. As you can see, I've had a pavilion erected to shade you and your soldiers, and I await your command."

Haridas looked at the tribune appraisingly. He was well favored in appearance—young, arrogant and privileged. Haridas was confident that the officer was too busy supervising two major projects to uncover the discrepancies in his daily logs.

Marcellus acknowledged him with a cold stare. "I was told that the man I left in charge had taken ill and a new stonemason had replaced him. I assume that is you."

Beads of perspiration gathered on Haridas's forehead, and one eye twitched nervously. "Aye, Jibade was struck by a stomach ailment and could no longer work." Haridas lowered his head and smiled to himself, thinking no one would ever guess he had been the one who'd added a poisonous root to his predecessor's food. "I feel privileged to be chosen to take his place, Tribune. We're glad you have come at last . . ."

Marcellus had been held up at another project, where the soil had proved too porous and the building site had to be relocated, but he was not going to explain himself to this man. "I'm here now."

The ingratiating smile froze on Haridas's face, and he licked his lips nervously. He'd been paid well to discredit the tribune, but apparently he—and the man who had paid him—had underestimated Marcellus Valerius.

This man was no fool.

The tribune's dark gaze swept across the project, carefully assessing each new addition with a scrutiny that momentarily disturbed Haridas. If Marc Antony had faith in the man's abilities, he must be a power to reckon with. The stonemason mentally shrugged. He was clever himself, and he had manipulated the books in such a way that it would take months to find the hidden errors.

He would bring this tribune down.

Tribune Marcellus Valerius rested his hands on his hips, surveying the progress that had been made on the aqueduct during his absence. To his surprise, the project had moved ahead of schedule; the bricks on the lower level were already in place, and he could plainly see the beginning of the arches. He should be pleased, but something was not right; he felt it in his gut.

Marcellus turned to Haridas and inspected him with the

same thoroughness with which he had inspected the aqueduct. He noted that the man looked shiftily away. Marcellus didn't care much for the man's smile—it was too sly, as if he were hiding something. The stonemason was thin and tall, with a ruddy complexion and close-set, dark eyes. Those eyes now darted about as if he were afraid someone was going to surprise him from behind. Although he wore a clean white tunic, he smelled of sweat and garlic.

"As you can see, we're ahead of schedule, Tribune Valerius. Does that not please you?"

"I have not yet decided," Marcellus replied, squinting against the glare of the sun, watching a slave slap mortar on the rough stone and position another row of bricks to the arch of the aqueduct. "How do you account for the progress?"

"Tribune, every day the workers are warned not to slack in their duties—if they do, they are whipped. They have been made aware that you would be arriving today. They've been informed that no man must displease you."

In the two months Marcellus had been away, the work had gone forward at a rapid pace. He frowned as he calculated how long it would take to complete the aqueduct. If the seasonal rains held off, it could feasibly be completed by early spring or, at the rate it was going, late winter. "What is your name, stonemason?"

The man bowed. "I'm Haridas."

Marcellus regarded him intently. "Well, Haridas, this project is close to Caesar's heart. I stopped by Aquila and the people there are in dire need—the wells have gone dry and the villagers are thirsty and forced to pay exorbitant prices for water to be hauled in by pack mule."

"Oh, Caesar will always remember the work done here, great Tribune. See how my workers labor. Each day they are reminded that they must please you and Caesar."

There was a falseness in the man's tone that caught Marcellus's notice. Something was not quite right about Haridas's attitude, and it irritated him that the stonemason avoided looking him in the eye. Yet his work seemed exemplary and beyond reproach, and that was all that concerned Marcellus. He did not have to like the man.

"I am amazed, Haridas," Marcellus stated, watching as a load of mud bricks was hoisted into the air by a pulley. "You had a task to do and a time to complete it, and as you said, you are ahead of schedule."

Haridas smiled. "Since I'm working for the most renowned architect in all of Rome, I must be worthy. Everyone knows you are the son of General Valerius, an honorable man, well respected by all before his untimely death. And look at you now," Haridas continued, unaware that the tribune had stiffened, "your mother is married to Senator Gnaeus Quadatus. It is an honor to work for a man from such a family. If there is anything you want of me, you have only to ask."

Marcellus glanced at the stonemason with distaste. "I don't care for flattery. For myself, I judge a man's value by what he accomplishes on his own, and not what his father or stepfather have done."

Haridas's right eye twitched. "To be sure, to be sure. I wasn't implying that you've not made the world take notice of you. No—nothing like that. I am but a stonemason whose fortune has been improved because your stepfather sent me to work for you."

Marcellus turned and stared at him. "What did you say?"

"I . . . do not know what you refer to."

"You said my stepfather sent you?" Marcellus demanded.

"Well . . ." Haridas said, mentally cursing himself for a fool. He should have known better than to mention Senator Quadatus's name. "Not him personally—a friend heard through him that you needed a stonemason. I was hired because of your stepfather's recommendation."

If his stepfather had made arrangements for the man to work on the aqueduct, there was reason to mistrust him. "To whom are you loyal, stonemason?"

"To none but you, Tribune," Haridas said hurriedly. "I hope my work will prove my loyalty."

Marcellus had to know he could trust the man he left in charge, and he did not trust Haridas. Caesar was depending on him, and he must depend on the men who worked under him.

Marcellus focused on the workers. Regardless of the fact that heat from the noonday sun struck against the thirsty land like fire against parchment, they plied their trades, pausing every so often to wipe sweat from their stinging eyes with grimy hands.

Haridas pointed to the huts that had grown up around the site. "It was a brilliant notion to have the ironworkers encamped near the project; thus, they can repair and build new tools as needed."

Marcellus nodded as he watched brick makers toil beside carpenters. "I can't take credit for that. It was Caesar's idea. He will be glad to hear it's working out well."

"You know the great Caesar personally?"

Marcellus drew in a wary breath. "We have met on occasion."

"Of course you have. I wonder if you could tell me some things about him?" The stonemason's face became flushed, and his voice excited. "What are his ambitions? Does he want to be emperor, or is he satisfied being elected dictator for life?"

Marcellus focused on the man suspiciously. He began to suspect his stepfather had sent this man to spy on him and, through him, Caesar. It would not be the first time Quadatus had set spies near him. "I am not in Caesar's head or even his confidence," he replied tersely. "The next time you see my stepfather, advise him to look to someone else if he wants information on Caesar."

"You mistake me," Haridas sputtered. "I was merely—"

Marcellus held up his hand to silence the man. "How many days did it take to cut through the rock cliff?" he asked, bringing the conversation back to the aqueduct.

"A week, maybe two. I was sick on my cot at the time, and when I regained my strength, it was done."

Marcellus removed his helmet and placed it on a camp stool. "So the work went forward without you?"

"Slaves are inspired when they fear the whip."

Marcellus looked closely at several of the workers, and noticed there were welts and dried blood on their backs. In anger his head snapped around to the stonemason. "You refer to the whip. Is it your habit to beat my workers?"

Haridas shrugged. "If you don't apply an incentive for them to toil, they slack off, and your aqueduct will never be built."

Marcellus's jaw tightened; then he turned his attention back to the workers. Sweat glistened on angry red whip marks on the back of one poor wretch. Marcellus watched as another man stumbled and fell under a heavy load of bricks. Before Marcellus could intercede, a guard plied the whip to the man's back, and he fumbled to gather his bricks.

"You there—guard!" Marcellus called out as he made his way down the embankment. "Give me that whip!"

The guard bowed his head and offered up the whip, his eyes downcast, his arms trembling. "How can I serve you, Tribune?"

Marcellus tossed the whip aside contemptuously. "He who serves me best does not apply a whip to my workers. Isn't their burden heavy enough without you adding misery to their toil?"

The guard, a hulk of a man, shot a glance at Haridas, and it was clear to Marcellus the man waited for some signal from the stonemason. When none was forthcoming, the man met Marcellus's gaze. "I was told you would expect it of your guards. This lot will not work if they are not prodded."

"Gather what belongings you have and leave."

The man's lips paled and his face reddened. "Master—"

"Do it now." Marcellus dismissed the gaping guard from his mind, concentrating on Haridas. "Call a meeting of all the guards immediately."

To the workers, Marcellus called out: "Everyone, stop what you are doing. Find shade and rest—replenish yourself. I will speak to you later."

A stunned silence followed the tribune's orders. One by one the men paused, but none was brave enough to abandon his work. They watched the architect as if he'd been too long in the sun.

"You there," Marcellus called out to the slave nearest him. "Spread the word to those who are not within hearing of my voice. They are to rest and fortify themselves with water and sustenance until I give orders to the contrary."

The man nodded. "It will be as you say, Master." He smiled, hurrying to tell the others before the tribune changed his mind.

The guards gathered to hear the tribune's orders. Many had worked for him on other projects; some he had never seen before. "It has never been my way to beat a slave to make him work. In my experience, you can get more labor from a well-fed, healthy man than a sickly, weak one."

Haridas's voice was argumentative as he stated, "Yet we are ahead of schedule; is that not a contradiction of your belief? Did not you compliment me on my accomplishment?"

Marcellus continued as if the stonemason had not spoken. "I'll have no man whipped unless he's done something to deserve it." He looked at the twenty guards who had gathered in the shade, and then he spoke to the stonemason. "Haridas, you will leave today with no recommendation from me."

Haridas's mouth flew open in disbelief, then he became angry. "You would not dare!" he sputtered. "You've no right to dismiss me—I am in the employ of Senator Quadatus."

"That is one of the reasons you will be leaving. My stepfather has no authority here. Gather your belongings and be gone before sundown." Marcellus turned his back on the stonemason and started to move away. He observed his soldiers standing nearby, and when he motioned to them, they stepped forward with their hands on the hilts of their swords. "Stand at ease," he instructed. "One of you go with this man and see that he leaves at once."

A murderous glint darkened the stonemason's eyes. "You'll be sorry for this."

Marcellus nodded to his centurion. "Perhaps you should help him on his way."

"You'll remember this day! I promise you, you will," Haridas threatened. But he hurried away to gather his possessions when the centurion moved toward him with a drawn sword.

Dismissing Haridas from his mind, Marcellus turned his attention back to the guards. "You saw what happened with the stonemason—if there are any among you who can't obey orders, or if you feel you have to enforce my rules with a whip, leave now. Should you choose to remain, the whip will not be used unless the man accused has had a fair hearing. Be warned: I will be leaving three of my soldiers to enforce my orders."

One of the guards stepped forward, lowering his head. "Tribune, may I speak?"

Marcellus nodded. "Go ahead."

"It was not Haridas who oversaw the building of the aqueduct."

"If not he, then who?" Marcellus demanded.

"The daily work was directed by a Greek slave. He is truly a man of insight, and most of us would be pleased if he was recognized for his work."

"You are saying that Haridas was not in charge?"

The guard shifted from one foot to the other, as if he were afraid to say more.

"No one has ever been punished for speaking the truth to me," Marcellus said. "Say what you will without fear of reprisal."

"Days would pass and we would not see the stonemason. He . . . there were several women who took up his time. There is more, but I dare not speak of it. If you ask the Greek, he may tell you."

"What is your name?" Marcellus asked.

"Gentimas, master."

"Well, Gentimas, because I appreciate your honesty, from this day forward you shall be in charge of all the guards. See that they do not unduly put their whips to the slaves."

The man grinned and bowed. "Your every command will be followed."

Marcellus looked at him speculatively. "Then bring the Greek to me."

Marcellus's personal servant, Planus, had cleaned and aired the tent that had been used by Haridas. The bed had fresh linens now, and everything that had belonged to the stonemason had been removed.

It was nearing evening before Marcellus finished inspecting the aqueduct and made his way wearily to his tent. The heat inside was sweltering as Planus helped him out of his heavy armor. The servant, who had a plain face and a thick, solid body, had been with the tribune for fifteen years—certainly long enough that he needed no instruction as he set about polishing his master's bronze breastplate.

As he waited for the Greek, Marcellus grew impatient, and he had time to think. Since his stepfather had controlled the stonemason, he would have to discover how much damage had been done by the man.

He dismissed Planus and dropped down on the cot. Tiredly, he fell back and closed his eyes, soon falling asleep.

A short time later something woke Marcellus. Whether it was a sound or a feeling, he could not have said, but he glanced up to find a stranger standing over him. The man was huge, at least a head above Marcellus in height. He had black, curly hair and sharp blue eyes that were blazing with anger.

Marcellus went for his dagger, only to realize it was across the room with his armor. "What do you want?" he demanded, rolling to his feet, realizing that the giant could easily kill him before he could reach his weapons.

"You sent for me," the man said gruffly.

"Ah." Marcellus rubbed his eyes, trying to focus on the man. The blue eyes held a jaded look, though if Marcellus were any judge, the man was not much older than he. "I suppose you would be the Greek."

Despite the slave collar the man wore around his neck, he was not in the least subservient. "I am Greek. My name is Damianon."

Marcellus's eyes narrowed. "You took your time getting here."

"I was in the mountains adjusting the drainage pipes when they brought word you wanted to see me. I assumed you'd want me to finish the task before seeking you out."

"I was told that you are responsible for much of the construction—it that true?"

The Greek's gaze bored into Marcellus. "I have some knowledge of the project."

"Do you read?"

"In several languages." This was spoken matter-of-factly, as if the Greek didn't expect to be believed and didn't care whether he was or not.

Marcellus motioned him to the table where the plans had been spread out. "Do you understand what is written here?"

"I do. And if you will look, you will find I've made changes."

Marcellus was more curious than angry about the man's behavior. "Why would you change my plans?"

"If these are your plans, they call for inferior materials; the aqueduct would not have stood past a decade. Was it you who specified the clay piping?"

Marcellus was studying the plans, his frown deepening. "I did, but not of this poor quality. These are not my designs." He flipped to another scroll and found the same discrepancy. Inferior supplies had been specified here as well, though he hadn't noticed when he'd looked at the plans earlier.

"I wasn't certain if the graft was the stonemason's doing, or if it was you who was cheating." The Greek shrugged. "It didn't much matter to me—but I don't like to waste my time using inferior supplies." He met Marcellus's steady gaze. "So I changed the plans. It was not difficult, since Haridas was occupied elsewhere and paid little attention to what went on with the work."

Marcellus dipped his head and studied the accounting. He traced a column of figures with his finger and glanced back at Damianon. "I see what you mean."

The Greek nodded. "In truth, I had heard only good of you. Hence, I suspected the cheating wasn't of your doing, but it is your fault nonetheless. With a project of this importance, you left the work to lesser men when you should have overseen the progress yourself."

Marcellus nodded. "I agree with you." He set one scroll aside and studied several more. "None of these are my specifications."

Damianon stared in the distance. "I was told you dismissed Haridas."

Marcellus suspected the stonemason had been attempting to increase not only his own wealth but, in all likelihood, Quadatus's as well. "Not soon enough, it would seem."

"Perhaps the damage is not irreparable. I have taken precautions."

"And I thank you for that. Obviously, you have some knowledge of building aqueducts."

"My father was a master builder in Macedonia—he passed that knowledge on to me and my three brothers."

"Yet you are a slave. How did that come to be?"

"Rome," Damianon said dully. "Rome conquers, and Rome takes prisoners."

Marcellus was lost in his own thoughts for a moment. Then he asked, "Would you be willing to take Haridas's position?"

"I have already been doing his work, and yours. Why should that change?"

Marcellus gave a slight smile, and then he laughed at how easily the Greek could deliver an insult. "Why, indeed? Except, as of today, you are no longer a slave. I will have your collar removed at once. And you shall be paid well for your work."

Mistrustful blue eyes stared back at him. "I have heard that your name is an old and honored one. I am pleased to find you are not the fool I thought you were."

Marcellus laughed long and deep. "I will never have to worry that you won't tell me the truth. But explain what I have I done to redeem myself in your eyes."

"You saw through Haridas. And you put a stop to the beatings."

"Go to the smithy and tell him I want your collar removed. Then wash yourself, and we will sup together," Marcellus said, smiling. "Perhaps I can convince you that you can trust me."

Marcellus watched Damianon leave and then refocused his attention on the scrolls. His jaw hardened when he thought of his mother's husband, who had tried to ruin him. And Quadatus might have succeeded if not for the Greek.

His mother was no better than her husband, and maybe even worse, since she had betrayed Marcellus's father. He could hardly think of her without contempt. He remembered happy days when he'd thought she loved his father, and they had been a family—or had he been a blind fool even then?

No—they had been happy—he knew they had.

His mother had sent a messenger with a request for him to visit her and his stepfather. Marcellus had ignored the invitation, but now he thought it was time he paid them a visit.

Egyptian Desert

Adhaniá's horse was racing full-out toward the target some hundred paces away. She took careful aim and let loose her arrow, watching in disgust as it landed on the third ring and not on the center.

Slipping off her horse, she pulled the arrow from the target. "I missed three out of four. I'll never be good enough to enter the contest if I do not improve."

Heikki, who had stretched out on the sand, shook his head. "Better not to enter at all, then. There is no praise for those who come in second or third."

She stomped her booted foot petulantly. "I can do it—I know I can! I just need more practice."

Heikki gazed at the waning sun. "You have been at it all day. Let us return to the encampment before dark."

"Not yet. I want to make another try." She gathered the reins and leaped onto her saddle. Racing some distance away, she whirled her horse and galloped forward, taking aim. She watched the arrow sail through the air and slice through the center of the target.

Leaping off her horse before the mare stopped, she ran to the target and fell joyously to her knees. "I know what I have been doing wrong!" A smile lit her face, and she swung around to glance at Heikki. "I was firing into the wind, and I should have compensated. I will need to pay heed to what direction the wind is blowing on the day of the contest."

Heikki leaned on his elbow, observing her next attempt. Disheartened, he watched her arrow hit true. She tried it again, and again it struck the center of the target. He sat up, his spirits sinking lower—she had mastered the bow.

There would be no stopping her now.

CHAPTER THREE ✗

Rome

Marcellus dismounted, and a young slave gathered the reins
and led the horse toward the stable.

"Give him water and rub him down, but do not stable
him. I won't be staying that long."

The front door swung open, and Marcellus's mother
stood hesitant, her eyes giving the impression of eagerness.
"Marcellus, my son," she cried, stepping forward, placing her
hand on his shoulder and gazing into his eyes as if she was
looking for some response from him. "It has been too long
since your last visit. One would think you had forgotten that
you have a mother."

Yes, he thought, she was his mother. At least she had given
birth to him, but the tenderness he'd felt for her as a boy had
long since vanished. The day she had married his father's
sworn enemy was the day he started to distance himself from
her. "Has it been long?" he asked, brushing her hand away
from his arm. "I hadn't noticed."

He thought he saw a sudden flash of hurt in her eyes, but
she was good at playacting, he reminded himself.

Sarania's arms dropped stiffly to her sides. "Come in the house and pay your respects to your stepfather."

His mother was still a beautiful woman, with cinnamon-colored hair and soft brown eyes. But there were dark circles under those eyes, and she was thinner than he remembered. Though there was still no flaw on her smooth skin, she seemed to have aged since the last time he'd seen her. When she had been married to his father, she'd worn gowns of the finest imported materials and jewels that had been the envy of her friends. Now there were no jewels on her fingers or at her throat. He'd heard she'd had to sell them to pay his stepfather's debts.

"I have no respect for your husband, Mother."

She ignored the insult and pretended not to notice when Marcellus stiffened as she linked her arm through his. He was certain she wanted something from him—he would wait until she was ready to tell him what it was. He saw her face whiten as she glanced over his shoulder and focused on the man who had just entered the room.

Marcellus turned to meet his stepfather's dark gaze. Quadatus was of medium height, with thinning hair and a nose that looked as if it had been broken several times. His chin was strong, but his eyes were small and watery, and his girth was wide, as if he indulged in too much food and wine. But the man's appearance was not the reason for Marcellus's dislike. Quadatus was a vulgar man of little honor and big ambition; Marcellus had never understood how his mother could have married such a despicable man after having been married to his father.

Quadatus had the ability to mask his feelings, and he tried to do so now, but Marcellus realized by the stiffness of the man's body that his stepfather had overheard his unflattering remark about him.

"Marcellus, it's always good to see you in our home,"

Quadatus began jovially. "Your visits are too few and too far apart."

Marcellus would never forget, nor forgive, the day he had found his mother and Quadatus in a lover's embrace a week before his father died. There had been speculation at the time that his father's death had not been an accident, although nothing had ever been proven. His father had been strong and surefooted, and it seemed unlikely he'd fallen to his death from the second-floor balcony of their home. One fact was certain: The widow's tears had hardly dried before she became Quadatus's wife. Marcellus had never pretended to like the man he suspected of murdering his father. If he ever discovered his suspicions were correct, that would be the day his stepfather breathed his last.

"Caesar has kept me busy."

Quadatus took his wife's hand and pulled her away from Marcellus, almost as if he was jealous of her attention to her son. "It seems to me you could take time out to visit your mother. She misses you."

Marcellus met Quadatus's gaze, but his words were for his mother. "The needs of Rome must take precedence over family reunions."

Quadatus stared at his stepson for a long moment. "You are gifted, growing in power, and for whatever reason, you have won Caesar's respect. You have powerful friends. It is said you are often in the company of Marc Antony."

Now, Marcellus told himself, he was about to discover the reason he had been summoned to this house. He glanced at his mother, then back toward her husband. "Antony is a good friend. We do see each other on occasion. In fact, I am on my way to his home now."

"And Caesar?"

"I see him but rarely."

Quadatus's smile did not quite make his eyes. "The word

in the Senate is that Caesar watches your career with interest. I would imagine you are on the rise."

Marcellus said nothing, merely waited.

Quadatus regarded his stepson intently. "I would like very much to be your guest when Marc Antony is dining at your home."

"Marc Antony is particular about with whom he associates."

The veins popped out on Quadatus's forehead and his face reddened, but still he smiled. "I heard he willingly dines with women of questionable reputation."

The air became charged between the two men. It was Marcellus who broke the silence. "And I have heard you associate with *stonemasons* of questionable reputation. Have you seen Haridas lately, Stepfather?"

Like a snake coiled and ready to strike, Quadatus hissed, "I don't know what you mean. Haridas is worthy of his craft, else I would not have recommended him."

"One of my workers caught him at thievery. And I have proof he altered the plans for my aqueduct."

"I am sure there must be some mistake." The senator's fists were balled at his sides. "I was told the man was honest and dedicated."

"Perhaps whoever told you that set his standards too low," Marcellus suggested. "In any event, the man no longer works for me."

Sarania, seeing the friction growing between her son and husband, tried to turn the conversation in a different direction. "Will you lunch with us, Marcellus?"

Glancing toward the door, Marcellus moved in that direction. "I'm sorry, I must decline your invitation. Antony is known for his punctuality, and he will expect me to be on time."

"I—I wonder if you could lend me some money, Marcellus?" his mother asked, her cheeks flushing with embarrassment. "I saw a bracelet I admired when I was at the Forum."

Marcellus had heard the money lenders were hot on Quadatus's heels, and he did not want his mother to suffer because of the man's debts. "I'll send a man around tomorrow and you can tell him what you need."

Her head snapped up and her eyes suddenly became sharp and piercing. "Wouldn't you have thought your father could have left better provisions for me? My only inheritance from him was this house, and not even enough money to pay the servants."

Marcellus had heard this complaint many times. "As his widow, you would have received a great fortune. When you became another man's wife so precipitously, the endowment stopped before it could even begin."

"Was that your doing, Marcellus?" she asked, hurt in her voice. "Quadatus said you could change the provisions in your father's will."

"As head of the Valerius family, I command all properties and holdings. I could even have taken this house, but I allowed you to keep it because I thought my father would want you to have it. It is your new husband's duty to provide for you now."

"I have never known you to be so cruel, Marcellus."

He felt her words like a stab to his heart. "Circumstances have taught me to be hard, Mother."

When he stepped toward the door, his mother intercepted him and stood in his path. "Will you not reconsider and invite Quadatus to one of your banquets?" she pleaded.

He gazed down at her. "And I'd hoped you asked me here because you wanted to see me."

She dropped her gaze. "The hard fact of life is that circumstances change people's lives, and we must change as well to help those we love."

He sensed a double meaning in her words, but he did not understand what she was trying to tell him. He ached when he remembered how much he had loved this woman as a child. "Would you embroil me in a lesson in philosophy, Mother?"

"No—I . . ."

"Why not tell me the real reason you asked me here," he insisted.

She met his gaze, and for a moment Marcellus thought he saw fear reflected in the shimmering depths—and could those be tears in her eyes?

"It is as I have already told you—your stepfather would like to be invited to dine with you when you have important persons in your home. And perhaps you could even arrange it so he could be presented to Caesar."

She had taken him by surprise, and he turned and looked at Quadatus. "I assumed since you are in the Senate, you would be acquainted with Caesar."

Quadatus looked annoyed. "I have spoken to him in passing, but Caesar never acknowledges me unless I speak to him first. I am not certain he even knows my name. But with your help, that could change."

Sarania's glance darted up to her husband's face. "Perhaps such an introduction would help advance your stepfather's career," she suggested. "Can you not do this for him?"

Marcellus felt sick inside that his mother would use him to further her husband's ambitions. "There are many in Rome who covet an introduction to Caesar. But only a select few are afforded that privilege. I will not take advantage of my friendship with him."

Quadatus was growing more agitated, his face redder. "Would you at least attend a gathering at our home if we invited Senator Cassius? Perhaps you could bring Marc Antony with you? Cassius has expressed an interest in meeting you."

"I have no liking for Cassius—nor do I trust him."

"Marcellus, put your dislikes aside and use your head," Quadatus told him. "You are Rome's most talented architect, and there are many who would court your favor because they are interested in your talent. There are those, Cassius included, who could help further your career. You must choose your friends wisely. Caesar may not always be in power."

Where Marcellus had merely been annoyed before, he now felt hot fury course through him. "I have neither the time nor the inclination to curry favor with your friends. My skills are dedicated to Caesar and the Senate."

Quadatus's eyes narrowed. "Then you are a fool."

"And you play a dangerous game, Quadatus. I will be watching you . . . and your friends."

Sarania suddenly clutched her son's hand, and his eyes widened when he felt her press something into his palm. She gave her head a small shake, as if she did not want her husband to know about it. "How can you refuse such a small request?"

Marcellus was puzzled—his mother's words said one thing while her eyes hinted at another meaning. "Our friends and acquaintances don't have the same interests, Mother."

Without allowing either his mother or Quadatus to respond, he turned, wrenched the door open and stepped outside, taking in a cleansing breath. He knew his mother had walked out behind him and stood on the steps, but he did not glance back as he headed for the stable.

He mounted his horse and rode down the tree-lined road, out of sight of the house, before he halted his horse and looked at the small papyrus written in his mother's hand.

My son, you must act quickly. There is a plot against Caesar.

He reread the small scroll several times. What game was his mother playing?

He didn't trust her.

But he must show the message to Antony all the same.

Sarania watched Marcellus ride away, her heart aching. "My son has not forgiven me for the time he found us together," she said, tears blinding her. "And who can blame him? He thought I had invited your attentions—how could he know you forced yourself on me?"

Quadatus grasped her arm and turned her to face him. "None of that matters now. You are my wife and will be until death takes one of us."

Her voice was no more than a whisper. "I will never understand why you wanted me for your wife, knowing I loved my husband and have no room in my heart for another."

"Call it desire—call it blind ambition. Perhaps it was a little of both . . . or neither. I wanted you, and I took you."

Quadatus had already proved he could be ruthless. There was nothing he wouldn't do to obtain what he wanted. Sarania no longer feared for herself, but she lived in fear of the threats Quadatus made against Marcellus—threats she knew he would carry out if she did not do everything he asked of her. Sometimes her burdens were so heavy she wished death would take her and free her from this prison Quadatus had created for her.

But she must remain strong so Marcellus would be safe. "I die inside when my son looks at me with such contempt. Why do you humiliate me by forcing me to ask favors of him?"

"Your son is a patrician from one of Rome's most esteemed families. As a result, he has influence and powerful friends."

Sarania's brow knitted in a frown. "He will never accept you into his social life."

Quadatus's heavy gaze fell on her. "Let us not speak of that. I would rather speak about why you deliberately tried to antagonize Marcellus so he would leave."

"Nay," she said, trembling with fear. " 'Twas his dislike of you that prompted his departure."

"If I thought for a moment that you baited him by design, you would curse the day of your birth."

Licking her dry lips, she dropped her gaze. "Did I not do everything you asked of me? Marcellus does not like you, Quadatus—he never will."

He yanked her to him, his snarling lips only inches from hers. "I suspect what you are trying to do; you want to make him despise you even more than he already does."

She winced when he tightened his grip on her arms. "Why would I do such a thing when I want only his love and respect?"

"I have not yet decided what game you play. But if you try to thwart me, you will regret it." He slapped her with an open palm. "Is that understood?"

Sarania winced and fell to her knees. "I gave birth to Marcellus—he's my son."

"And you are my wife." He gave her a triumphant smile. "I saw you and wanted you, and I took you."

"And you forced me to marry you by threatening my son's life. You know that is the only reason I stay with you."

"Never forget I could have Marcellus's life snuffed out like that." He snapped his fingers. "And I never make groundless threats."

Quadatus had used threats and lies to force Sarania to marry him, and as a result, he had a cold woman in his bed. Each time he took her in his arms, he felt her withdraw into her own private thoughts, and no matter how skilled he was as a lover, he had never made her moan with passion.

Quadatus thought back to the day he had arrived at the

Valerius villa and found Sarania alone in the garden. He had not intended to rape her, but his desire for her had been so great, he had forced himself on her behind the huge fountain. She had fought and clawed at him, but he had overpowered her and clamped his hand over her mouth to silence her screams. He had feared the worst when Marcellus had come home unexpectedly and found them together.

How Sarania had struggled and twisted, trying to get free, but he had kept her against him, even while her eyes beseeched her son to help her. Quadatus remembered the horror and disgust in young Marcellus's eyes that day. He'd believed his mother had welcomed the advances.

He did not know whom Marcellus despised more, him or his own mother.

"I will never love you," Sarania whispered.

"Do you think I care? You know me well enough to realize I always obtain what I desire." He turned away and stopped at the doorway. "You might think about this—I also get rid of what I no longer want."

CHAPTER FOUR ✦

Marcellus's sandals echoed across the blue and white mosaic floor as a servant led him through a side door into Marc Antony's garden. Antony was in conversation with his gardener, and Marcellus waited until he had finished before making his presence known.

Antony was of medium height, with black curly hair and a face and body that drew the women to him. There were scars on his forearms from old battle wounds, but that only intrigued women all the more. His title was Caesar's Master of Horse—while, in fact, he was Caesar's most trusted friend and bodyguard.

He looked up and smiled, motioning Marcellus to him. "You are an architect—what do you think of the layout of my new garden?"

Marc Antony's gardens and house had once belonged to the Great Pompey, who had been beheaded by the Egyptians. As a reward for his loyalty, Caesar had given Antony the holdings of the former Proconsul of Rome.

The scent of pine trees dominated the air, along with a slight aroma of lavender. Lush climbing plants arched their way across brick walls, and an enormous fountain depicting Athena pouring water from an earthen jar vied for space with the trees. Marcellus smiled. "I have always admired this garden. I see you have made many changes."

"I'm glad you noticed."

Marcellus nodded at a grove of trees. "Those Spanish orange trees will never bear fruit in this climate."

Seemingly unconcerned, Antony folded his arms over his chest. "So I am told. But I am determined to prove you, and my gardener, wrong. It cost me a fortune to have them shipped from Spain."

Marcellus grinned. "The day they bloom, send for me. I will want to see such a phenomenon."

Antony shrugged. "You are saying I did not spend my money wisely?"

"You did if you enjoy the trees and don't care that they bear no fruit."

Antony laughed and clapped Marcellus on the back. "I did not send for you to discuss my garden. Caesar has a mission for you to undertake."

"I am his to command."

"Aye, you always have been. Do you know how Caesar refers to you? Of course you don't; hence, I'll tell you. He calls you his tribune who builds instead of destroys."

"Which could refer to the fact that I have only fought in the battle of Pharsalus."

"Worry not, my friend—you covered yourself with glory that last dreadful day. But Caesar would leave fighting to lesser men. He does not want his most prized architect in the path of danger."

"He is on a mission to improve Rome."

"Precisely."

Marcellus gazed up at the white-hot sky. "What is it that he wants of me?"

"You are to go to Egypt."

Marcellus jerked his head in Antony's direction. "Egypt?"

"Aye. Queen Cleopatra wants her sister with her here in Rome. And Caesar is predisposed to grant the queen her slightest wish."

"I had heard the Egyptian queen had no sisters left. That they were all put to death for craving her throne."

"This sister lives because she is no threat to the queen's throne, although they share the same father. As Caesar tells it, this sister risked her life to save Cleopatra." Antony frowned. "But you know the sister's husband. Remember Lord Ramtat, who led the Egyptian troops at Pharsalus?"

"I did not actually meet him, but his name is not unknown to me." Marcellus's mind moved to other matters. "All Rome is talking about Caesar and the Egyptian queen. I have overheard some dangerous murmuring."

"Caesar is a man in his fifties, besotted by a young, powerful and highly intelligent woman. If you saw her, you would understand the attraction. She is not the first you would notice if you walked into a room of beautiful women, but she would eventually draw your attention, and the others would fade into nothing." Antony took a deep breath. "I have never seen eyes as green as hers. When she looks at me—" He looked a bit embarrassed. "She is most remarkable."

Marcellus grinned. "If I didn't know better, I would think you were besotted by this foreign queen yourself."

"Just to be near her is a privilege. But she sees no man other than the great Caesar." He gazed back at the orange trees. "A man would do a lot to possess such a woman."

"If I did not know that you are frequently enamored by a pretty face, I would believe you had lost your heart."

"It is not her beauty—it is—" Antony struggled for the right words. "It is her whole being, her essence." He shook his head. "But no matter. How soon can you be ready for the voyage to Egypt?"

"The work on the aqueduct is nearing completion. I have a good man on site, and he will see it finished."

"Good—very good. You will be traveling with Cleopatra's most trusted guard, Apollodorus, the Sicilian. You will find him an extraordinary individual."

"I have had few dealings with Egyptians."

"My friend, you are about to view a way of life one can only imagine. No one can be unaffected by the beauty and grandeur of Alexandria."

"Why would Caesar choose me for this mission?"

"The official story is that he wants a diplomat to convince Lord Ramtat to accompany his wife to Rome, and you, my friend, are highly intelligent, from an aristocratic family— someone he will respect." Antony turned his head to look at Marcellus. "In truth, Caesar wants a man he can trust."

Marcellus nodded. "I need to speak to you about another matter." He related to Antony the details of his visit to the home of his mother and stepfather and gave Antony the note his mother had slipped into his hand.

Marc Antony, always one to sniff out trouble where protecting Caesar was concerned, nodded. "This matter must be examined closely. I will let you know what I discover." He smiled. "Now make ready for Egypt. The queen is anxious to see her sister, and we have not a day to lose."

Apollodorus turned out to be a surprise. The man was at least a head taller than Marcellus, had curly black hair that hung to his shoulders and black eyes that seemed to see deep within a person. Happily, he spoke Latin and seemed willing to answer Marcellus's questions—and he had many.

The voyage to Alexandria had been smooth, blessed by a strong wind that blew in the right direction. But Marcellus and Apollodorus did not linger in Alexandria, for they discovered that Lord Ramtat and his wife were in the desert. The Sicilian had turned out to be an enjoyable traveling companion, and patiently pointed out the sights of Egypt. Marcellus was startled to learn that Lord Ramtat, a trusted friend of Caesar's, was of half-Bedouin lineage, and sheik of the Badari tribe.

As an architect, Marcellus was impressed by Alexandria, with its towering marble and granite buildings so different from the brick structures of Rome. He wanted to spend time on Pharus Island and inspect the great lighthouse that continuously sent its beacon thirty leagues out to sea, but Caesar's mission would not wait.

At Apollodorus's suggestion, Marcellus agreed to exchange his uniform for the less conspicuous robe and trappings of the desert dwellers.

"Before the mission has ended, you will be glad you abandoned your Roman uniform. That metal breastplate and helmet would grow hot beneath the scorching desert sun," the Sicilian advised him.

As they left the city of Alexandria behind, Apollodorus noticed that Marcellus kept looking over his shoulder. "Think about this, Roman—while your ancestors were digging with wooden hoes and living in wooden hovels, the Egyptians dwelled in great cities ruled by pharaohs in marble palaces and were bedecked in gold and gemstones. They had created a written language and become a center of knowledge before your city of Rome was even built."

"It is a wonder without equal," Marcellus agreed.

Marcellus and Apollodorus rode on fine Badarian horses that traveled over the desert sands with ease. Three Bedouin from Lord Ramtat's tribe had been sent to accompany them to the Badari encampment.

When they made camp the last night out, Marcellus took a bite of roasted goat meat and leaned back on his bedroll. "I have heard of Lord Ramtat but know little of him," he said to the Sicilian.

"He is Queen Cleopatra's general and trusted adviser. His father was a noble of the court, and his mother is a Bedouin princess. The Ramtat you will meet here in the desert will be Sheik El-Badari. Though the outer garments will be different from those he wears as a high lord of Egypt, the man himself is the same one who is well respected by your Caesar and my queen."

They sat in silence for a while, each lost in his own thoughts—then Apollodorus spoke again.

"When we reach the Bedouin village, you will see their women only from a distance. They will be heavily veiled and guarded by their men. Do not attempt to speak to them if you value your life," he advised Marcellus. "The only exception will be Lady Danaë, Lord Ramtat's wife. She may, or may not, be veiled, and you will be allowed to speak to her at the encampment since we are on the queen's business."

"I saw women in Alexandria who were dressed no different from Roman women; they wore no veils."

"Ah, my friend, you are about to enter another world. In most of this country, as in Rome, women can own property; but unlike Rome, a woman here can rule the land, and even be a goddess." Apollodorus nodded in the direction they were headed. "But where we are going, Sheik El-Badari is the law, and the women are not even allowed to eat with the men. I just wanted to warn you so we will not offend our host."

"What a strange and enchanting country this is," Marcellus mused. "I would like to spend more time exploring it."

"It would take many lifetimes to see all Egypt has to offer. And we have only a few weeks."

Marcellus stared up at the night sky, which was studded with stars and a brilliant crescent moon. The sky, like the desert, seemed to stretch on forever. There was a strange stirring within his blood—an excitement he could not understand. He fell asleep to the soothing sound of one of the Bedouins playing a flute.

Just after sunrise Marcellus halted his horse atop a sand dune and glanced down upon a huge encampment. At last they had reached the home of the desert dwellers. Wild Bedouin tribesmen raced their horses down a course that had been built for the upcoming games—banners flew above the main tents and music filled the air. Driven by excitement, Marcellus nudged his horse down the steep incline, anxious to witness a way of life that few outsiders ever saw—a wild, untamed existence that had gone unchanged for thousands of years.

"There are so many people," Marcellus observed. "The head count must be in the thousands."

"There will likely be more before the week is out. You are fortunate that you arrive at a time when the Badari gather to pay homage to their sheik." The Sicilian smiled, something he rarely did. "You will see horsemanship unequaled anywhere in the world."

Marcellus could not quell the exhilaration that stirred within.

He was stepping back in time.

CHAPTER FIVE ✚

For the past week Adhaniá had thought of little else except the upcoming games. But now that the time was upon her, she was experiencing doubts. Her heart was racing, her palms were sweaty and she wondered if her brother would be angry or proud of her.

"You don't have to do this," Heikki reminded her. "It's not too late to withdraw."

"I would like your encouragement and for you to have faith in my ability," she said haughtily.

"I don't question your ability, just your sense. What you are planning is unseemly for a woman. Would you not try to stop me if you saw me doing something that was not right?"

"I would trust you," she told him in a subdued voice. Her hands were trembling, and she gripped them to her sides so Heikki would not notice how nervous she was. In truth, if he continued to press her, she might heed his warning and give up her dream of competing. Regret and indecision were creeping into her mind, growing rapidly.

"Even though I watched you practice every day, I never

thought you would really ride in the contest. Would you shame your brother before all his tribesmen?"

These were her people too, and there was nowhere she'd rather be than with them here in the desert. Although most of her time was spent at one or the other of her family's villas, if she had the choice, she would never leave the desert. Her chest felt tight and she was having difficulty drawing a deep breath. When her father had died, Adhaniá had been very young, and Ramtat had become her father figure. Most of the time he allowed her to have her own way, although their mother accused him of being too indulgent. Surely he would be proud of her accomplishments, even if she did not win the Golden Arrow.

It was her mother who treated her like a child, accusing her of being headstrong, and Adhaniá admitted she sometimes acted before considering the outcome. She stared down at the toe of her red boot, gathering her courage. Regardless of the consequences, she would participate in this contest.

Could she not shoot an arrow with more accuracy than most of the tribesmen?

Why should she be excluded just because she was female?

She set her jaw in a stubborn line that reminded Heikki of the sheik at his most formidable. He watched her hoist herself onto the mare and wrap the reins around her hand.

"Hand me the quiver of arrows," she said, threading her arm through her ebony bow.

"It will mean trouble for us both if you do this."

"You have no cause to worry; I shall explain to my brother that you had no part in my plan." She lifted her brow and sent him a smile that rocked his world. "If Ramtat becomes annoyed with me and sends me to my mother in Alexandria, I will ask if you can come with me."

His shoulders slumped as he thrust the arrows at her. Then he turned and stalked away.

Adhaniá called on all her courage. Heikki was right, of course—Ramtat was going to be angry with her. And yet, her competitive nature would not allow her to back down now.

She nudged her horse forward, determined to win the Golden Arrow.

Lord Ramtat stood beneath a canopy of green staring into his wife's equally green eyes. Danaë, half-sister to Queen Cleopatra, was his shining jewel. At the moment she held their two-year-old son, Julian, namesake to Julius Caesar. The child feared nothing and was clapping his hands gleefully as the long line of mounted tribesmen rode past, dipping their spears in homage to their sheik. His son would make a worthy sheik on the day he inherited his titles. He had his mother's courage and her illustrious lineage, as well as the wild Bedouin spirit of Ramtat's ancient bloodline.

Ramtat felt his heart swell with love and pride as he looked into Danaë's eyes. The gods had given him the one woman who could make him happy and a son to walk in his footsteps. There was nothing in the world he wanted that he did not have. His life was divided between his duties as sheik to his wild Bedouin and his duty to Queen Cleopatra. He was, above all, a son of Egypt.

Danaë was talking to Cleopatra's emissary, Apollodorus, and the Roman officer who had accompanied him to the encampment. Ramtat was curious as to why the men had sought them out in the desert. But they had only arrived that morning, and his duties as sheik had kept him occupied and unable to confer with them.

"I am glad you have arrived on a day when the games are being held," Danaë told them.

"I, too, am glad," Apollodorus said to the queen's half-sister. "But that is not why we are here."

"You have already assured me that my sister is in good health."

"She is, indeed," Apollodorus answered. "But she is in want of company and has asked if you could possibly come to her in Rome."

Danaë was thoughtful for a moment, and her gaze locked with her husband's. She saw the concern in his eyes and shook her head. "I cannot make such a journey at this time. I will give you a scroll to take to my sister so she will know the reason."

Apollodorus looked thoughtful. "The queen will be disappointed."

Danaë smiled at the fierce-looking Sicilian. "She will understand when I tell her my reason." She noticed both relief and curiosity in Ramtat's gaze. He would not have wanted her to make such a journey in any case, but he speculated on the cause of her refusal.

"I am curious as to why Caesar sent you, Tribune Valerius," Ramtat said, turning his gaze on the Roman officer.

"I was sent to try to convince you to accompany Lady Danaë to Rome. But I see my persuasive skills will not be needed."

"In any event," Danaë stated, looking at the handsome tribune, "I hope you will enjoy the games. And the feasting will rival anything you have experienced in Rome."

"I can assure you, I am enjoying myself already. I will have much to tell my friends when I return to Rome."

Ramtat turned his attention back to his tribesmen and nodded in recognition to those who were known to him as they passed. Excitement thrummed through the air as old friends greeted one another, and the tribe became one again.

To begin the festivities, there was a contest to demonstrate who could throw a spear the farthest and with the most accuracy. Then there was swordplay, the winner being the last man standing. Ramtat laughed when he saw Danaë cringe and look away.

"Fear not, no one ever dies of wounds received in this game—although there will be cuts and bruises aplenty."

Ramtat arched his brow and smiled at the beauty beside him. He reached out to touch the hand of his son and the baby giggled up at him. He turned to Marcellus and explained, "This celebration goes as far back as our history is recorded."

"I am most anxious to see the contest for the Golden Arrow that Apollodorus told me about."

Danaë watched as the contests progressed, smiling as Ramtat rewarded the winners. Sometimes the gift was a bow and quiver of arrows, a hand-carved spear or a jewel-handled dagger. Later, the greatest prize of all would be awarded—the golden arrow for the most skilled warrior of them all. Already young men were lining up to participate in the final contest.

When the morning games were finally over and the feasting had begun, Danaë had been presented to so many tribesmen, she doubted she would remember any of their names. She handed a very tired Julian over to his nurse, Minuhe, so he could be put down for his nap.

"I have not seen Adhaniá since early morning," she observed, looking about the banquet tent.

"Nor have I," Ramtat replied. "I am certain she is becoming reacquainted with old friends. She is a favorite with everyone."

Danaë nodded. "I have little doubt of that. She is a favorite of mine as well." She slid her arms around his waist. "When will the Golden Arrow competition begin?"

"As soon as I say the word." Ramtat took her arm and guided her out of the tent and underneath the shade of the pavilion. A short time later, smiling at Danaë, he raised a red linen cloth over his head and released it, watching it flutter to the ground. "Now," he said, listening to the roar of approval from the crowd, "let the contest begin!"

Ramtat turned to Marcellus. "Some men have trained for years to compete this day. But only the most worthy will actually finish the grueling task, and of that handful, only one will be the winner. It is a great honor to win the Golden Arrow—the man who succeeds will be revered by all, and his name will be entered on a golden tablet alongside many great warriors of the past.

"One of the keys to winning is having a horse with stamina that can jump over the obstacles." He pointed in the distance. "First they must complete the course with the red flags, and then the harder course with the golden flags. They must jump the high rails and race to the tall sand dune you see in the distance. Once that is accomplished, those remaining will enter the compound and each will show his mastery over his horse by performing difficult tricks. Then he must string his bow while galloping at full speed, and the arrow must go through those narrow rings you see there and hit the center of the target."

"I can see why only your best warriors compete. It is a daunting course."

"There is always a winner. My Bedouin raise the finest horses in the world—at least we think so. And you see before you the greatest horsemen in Egypt, perhaps in the world."

Apollodorus watched with great interest. "This reminds me of the games of my own village." A brief sadness flashed across his face. "Sometimes I miss Sicily," he admitted.

Marcellus watched a young warrior riding a stark-white

horse—the beautiful animal pranced and tossed its head, instantly obeying the nudge of a heel or the tightening of the reins in the rider's hand. Marcellus was caught up in the excitement along with the others. The young warrior was already two horse-lengths ahead of the other competitors. Three of the horsemen had fallen behind, and two horses knocked over a rail by missing their jumps and were disqualified. There were only six contenders left, and it was easy to see that the one on the white horse was pulling even further ahead. Marcellus found himself cheering for the leader riding the white mare.

Ramtat was watching the same rider but with a totally different feeling. He stiffened, his dark gaze sweeping over the horse from its rippling mane to its flying hooves. His jaw came together in a hard line as he recognized his sister's mare, and it was only moments before he realized the identity of the slight rider.

As Adhaniá bent low over her horse, she was cheered on by the enthusiasm of the crowd. Her horse, Sabasa, was running full out as she performed one difficult maneuver after another.

Marcellus watched in admiration. He turned to Ramtat, smiling. "That is the most extraordinary horsemanship I have ever witnessed."

Ramtat stared at the rider, his voice heavy. "Indeed."

A great roar of approval reverberated through the crowd as Adhaniá galloped toward the last obstacle while artfully stringing her bow. When this was accomplished, she reached into her quiver for an arrow. Silence settled over the crowd as her horse galloped forward and the onlookers held their breath. Adhaniá sent her arrow slicing through the air.

It whizzed through the three rings.

It flew with wings of accuracy and landed true, quivering in the center of the target.

The crowd fell silent.

Adhaniá brought Sabasa to a halt and nudged the horse; the animal bent forward into a bow.

The crowd went wild with admiration. Even the other participants raised their voices in praise.

With her head held high, Adhaniá turned her horse and rode in the direction of the pavilion. She could feel her horse quiver with anticipation, as if the mare knew she had done well. The animal pranced and tossed her mane, bringing more ripples of approval from the crowd.

Slowly Adhaniá rode past a sea of faces without seeing them. Her brother stood just ahead, and her glance settled on his face.

He was not smiling.

When she drew up before Ramtat, he did not cheer her as everyone else had.

He was angry.

His dark eyes were filled with displeasure that went right to Adhaniá's heart.

"Dismount," Ramtat said in a clipped tone.

Meekly now, her heart pounding in her chest, Adhaniá slid off her horse and bowed low before her brother. She looked at Danaë, her gaze asking for pity, but she saw that Danaë had not yet guessed who she was. She recognized Apollodorus, whom she knew very well, but he was not smiling, although she was sure he had recognized her.

Her gaze lifted to the stranger who stood beside her brother. She met his admiring gaze and looked away quickly.

Everyone was watching and waiting for the sheik to honor such a gifted warrior. Ramtat raised his hand to ask for quiet. "The remaining three contenders will make another run from the sand dune and complete the competition. The winner among them will be awarded the Golden Arrow."

The onlookers were stunned and began murmuring among themselves.

Danaë shook her head and grasped Ramtat's arm. "But why?" And then she met her sister-in-law's tear-filled eyes and recognized her. Glancing quickly from brother to sister, she understood what had happened. Her heart was breaking for Adhaniá, who was being humiliated. Ramtat could not award his sister the prize—it was a contest for men alone.

For a long moment no one moved, and there was much speculation as to why the true winner had been disqualified.

Ramtat's gaze was unrelenting as he stared at his sister. "You will go to my tent and wait until I come to you there."

Adhaniá reached out and clasped Danaë's hand with tears swelling in her eyes. "I hoped he would be proud of me."

Danaë slid her arm around Adhaniá. "I will go with you."

"No," Ramtat said, his gaze already on the other challengers. "You will stand at my side and pay honor to the man who fairly wins the Golden Arrow."

Marcellus was stunned; he could not guess why the young rider had been stripped of the glory he had so deservedly won. He had seen the tears in the lad's eyes before he'd lowered his head and, dejectedly, led his horse away.

"What has happened?" Marcellus whispered to Apollodorus.

The Sicilian watched the sheik's sister leave, still astounded by her daring. He wondered what her chastisement would be. In his village such a deed would be severely punished. "It is but a family matter," he told Marcellus. "Let us leave it at that."

CHAPTER SIX ⚔

Adhaniá paced across the tightly woven rug, her mood vacillating between wounded pride and fear. Ramtat had never
spoken to her in such anger—he had never dismissed her so
abruptly in a way that embarrassed her before everyone.
Shoving aside the heavy curtain that was draped over the
tent opening, she focused her gaze on the spidery shadows
beneath the palm tree. It was growing late, and soon the real
celebration would begin. Of course, the women were never
allowed to enjoy the events that were provided for the men
alone. And she had so wanted that Golden Arrow.

She deserved it!

Adhaniá berated herself as she moved back inside the tent,
dropped down on a cushion and buried her head in her
hands, fully realizing what she had done. She had shamed
her brother before all his tribesmen. Heikki had tried to
warn her; she understood that now. A servant brought her a
meal of figs and cheese. After the woman had gone, Adhaniá
frowned, shoving her food away untasted. She couldn't swallow past the thick lump in her throat.

In Alexandria, where she was known as Lady Adhaniá, she

was a young woman who commanded respect. Women were valued in Alexandrian society and were not merely an extension of the males in their household. Was not the ruler of Egypt a woman—glorified as a goddess, revered as the most high? But here in the Bedouin camp, most of the women wore their heads covered, standing behind their husbands rather than beside them.

With her two heritages warring within her, how could she help being confused?

Adhaniá thought of the coldness in Ramtat's eyes. She had done well, she reasoned. She should have won, no matter that she was a woman—she had been the best.

She leapt to her feet when the curtains were pulled aside, thinking it would be her brother arriving to tell her about her punishment. Her heart flooded with relief when she saw it was Danaë.

Her sister-in-law came to her and pulled her into her arms. "Sweet sister," was all the comfort she could offer.

Too proud to cry but aching inside, Adhaniá laid her head on Danaë's shoulder. "Is my brother still angry with me?"

Danaë looked at her with pity. "I am afraid he is."

"It is no more than I deserve."

"I think it was a very brave thing you did, but very foolish, little sister." Danaë smiled. "I have never seen anyone who could match your horsemanship. I am sure you will get no more than a scolding," she said comfortingly. "I will speak to your brother and try to lighten his anger."

Adhaniá did not realize she'd been holding her breath until she let it out in a sigh. "I believe he will send me back to Alexandria."

"Would that be so bad? Alexandria is also our destination when we leave here in a few days. You will be reunited with your mother—I know how much you miss her."

Adhaniá had adored Ramtat's wife from their very first

meeting. Danaë never flaunted the fact that she stood close
to the throne of Egypt, and everyone loved her, from
Bedouin tribesmen to the servants in Alexandria. "I do miss
my mother," she admitted. "Although I'm happy here, I will
not be so sorry to leave. It will be difficult to face everyone
after my shame today."

At that moment the curtains were thrown aside, and
Ramtat entered. His gaze went first to his sister, noting that
she still wore the *kiffiyeh* and robe of a man. "You have not
changed your clothing," he said angrily. "I will not speak to
you until you are properly attired."

"Ramtat," she said, hoping she could make her brother
understand why she had entered the contest, "I wanted you
to know that I am as capable as any of your tribesmen—I
wanted you to be proud of me."

There was no softening of his expression. "You will never
behave like this again, for you shamed me before all, and
mostly, you shamed yourself. Go to your tent and do whatever women do to pass their time."

She felt as if he'd slapped her. "Most women my age are
married."

"And you should be as well," he told her in a brittle tone.
"I see that now. I will make certain your marriage is
arranged as soon as possible. Leave me."

"Ramtat," Danaë said, seeing the stricken look on his sister's face, "now is not the time to—"

Ramtat held up his hand to silence his wife. "Do not
plead her case, Danaë. She should be learning how to please
men, not how to humble them. After today, I will have a hard
time finding a man who will consent to take her as his wife."

Both women gasped, but it was Adhaniá who lowered her
head to hide her anger. Her brother had said nothing about
the fact that she'd beaten all of his most worthy warriors—
instead of praising her accomplishments, he belittled her.

"I will go." She tore the *kiyffiyeh* from her head and threw it at her brother's feet. "I shall show you that I can please a man," she said, striding out of the tent with her head held high and her shoulders back.

The anger drained from Ramtat, and he met his wife's sympathetic gaze. "She is young. She will learn." Then he sighed. "I hope."

"Was it so very bad what she did today? I thought she was magnificent."

"It was very bad."

Ramtat pulled his wife into the shelter of his arms, trying to think how to say what was in his heart. "I am happy that you did not consider going to Cleopatra in Rome. I could not be parted from you, so if you had gone, as our new Roman friend suggested, I would have accompanied you."

"I have no wish to face the day when I am not with you." She laid her face against his chest, listening to the steady beat of his heart. "But there is another reason I must limit my travels."

He looked at her, his lips curving into a smile, and he waited anxiously for her to confirm what he already suspected.

"I am with child." She watched his eyes soften and laid her hand on his arm. "You have impregnated me yet again."

Pride, happiness and softness chased each other across the planes of his face. "It is as I hoped, beloved."

He fell quiet for a long time, thinking about the happiness in his life, but there was a dark cloud of doubt that plagued him as well. "Perhaps I was too hard on Adhaniá. In truth, you saw how everyone cheered her, even when they discovered her identity. I had several of the tribesmen beg me to award my sister the prize." His arms tightened around her. "You left before you heard what the winner of the Golden Arrow said to me." He rested his chin on the top of her head. "He said that Adhaniá was the true winner of the contest."

She touched his face. "You will tell her this. But do not wait too long—I know why she did what she did."

He smiled down at her. "And why is that?"

"Because she thought it would please you."

His frown turned into a reluctant smile. "She was very good," he admitted.

"And at this moment she is very hurt."

He smiled, his hand caressing her arm. "How did you become so wise?"

"I am not wise. I merely know the man I love, and I know the love you have for your sister."

"What should I do? Even though she prefers it here in the desert, I cannot allow her to remain under the guidance of my aunt, who spoils and indulges her."

Danaë was certain they all spoiled his sister, but none more than Ramtat himself. She decided not to call his attention to that fact. "Will you send her to your mother?"

"It is time that she stopped behaving like a child and became a woman. This she will do under the guidance of our mother."

"Perhaps that would be best."

"Let us speak of Cleopatra. I know you are worried about her."

"Apollodorus told me of her loneliness and isolation. She has not been well received in Rome."

"But she is surrounded by a multitude who live to serve her."

Danaë raised her face to him. "But one can be lonely even among hundreds if the one you love is not with you."

He breathed in deeply, and his hand tightened about her. "Yes. I have discovered that for myself."

She closed her eyes. "There is trouble there—I can feel it."

"Perhaps the queen will soon return to Egypt."

"I hope she will. I have a feeling—" She broke off. "Go and rejoin our guests. Marcellus Valerius seems a worthy Roman, and he has traveled far. You should entertain him."

Marcellus watched a wrestling match, cheered on his favorite and lost fifteen pieces of silver when the man was defeated. He ate with the tribesmen, who graciously treated him as if he were one of their number. But his mind kept going back to the contest of the Golden Arrow. Apollodorus had finally admitted to him that it had been the sheik's sister who had been disqualified.

All he could think of was a pair of amber eyes that sparkled with tears.

CHAPTER SEVEN ✗

Adhaniá had gone from the depths of despair to frustrated anger. If Ramtat wanted her to act in a way that would please a man, she certainly could do that. She stalked across the soft woven rug in her tent, forming a plan. She had something in mind that would surely make Ramtat even angrier, but what did she care—she could be in no more trouble than she was at the moment.

She froze in midstep when she heard someone at the entrance of her tent and saw her grim-faced aunt.

"Child, child, what have you done?" Zamah asked dourly. "I was with the women helping prepare the feast for tonight and have only now learned of your rashness."

Zamah was tall and willowy, with dark eyes that were her best feature. She had been married and widowed, and her only son was one of Ramtat's most trusted warriors. She carried herself in a regal manner Adhaniá wished she could emulate.

"I do not want to talk about it anymore."

"Of course you don't, because you know you were

wrong. How could you have done such a thing to your brother?"

Adhaniá kicked at the red boots she had just removed. "If you have come to scold me, you needn't bother." She lowered her head into her hands. "Ramtat has already done that . . ."

"I will be blamed for your actions. I promised my sister, your mother, that I would look after you and give you proper instruction. She gave you into my care so I could teach you the healing herbs, and I have done that. But I neglected to teach you the first thing a young woman must learn. What will become of you—the wildness in your blood must be curbed." She sighed, and her frown deepened. "You must be taught skills that will make you appealing to a future husband."

"What else should I learn?" Adhaniá replied defensively. "I am an accomplished horsewoman, and I proved today that I can wield a weapon as well as any man. I can speak four languages, as well as read and write them—what more do I need to know?" She raised her face to her aunt. "What more can you teach me?"

"It seems I cannot," Zamah said tiredly, sweeping a strand of ebony hair back beneath her green headdress. "I leave it to your mother to settle your restless spirit." There was a deep hurt in the tone of her voice. "The naked truth is that Ramtat has accused me of allowing you to run wild."

Adhaniá turned away so her aunt could not see the tears that dampened her cheeks. "He should not have said such a thing to you. You are blameless."

"He has every right to fault me. He was not speaking as my nephew—he made his judgment as my lord and sheik. He has decreed that you will be married, and that will be the end of it. Take every chance to show him you know how to please a husband."

Adhaniá's mouth flew open in shock. "Has he already chosen someone for me?"

There was misery in the older woman's eyes. "He has not, but he will. Obey him in this. There is nothing else you can do."

Scowling, Adhaniá stalked across the rug and back again, clenching her fists impatiently at her sides. "Oh, yes, there is! I will show my brother that I know very well what a man likes." For a moment she could not breathe for even thinking of the daring scheme that was hatching in her brain. "If that is what he wants from me, that's what he'll get."

A chilling breath of cold air swept over her, a warning whispered in her ear, but she ignored them both.

CHAPTER EIGHT ⚶

Adhaniá shoved the curtain aside and stalked into the tent where the dancers had gathered to prepare themselves for the night's entertainment. The sound of their giggling and twittering grated on her ears. The dancers, twelve in all, fussed with bracelets and shimmering veils, some tugging over a pretty bauble like a dog with a bone.

Filicia, the head woman who looked after the dancers, called for silence and ordered the women to cease their bickering. When quiet settled over the tent, she turned her attention to Adhaniá. "You see how the women chatter. They have heard that the queen's man, Apollodorus, will watch their dance."

"And that handsome Roman," one of them said, her lashes sweeping across her dark eyes.

"I heard he was Caesar's envoy and a high-ranking officer in the Roman army," someone added.

"I saw him from a distance and thought him quite handsome," another simpered. "I shall dance for him tonight."

Once again the squabbling started, and Filicia held up her

hand. "Be quiet, you squalling crows. You will never dance tonight if you do not attend to your garments."

Over the years Adhaniá had often sneaked into the dancers' tent to watch them, and even to dance with them, unbeknownst to her brother or her aunt, of course. It had been only a matter of time before she learned every dance. Filicia had often told her that if she were not from a high-born family, she would have been a great dancer and would have broken men's hearts.

Adhaniá gazed about at the couches strewn with brightly colored costumes and touched a vibrant yellow garment, wondering if she dared wear such a revealing costume. She gathered up a white veil and ran it through her fingers. If she kept her face covered throughout the dance, no one would recognize her.

The biggest obstacle to her plan was standing with hands on hips and looking at her suspiciously.

Filicia.

Adhaniá must convince the head woman to allow her to join the dancers tonight, and that was not going to be easy.

A shadow crept across Adhaniá's heart as she approached Filicia, who was busy fastening a bracelet on the wrist of one of the dancers. The woman's dark skin was wrinkled with age, and although it was said she had been an unequaled dancer in her younger days, her hands were now misshapen, and her eyes had been dulled by the passing years. But on occasion as she had watched the others dance, Adhaniá had observed the woman's hips swaying to the music.

Adhaniá cleared her throat nervously and quickly blurted out before she lost her nerve: "I want to dance tonight."

Filicia's hand went to her mouth. "Aiee! Sheik El-Badari will never allow his own sister to do such a thing. Nay, nay," the woman croaked in protest. "You must not ask such a thing of me!"

Adhaniá tilted up her chin stubbornly. "You often allowed me to dance with the women in the past."

"But that was only in secret. No men were present. Nay. I will not allow it."

"My brother will never know. I will wear a veil. Did you, yourself, not say I was as good, perhaps even better, than most of your dancers?"

Filicia clicked her tongue. "Being able to dance and being allowed to dance are on opposite sides of a camel."

Adhaniá looked at her pleadingly. "I *must* do this."

The woman's face whitened, and it took her a moment to find her voice. "But your brother—"

"If Ramtat finds out, he will be told that you had nothing to do with my decision. Indeed, you can go to your own tent now and tell everyone you suffer with a sour stomach and cannot be present for the dancing."

Filicia pursed her lips. "I cannot do that."

Adhaniá slipped out of her shoes and reached for a bright blue costume. "I am determined."

Two of the dancers swirled around Filicia, adding their pleas to Adhaniá's. "It would be such fun to have her dance with us, and she is a very fine dancer."

"She is worthy," said another. The others joined in the chorus. "Allow her to dance."

Determined amber eyes stared into Filicia's dark ones. "I *will* do this. You cannot stop me unless you go to my brother and tell him. Then Ramtat would want to know how I learned to dance."

Filicia looked troubled. "The sheik will demand the truth from me, and I will never say anything to him that is untrue."

"I *will* do this."

The dance mistress raised her hands and shook them at the heavens. "I am too old for this—I am at an age when I should retire; then I would no longer have to listen to the chattering of women."

Adhaniá smiled, knowing she had won. A moment of doubt twisted inside her, but she ignored it. The dancers swarmed around her—one woman tied bells to Adhaniá's ankles and wrists, while another dyed her palms and the soles of her feet with henna.

"Aiee! Aiee!" Filicia cried, her lips pursing tightly when the women would have dressed Adhaniá in a thin costume such as they wore. "If the sheik's sister is to dance, she must be covered." She turned with displeasure to Adhaniá. "I insist that you wear thick robes and cover your face. Do not think I will allow you to show your skin. The truth is, when a woman wears more clothing, she is a mystery, and a man will be intrigued, wondering what lies underneath."

Adhaniá agreed with a nod. She had no wish to wear a revealing costume.

When at last the dancers filed out into the night and approached the huge tent where important tribal leaders were being entertained, Adhaniá felt as if she were going to be sick. No man had ever seen her dance before. She tried not to dwell on her nervousness and, instead, went over in her mind some of the dance steps. Let it be on Ramtat's head—he had challenged her to learn how to please a man, and that was just what she would do.

The essence of some exotic scent curled through the air along with the aroma of food and drink. The boisterous laughter of the men became louder as they relaxed after having eaten well and drunk their fill. One of the lesser sheiks from the north stumbled to his feet and drunkenly recited a glowing tribute to Sheik El-Badari's wondrous hospitality.

Ramtat stood, wishing all a good night and encouraging them to enjoy the entertainment that had been provided. As he made his way to his tent, he frowned, thinking of his sister. What she had done today had been unacceptable and daring, but he had decided to forgive her. She had been humiliated enough, and surely she had learned the error of her ways. She was young. It would not happen again.

He entered his tent and made his way to the small curtained area where his son slept. Bending, he touched his mouth to the child's forehead, then stood back to watch the steady rise and fall of his chest. Did every father think his child was the most beautiful? He dropped the curtains and moved across the soft rug.

He found Danaë in bed but still awake. No words passed between them, just the passion that shone in their eyes. He went down to her, and her arms slid around his shoulders.

"You did not stay for the entertainment?"

He smiled. "I came to you for that."

Adhaniá was so nervous, she stumbled and would have fallen had not one of the women steadied her. This drew a giggle from the other girls, and her cheeks became stained with embarrassment.

"How can I dance," Adhaniá asked, smiling, trying to appear lighthearted, "if I cannot even walk?" Her stomach was in a knot. What had made her think she could do this?

The light from well-placed lanterns flickered brightly as she stepped inside the tent. She reached up, making sure her veil covered the lower part of her face so she would not be recognized. No one would notice her among the dancers, especially if she stayed behind the others. Later, she would take great satisfaction in telling Ramtat exactly what she had done to please a man.

Two flute players were seated in the shadows, their legs folded, their music blending with that of the drummer who knelt beside them. Their melody was haunting, and the men's attention was riveted on the dancers. Adhaniá swept forward just behind the others and slowly began to sway her hips to the rhythm of the music.

Sickening bile rose in her throat when she saw the lustful glances on some of the men's faces, and she blushed at their crude comments. She felt ashamed that the men might be focusing on her body. She tried to think about the dance steps, to concentrate on the feel of the soft carpet beneath her bare feet—the sound of the silver bells on her wrists and ankles.

In truth, she was trembling with fear. Raising her head the merest bit, she scrutinized each face in the crowd, and it was with relief that she realized her brother was not among them.

All she had to do was get through this first dance, and then she would leave. With luck, Ramtat would never discover what she had done. One of the dancers bumped into her, and Adhaniá realized she had missed a step—she must concentrate on what she was doing or she would draw every eye in the tent. She hung back, hoping to be inconspicuous.

No one must learn of her shameful behavior tonight. The dancers might talk about it, but they would not betray her to Ramtat. Of course, there was no fear the dance mistress would tell anyone—she did not want to be reprimanded by Ramtat.

Her hips swirled to the beat of the music, and she swallowed deeply.

All she had to do was make it through this dance.

Her frightened gaze fell upon the Roman, and she almost missed another step. Peering at him through half-lowered lashes, she thought he was indeed handsome—she wondered what he would look like in his Roman uniform. He was tall, his skin bronzed—he had a proud, haughty look, almost as if he was indifferent to everything around him, but his eyes said otherwise. She felt his gaze sweep down her body, and she whirled behind one of the other dancers so he could not see her.

She promised herself she would never again be so foolish.

CHAPTER NINE ⚡

Marcellus was seated next to Apollodorus, enjoying the entertainment. He had never met friendlier people, and they often spoke to him, although the Sicilian had to translate. One tribesman spoke of increasing his herd of goats, while another spoke of increasing his harem. These were happy people, and they made Marcellus feel carefree, if only for tonight.

He glanced with interest at the dancers in their filmy costumes. They were all comely, and he had never seen dancers move with such abandonment. The swaying of their hips and the weaving of their hands was almost hypnotic. He looked at each woman individually before moving on to the next. His gaze halted, and his attention centered on a dancer in blue who seemed more modest than the others with her movements. Her hands circled above her head, and her hips moved only slightly.

Clingy blue material swirled around her, and it seemed she was suddenly taken by the music. Marcellus watched her spin and whirl, her hips moving like an invitation to every man in the tent. She was the only one who wore a veil, and that somehow made her more beguiling than the others.

The bells she wore jingled in time with the flute, her arms wove in the air with the beat of the drum, and Marcellus was entranced. He wondered what beauty lay hidden behind that veil. The lantern light flickered across amber, kohl-lined eyes. His gaze swept across the outline of her body—she was young, firm and beautiful. When she turned, dipping her head back, he inhaled the haunting aroma of some exotic flower.

He smiled to himself. No female he'd ever seen could seduce like these Bedouin dancers, and the veiled one more than the rest. She was incredibly alluring, reaching inside him to a place no woman had ever touched.

It took Adhaniá a moment to realize the other dancers had dropped back behind her, and she alone was dancing. They either thought it was a good joke on her to let her dance alone, or perhaps they were paying her an honor by allowing her this solitary moment to display her skills.

The music wound through her mind and circled her heart, and she forgot everything but her dancing. As she whirled by, her gaze settled on the Roman. He seemed to be enjoying her dance; hence, she would give him something to take back to Rome with him. Circling her hips, she began to dance for him alone. Adhaniá knew the moment she had captured him, the moment his gaze locked with hers and his lips curved into a long, slow smile.

She had not noticed the young man who was serving the guests. She did not see him carefully place his tray on a cushion and stalk toward her. She was taken completely by surprise when he grabbed her wrists and pulled her toward the tent opening.

"Come with me!" Heikki hissed through gritted teeth. "Have you not shamed yourself enough today?"

Adhaniá saw the shocked look on the Roman's face as Heikki pulled her across the rug. She heard the protests that rose from the other guests as he led her into the night.

"No doubt the man is a jealous lover," one remarked.

"Or a jealous husband," added another, who was not familiar with many of the younger people of the sheik's encampment.

"Too bad," another man said. "She was a feast for the eyes—surely the youngest and most delectable of all the dancers."

Adhaniá wanted to flee into the night. She pulled back and twisted, but Heikki held her tight. She heard the music fade in the distance and knew she had been foolish.

Ramtat would never forgive her.

Marcellus, looking puzzled, bent toward Apollodorus. "What was that about?"

The Sicilian had the power to observe and discern. Many times his astuteness had kept him, and sometimes even Queen Cleopatra, alive. He had known the moment he saw the young dancer who she was. He also knew she would be punished severely for her actions tonight.

"That was Lord Ramtat's sister," he told the Roman.

Marcellus sobered. "The one who rode for the Golden Arrow today?"

"Ramtat has but one sister."

Marcellus shook his head. "She seems to cause quite a stir wherever she goes."

Heikki whirled Adhaniá around to face him. "You have gone too far this time. Since you never heed my words, I am taking you to Sheik El-Badari," he growled, furious with her for exposing herself to the gaze of other men.

She shoved his hand away. "You are not allowed to touch me if I do not wish it. And I do not wish it. Leave me alone."

He gripped her arm, sliding his hand to her wrist. "It is my duty to keep you safe."

Hot tears scalded her eyes and she began to tremble. "No, Heikki, do not do this. I know I did wrong. Let me go."

"I will not." He jerked her forward, and she had no choice but to run along beside him to keep up with his hasty steps. "You are not the woman I thought you were," he said angrily. "If you keep up this behavior, no man will want you for his wife."

She said nothing because she had no defense.

When they reached Ramtat's tent, Heikki called out, "Sheik El-Badari, may I enter? I have a matter to discuss with you that is of great significance."

After a moment, Ramtat bade him enter.

With his hand still gripping Adhaniá's wrist, Heikki led her inside the dimly lit outer room of the sheik's tent. There was a long moment of silence as Ramtat stared at them. Then he angrily grabbed a robe from one of the couches and threw it over his sister's shoulders.

"You had better have a good explanation for this," he told Heikki, pulling Adhaniá to his side. "What are you doing with my sister?"

The young man dropped his head. "I am to blame, El-Badari. I knew she was going to try for the Golden Arrow today, and I did not tell you. Then I was asked to serve the headmen tonight, and on entering the tent, I found your sister like this." He lowered his head, as if he could say no more.

"And—?" Ramtat said through gritted teeth.

"She was dancing with the other women."

Ramtat looked at his sister in disbelief, unmoved by her tears. "You dared display yourself in front of my tribesmen?"

Adhaniá grasped her brother's robe in a pleading gesture. "I know I was wrong. I thought I could show you I knew how to please a man. Was that not what you said you wanted?"

The silence was heavy, and she could hear every breath her brother took.

"You deliberately misunderstood me," he said quietly—too quietly. "You are reckless and spoiled, Adhaniá. Too long I have let you have your way. Tonight that stops. You will go to Rome to join Cleopatra. Perhaps under the guidance of the queen, you will learn your place."

Fresh tears streaked down Adhaniá's cheeks. "Am I to be banished?" She dropped her head. "It is no more than I deserve," she said with a heavy heart. "But must it be so far away?"

"Queen Cleopatra will welcome your company, and you may well benefit by her instruction."

Adhaniá stared at her brother hopelessly. "Do not send me out of Egypt. If you will give me another chance, I'll retire to our mother's house and work hard to become a proper lady."

"The matter is settled. Go now to our aunt and tell her to make you ready for an early departure. You will go first to our mother in Alexandria so you can be properly attired before traveling on to Rome."

Adhaniá buried her face in her hands and ran from the tent. She had gone too far—she knew that. Had she so shamed the family that her brother would never want to see her again?

Ramtat next turned his attention to the young Bedouin. "You will be going with her."

Heikki bowed his head. "My Sheik, am I to be banished as well?"

"Indeed you are." The muscle in Ramtat's jaw tightened. "I give you the task of guarding my sister. You are to make certain she does not further disgrace herself. This will be your only chance to redeem yourself in my eyes."

Heikki bowed his head once more. "I failed in that today."

Ramtat's voice held the hint of a threat. "That is why you will not fail the next time." He motioned to the tent opening. "I will have a message for you to take to my mother, since she will need to be informed why I have made the decision to send my sister to Rome."

Heikki bowed and backed out the tent opening, feeling like a traitor to Adhaniá, but what else could he have done?

After Heikki left, Danaë came to her husband's side and slid her arm around his waist. "I heard what happened. Please do not send her away. She is young and unthinking, as we all were once. She just needs guidance."

Usually Ramtat gave his wife whatever she asked, but not this time. "She needs a strong hand."

"And you think Cleopatra will be that hand? I think not, Ramtat. My sister sees only Caesar and the ambition they share to rule the world."

"I will send Cleopatra instructions."

"Only you, my husband, would dare to instruct a queen."

"My sister will learn obedience. I will bring her home before the year is out, and she will be ready to become a worthy wife."

"Perhaps you are right. Adhaniá may enjoy joining Cleopatra's household."

But she doubted it.

Marcellus stood beneath a star-capped night, breathing in the desert air that had a perfume all its own. It was peaceful here, like nowhere he had ever been. His mind drifted back through the day, and he thought of Lord Ramtat's sister. The girl was unruly. Even in Rome's more lenient society, her behavior would not be tolerated.

But thoughts of her wound their way inside his mind. She was a mystery, exotic and beautiful. At least he thought she was beautiful from what little he had seen of her.

He had just decided to go to his bed when a shadow emerged from one of the tents. He watched the slight figure move toward him, knowing it was a woman covered by a heavy robe. He was surprised when she stopped very near him, seeming totally unaware of his presence.

Light from a passing torch streaked across her face, but her heavy head covering hid everything but her eyes. The same exotic fragrance he had smelled on Ramtat's sister when she had danced near him drifted through the air, and he knew it was she.

"I saw you ride in the contest today," he said in Latin, not sure she would understand him.

She whirled around, almost colliding with his powerful body, and when she regained her composure, replied in Latin, "Much to my shame, everyone saw me ride today."

"And I saw you dance tonight."

She shook her head, backing away. "Roman, you saw too much today. I beg you to forget my disgraceful actions. I only wish I could."

In that moment she stepped back and stumbled over the rope that secured his tent. Instantly, he reached out to steady her and found her in his arms. The sweet scent that clung to her was intoxicating, and her skin was soft to the touch. Marcellus found himself pulling her closer. "Sweet little dancer, what is that mysterious fragrance you wear?"

"It is a scent extracted from the jasmine blossom," she said breathlessly.

"I think I will never forget you, although I have not seen your face."

At first she did not realize what she was doing. Something about the Roman made her feel safe. He was a comfort to her, his chest solid to lay her head against. His arms tightened around her, and she allowed it.

A lock of her hair had escaped the veil, drifting across his face. "I think I would die if your brother caught us like this." Reluctantly, Marcellus set her away from him. "And I have heard you are already in trouble."

Adhaniá took a hasty step away from him, wondering how many times she could shame herself in one day. "Please. I must go."

With a soft stirring of her robe, she moved away, leaving him staring after her. He wondered what the young girl's punishment had been at the hands of her brother.

Apollodorus, having just left Lord Ramtat's tent, had viewed the exchange between Marcellus and Ramtat's sister. "What you said was true. You could lose your life for touching her."

Marcellus watched the young woman disappear into the shadows before he answered. "There are some things in this world that are worth the risk."

"This is not one of them. You are a guest here . . . and an emissary for Caesar."

"Aye. But I would give up two years of my life to see her face and know what she looks like."

"Put those thoughts aside. We leave in the morning at first light, and Lord Ramtat has asked me to escort his sister as far as Alexandria. While she is under my care, no man will go near her."

"We leave so soon?"

"We must. Lord Ramtat has asked that I pave the way for his sister to join Queen Cleopatra's household in Rome."

Marcellus drew in a shallow breath. "So that is to be her punishment."

"It would seem so."

"What a strange young woman she is. Is she always so rash?"

"That I do not know. But she is little more than a child. Perhaps she will learn her place in this world."

Marcellus stared toward the water well, and he watched the palm fronds sway in the night breeze. "She carries with her the essence of this place on the softness of her skin."

Apollodorus gazed into the night. "If you are beginning to think this way about Lord Ramtat's sister, you could easily find yourself at the wrong end of a sword."

"It's just that she is a mystery."

"Some mysteries are better left unsolved," Apollodorus advised. "I will wish you a good night, Tribune Valerius. Make ready for the homeward journey."

Marcellus nodded absently. The desert called to his spirit, and when he left, he would leave a part of himself behind. He was enchanted by a young woman whose face he had never seen, and though he would be traveling with her to Alexandria, he would probably not even be able to speak to her.

If he lived for endless years, he would never forget the sight of those sad amber eyes swimming with tears.

CHAPTER TEN ✗

Makana, the personal servant Ramtat had chosen to accompany Adhaniá to Rome, was red-eyed from crying. Adhaniá judged the girl to be about her own age, but from the way Makana carried on, it was obvious she had never been away from her family. As the maid helped Adhaniá dress for the journey, she kept sniffing and drying her eyes.

Once she was dressed in her leggings and a heavy robe, Adhaniá could no longer endure Makana's whining. "Stop crying in my presence. Do you think I look forward to this journey with any more enthusiasm than you? Yet I do not give in to my feelings and annoy others." She jerked the heavy veil she was to wear about her shoulders, then drew it across her hair. "Get to your horse lest I ask my brother to choose another to take your place." She waved her hand dismissively. "Go now!"

The girl ducked her head and hurried from the tent, sobbing as she went, further annoying Adhaniá.

Moments later Adhaniá emerged from the tent and found Ramtat waiting for her. He stood rigid, his expression uncompromising. There was no sign of her loving brother, only her sovereign lord who had passed judgment on her. There was no softening in his eyes, and she knew by the fierceness of his countenance that his judgment was final.

Danaë looked at her with sympathy. "You must be brave, Adhaniá—all will be well in time. Take comfort in the fact that I have given Apollodorus a message to the queen, asking her to see to your welfare. Look upon this as an adventure, and the time will pass quickly. We will soon be reunited. When you return, there will be a new baby for you to hold and spoil."

Adhaniá's grief was momentarily pushed aside until realization hit her that she would not be with her family when the baby was born. Trying to hold back her tears, she looked at her brother. "I am happy for you," she murmured.

He nodded, although he did not change his rigid stance. "A child is always a blessing. I recall the night you were born—I thought I had never seen anything so beautiful. You brought joy to our family."

The color drained from Adhaniá's face as she met Ramtat's softened gaze. "I will attempt to overcome my willfulness," she told him. "I will make you proud of me."

He touched her cheek. She saw his chest rise and fall, and she knew he was having difficulty sending her away. "Look well to Queen Cleopatra for guidance. Obey her in all things."

She bowed her head, a shivering chill moving through her body even though the day was sweltering. "I shall. Her majesty's word is law." Suddenly she was hit by a great fear: Soon she would be going into the unknown. Grasping her brother's hand, she tried to hide her trepidation. "You will send word to me when the baby is born?" Panic lingered on the edge of her mind, and she struggled to keep it from showing.

Danaë answered her because Ramtat seemed unable to find his voice. "You can be assured we shall."

Adhaniá sighed and then turned to her nephew, who was twisting in his nurse's arms and reaching out to her. Grabbing him up and holding him close, she laid her cheek against his, inhaling the sweetness of his soft skin. Then she reluctantly handed him back to his old nurse, Minuhe.

"He will forget me," she said, looking at her sister-in-law woefully.

I will not allow that to happen," Danaë assured her. "I will speak of you to Julian each day."

Heikki led her horse forward, and Adhaniá saw Apollodorus some distance away, mounted and waiting for her. Her glance rested momentarily on the Roman at his side, still dressed in a Bedouin robe. He did not look in her direction; she was sure Apollodorus had warned him against it. There were twelve mounted warriors who would be her escort as far as Alexandria, and, of course, there was the ever-woeful Makana, who Adhaniá was determined would not ride at her side if she kept sniveling.

She wrapped her headdress about the lower part of her face and quickly turned, mounting her horse. With a stabbing ache in her heart, she rode away from the encampment. She was not happy that Heikki would be accompanying her to Rome, and she glared at him, then twisted her head so she did not have to look at him. Apollodorus rode beside her, and the Roman on the other side of him.

A subdued and silent Heikki dropped back behind Adhaniá to ride beside Makana.

Adhaniá could hear the girl's muffled sobs, and in exasperation, she nudged her mare forward to put some distance between them. The ever-watchful Bedouin warriors closed in around the rest of the party like a shield.

Smoke from early morning cookfires curled through the air as the encampment stirred to life. The celebration would continue for several more weeks, but Adhaniá wouldn't be there to enjoy it.

As they topped the first sand dune, the poignant smell of the desert filled her senses. She forced herself to look straight ahead, although she wanted to turn back to her brother. She knew he would be watching until she rode out of sight.

She would bear her exile as best she could.

The galloping hooves stirred the grains of sand into smothering dust. She gazed sideways to see how the Roman was faring. Most probably he was not accustomed to the arid desert heat—she did notice he drank more often from his waterskin than the others. She remembered how it had felt to be touched by him, and her thoughts were unsettling. The only man who had ever been allowed to lay a hand on her was Heikki, but he did not matter since he was like a brother to her. She mentally shook her head, not wanting to think about Heikki.

Adhaniá glanced at Apollodorus, who rode silently, his dark gaze moving over the land, ever watchful and ready for any trouble that might come. He knew, as did the guards, that there were warring tribes in the area who would like nothing better than to kidnap Sheik El-Badari's sister.

Intermittently Adhaniá could hear Makana sniffling, and her annoyance intensified. Makana behaved as if she were being punished rather than honored. In her heart, Adhaniá would have liked to turn her horse and ride back to the encampment, but she kept her eyes ahead, determined to make the best of her situation.

It was dusk when they stopped to make camp. Under Heikki's direction, three Badari tribesmen erected Adhaniá's tent, and Makana arranged the bedding. The rest of the party would sleep beneath the stars, and they began laying out their bedrolls in a protective circle around Adhaniá's tent. Apollodorus told Marcellus they would make camp away from the sheik's sister, so the two of them settled on a rise overlooking the distant sand dunes.

The setting sun spilled across the sand, painting it with a golden glow. Adhaniá stood just outside her tent, the evening breeze whipping at her robe. She was affected deeply by the beauty that surrounded her. Her family had many homes, grand villas and even two huge farms along the Nile. But she was always most at home in the desert—it called to her, it was where she had been happiest . . . until now.

The horses had been fed and hobbled, and she walked to her mare and laid her head against Sabasa's sleek neck. Her fingers drifted into her silken mane, and she ached because she would have to leave her mare when they took the boat to Alexandria.

She was so deep in thought she did not hear the bootsteps that approached her from behind.

"She is a real beauty," remarked Marcellus.

Adhaniá kept her eyes averted as a faint flush stole up her cheeks. "You should not be seen speaking to me," she warned him in perfect Latin. " 'Tis not wise."

His dark gaze moved over her, as if he were trying to see beneath the heavy veil that hid her face. "I only stopped to compliment you on such a fine animal."

She saw that he had removed his *kiffiyeh,* and his dark hair fell across his forehead. He was taller than Ramtat, and his eyes were the most expressive she had ever seen. Her heart fluttered when he smiled. "If you are caught, it will mean trouble for you, and I have enough problems without having to save you from my Bedouin's swords."

He bowed his head and stepped away, but she saw the

smile playing on his beautifully shaped lips. Adhaniá knew nothing about the man save that he was a tribune of Rome. She did not even know his name, or if he was married. But she did know he could mean trouble for her if she wasn't careful.

She wanted to walk up to him and press her mouth against his.

What was wrong with her?

She had never had such thoughts about a man before.

Why now? And why this man?

Pushing the Roman out of her mind, Adhaniá smelled the aroma of roasting meat that wafted through the air. She moved toward her tent. She was hungry, and she was weary.

Later in the night, when she sought her bed, she closed her eyes, seeking sleep. Makana lay on a bedroll at her feet, and Heikki was sleeping just outside the entrance of her tent. She rested her head on a soft cushion, and despite her resolve not to, she thought of the Roman. She remembered his smile, and her stomach tightened.

She warned herself it was too dangerous to think of him. But the warm glow in his dark eyes followed her into sleep.

Each day followed the same routine as the one before, and each night Adhaniá was forced to listen to Makana's mournful sobs. The woman complained because she missed her mother, and she lamented because she was saddle-sore, being unaccustomed to such rigorous riding. It was all Adhaniá could do to keep from sending her back to Ramtat.

It took them five days of hard riding to reach the Nile Valley. When Adhaniá saw the green strips of land that snaked along both sides of the river, she breathed in the damp air. From there, they would board a boat that would take them on to Alexandria.

She dismounted and laid her head against the neck of her

mare, wishing she did not have to send her away. Sabasa was her last link with her desert home, and she was loath to part with her. "Take good care of her," she told the Bedouin who would return Sabasa to the encampment.

He bowed his head. "I will be as gentle with her as you have been, mistress."

The small village where her family usually boarded a boat to ferry them to Alexandria was familiar to Adhaniá. She knew many of the people who dwelled within and acknowledged their greetings as she walked past. She absently watched fishermen casting their nets, and then focused on one old man as he sat with his back braced against a weathered boat, a net spread across his lap as he plied a fishbone needle with nimble fingers.

Her mouth quivered. Most young women would be happy at the prospect of joining their queen, but although Adhaniá revered Queen Cleopatra, she did not really know her all that well. She had spoken to her on occasion, but if the queen remembered her at all, it would only be because she was Ramtat's sister. She was leaving her friends and family behind, and the prospect was tearing her apart inside.

Rome, so far away. What would it be like?

The city of the masters of the world.

Like poor Makana, Adhaniá, too, wanted her mother.

Heikki touched her arm. "We can board now."

She glared at him and pulled away, still harboring anger toward him. "I don't want to talk to you. Just stay away from me." She saw his hurt expression and wished she could recall her cruel words. Did he not know he'd destroyed the trust she had in him? She was not yet ready to forgive him.

With her head held high, Adhaniá walked up the gangplank, looking neither to her right nor left. But Makana's hand flew to her throat, and her eyes darted about, nervous and frightened—she had a firm grip on the railing as the sails caught the wind and the boat shifted to the middle of the Nile. Adhaniá had to remind herself the poor wretch was a desert dweller and frightened out of her wits.

Heikki took up a protective stance near Adhaniá, and she purposefully moved away from him.

Apollodorus saw the misery in the young Badarian's eyes and said, "She will forgive you in time."

"I am not convinced she ever will." He looked at the Sicilian. "Even if I'd known Adhaniá would be banished to Rome, I would have acted no differently."

Marcellus overheard the conversation and glanced at the young Bedouin. "Is she promised to you?"

Heikki met Marcellus's gaze. "She is not, nor can she ever belong to me. She is a lady of great standing, and I am her servant."

Marcellus glanced across the deck of the small papyrus boat, observing Adhaniá. The afternoon breeze caught her green veil and tore it off her head, sending it fluttering across the deck. Heikki dashed forward and grabbed it, carrying it back to her, but not before Marcellus had caught a quick glimpse of smooth skin and delicate cheekbones.

"Poor Heikki," Apollodorus said. "His love for Lady Adhaniá is hopeless."

Marcellus remembered the Bedouin dragging the sheik's sister out of the tent the night she joined the dancing girls. "Will she really forgive him?"

"You have not seen Lady Adhaniá at her best. She is worthy, kind and joyful. I am accustomed to her laughter. I have not heard it of late."

"You sound like you have feelings for her yourself."

The Sicilian glanced at the disappearing shoreline. "I serve the queen."

There was a world of meaning in Apollodorus's words, but Marcellus did not ask him to explain. He suspected Apollodorus, too, could not reach so high as to touch the woman he favored . . . that woman being the Queen of Egypt.

When Adhaniá rewound her headdress, she spoke to Heikki. "You are now exiled with me. I hope that makes you happy."

"I don't apologize for seeing to your welfare."

"And I no longer look upon you as my closest friend. You betrayed me." Until she was ready to forgive him, she would rather not have him near her, and she moved away.

For more than a week the dreary little boat made its way toward the Mediterranean. Adhaniá paid little attention to the journey since she had made it many times in the past during happy and carefree times. She had long hours to dwell on how she had disgraced her family. She had brought Ramtat's wrath down upon her head, and now she would cause pain to their mother, who would blame herself for not being present.

As a Badarian princess, Lady Larania should have attended the festivities honoring her son, but she had declined so Danaë could take her rightful place at Ramtat's side and be recognized as the new princess of the Badari.

Adhaniá now saw that her heedless actions reverberated throughout the family. She was not the only one who would suffer because of her willfulness.

She was in a hopeless situation.

Her eyes met and caught the Roman's, and she looked away. She wished she was able to talk to him. There were so many questions she wanted to ask him about Rome.

She felt his presence at all times, and more and more, her gaze sought his.

The last evening onboard, Adhaniá could not sleep. She quietly dressed and left her cramped cabin. The boat was anchored near shore for the night, and it was hot and miserable. Even netting had not discouraged the swarming gnats from pestering Adhaniá. When she stepped on deck, she found Heikki had already sought his bedroll, and the captain of the ship acknowledged her with a nod but did not speak.

She sighed, standing at the railing, wishing herself back in the desert.

"A magnificent night," a clipped Roman voice said from the shadows near the bow.

A thrill went through her at the sound of the Roman's voice. Adhaniá knew she should go immediately to her cabin, but she foolishly lingered so she could talk to him. "Aye," she agreed. "Or it would be but for the swarm of gnats."

He came closer to her. "I am amazed at how well you speak Latin."

She felt him beside her and took a deep breath. "I had a worthy teacher."

"I will be saying good-bye to you tomorrow. I understand we will dock in Alexandria before nightfall."

His voice was deep, and it struck a cord within her. "That is what I am told as well."

She felt his nearness, and for some reason she could not understand, she wanted to touch him. That impression made her tremble inside. The thought of never seeing him again caused a sharp ache in her heart. "You are a tribune, Apollodorus tells me." She had not dared ask much about the Roman, not wanting to appear too interested in him.

"Aye."

"Then will you soon be off to war? That is what Roman tribunes do, is it not?"

His burst of laughter awoke something deep inside her— heat that flowed through her body—a yearning she did not understand.

"Nay. I will not be off to war."

She was hanging onto her composure by a mere thread. "What does a tribune do when he is not warring with his neighbors?"

"This tribune builds bridges, libraries, cities or whatever Caesar bids me build."

She digested that bit of information, then dared to speak of what was troubling her. "I don't suppose we will see each other after tomorrow."

His voice deepened even more when he glanced down into her eyes. "I don't think I will be invited to meet with your queen."

It hurt to think this was the last time she would ever see him. "I suppose not."

"So you will drift out of my life without my ever having seen your face," he said, his breath stirring the curl that had escaped her veil.

"My face is nothing that you would remember if you had seen me."

His raised eyebrow challenged her assertion. "I wonder if you might give me a parting gift—a remembrance?"

Her heart thundered inside her. He wanted to remember her? "If I can."

He daringly reached out and touched her veil. "I would like to have this."

She hesitated for only a moment before she unwrapped it, slid it off the lower part of her face and held it out to him. Their fingers brushed as he took it from her, and she wanted to wrap her hand around his, to hold on to him and to hold back tomorrow. "You will look funny wearing it," she managed to say, smiling.

For a long moment Marcellus was wordless. Soft moonlight illuminated the most unforgettable face he'd ever seen. His gaze swept across features that seemed to have been fashioned by the gods to please a man. She had not the soft beauty of a Roman woman, but an exotic, unforgettable, haunting beauty that would linger in a man's mind long after he had forgotten other women. "I shall carry your image inside me so I can remember." He looked at her intently. "You take my breath away."

Adhaniá had never had a man say such things to her. She could hardly catch her breath. "So you will not give my veil to another?"

Marcellus waved the silken cloth beneath his nose, inhaling the exotic scent. "No one will wear this—I shall keep it close to my heart to remind me of the beautiful, high-spirited young woman who once crossed my path."

His words thrilled her and saddened her at the same time. "And I would ask something of you," she whispered.

"Anything that is within my power to grant is yours."

She turned to fully face him, wanting so much from him but not knowing exactly what. "I would have you tell me your name."

He swept her a deep bow. "I am Marcellus Valerius, very much at your service."

She started to touch his arm but drew back. "Farewell, Tribune Marcellus Valerius, who builds libraries."

He daringly touched her cheek, tilting it into the moonlight. "Something I cannot explain draws me to you."

Her whole body was shivering, not from cold but from a strange yearning. With her heart beating wildly and her breath trapped in her throat, she turned away and fled.

Marcellus watched Lady Adhaniá hurry away, his imagination taking him in a dangerous direction. If they had been caught together, she would have been punished. But he could not stop thinking about the softness of her skin. He could still hear the sound of her deep, throaty voice; her accent when she spoke his language was like poetry. She was more beautiful than any women he knew, and certainly no other woman could match her in horsemanship. She was as untamed as the desert from whence she came.

His gut twisted as he thought about those intriguing dimples that appeared in her cheeks when she smiled, and the way she pursed her lips in thoughtfulness.

He had been wise to resist the urge to kiss those dimples.

Very wise indeed.

CHAPTER ELEVEN 🦎

Once the boat was tied up at the dock in Alexandria, Heikki immediately made arrangements for a litter to transport Adhaniá to her family's villa outside the city. She glanced around the deck for Marcellus, but he was nowhere to be seen. Going down the gangplank, she watched men straining their backs loading cargo, and the sails of ships catching the wind for voyages to far-off ports.

She searched for Marcellus among the working horde at the waterfront, and, with a sinking heart, realized he and Apollodorus must have left the boat soon after they'd docked.

With a dull ache in her heart, she climbed into the litter Heikki had ordered, and he mounted a horse to ride alongside. Now that they were in Alexandria, Adhaniá removed her head covering and felt the damp air against her face.

Alexandria, the marketplace of the world, was magnificent. In the distance, Adhaniá glanced at the splendor of the jewel of all cities. The turquoise color of the Mediterranean was reflected against marble temple walls. The city sprawled along miles of shoreline. The bright sunlight glancing off the white marble hurt her eyes, so she closed them and leaned back against the cushions.

She wished she had seen Marcellus one last time. Then she pushed him out of her mind and thought of her mother. This would not be the happy reunion it usually was when she returned from the desert. Her mother would be terribly displeased with her.

It was almost sundown when they reached the outskirts of the villa. Workers toiling in fields of golden grain paused in their work to wave and smile a welcome to her. Fruit pickers doffed their caps and bowed in her direction. Everything was dear and familiar to her.

Once inside the house her mother walked toward her with a happy smile. Lady Larania was a woman of uncommon beauty. She was tall and statuesque, with the golden skin of one who belonged to the Badari tribe. Her dark hair was barely dusted by gray at the temples, and it was from her that Adhaniá had inherited her dimples.

"Daughter," she said, touching Adhaniá's shoulder and then pulling her into her arms. "I was not expecting you so soon. Tell me quickly, did they accept my daughter-in-law in my place?"

"They loved Danaë, Mother, just as you said they would."

"Then all is well." Larania looked puzzled. "Are the games over so soon?"

Adhaniá lowered her head. "I have been sent away in disgrace. I am ashamed of what I have done."

Her mother smiled, thinking there was nothing Adhaniá could have done that would be very bad. "Tell me," she said, leading her daughter to the couch, where they both sat. She waited expectantly, and when Adhaniá said nothing, she asked, "What have you done?"

As Adhaniá related the two incidents, sparing herself none of the shame, she watched her mother's face whiten with disbelief. It hurt to see shock and disappointment harden her mother's expression.

"Must I go to Rome?" Adhaniá pleaded, clinging to her mother's hand. "Can you not convince Ramtat to relent—tell him how sorry I am? You have my word I'll mend my ways and become a proper daughter and sister."

The mother in Larania ached for her daughter, but the Bedouin princess in her stiffened with resolve. "You know very well I cannot go against your brother. He is not only head of the family but our sheik as well. We must both abide by his decision."

Adhaniá lowered her head. Her mother was right. "I will obey. What I did was wrong, and I was selfish to hurt my brother in such a shameful way. I am sorry for the pain I've caused you both."

Larania drew Adhaniá into her arms. "Daughter, I know this is hard for you—it is difficult for us all. I can only imagine what strength it took for my son to send you so far away."

Adhaniá wanted to cry, but she knew her mother would expect her to take her punishment without complaint. "His law is just."

But it was so difficult, so very difficult to think of leaving Egypt.

A swarm of needlewomen descended on the villa to make Adhaniá gowns worthy of the queen's household. Adhaniá cared little for the silken robes, veils and dresses made of every hue in the rainbow. She barely looked at the jewels or the soft leather sandals that matched her new clothing. It mattered but little to her that her hooded cloak was made of purple silk—the purple dye being rare since it took thousands of mollusk seashells to obtain such a hue. It was said purple was banned in Rome except to those of nobility. It was an appropriate color for Adhaniá since she was a Badari princess.

The days passed too swiftly, and the time soon arrived when she would depart for Rome.

The last evening an intense thunderstorm struck; the force of the wind rattled the doors and shook the ground. Adhaniá stood at the window, her body trembling with an unknown dread. She watched raindrops dissolve into the dry earth, and she wept.

Exhausted, she went to her bed and finally fell asleep.

It was a sad occasion when Adhaniá boarded a sea-going vessel for Rome. It had been difficult to say good-bye to her mother, but she'd managed to do it without giving in to the tears that stung her eyes.

This time instead of a small papyrus boat like the one that had transported her down the Nile, the *Parnethous* was a large ship with well-appointed cabins, many comforts and thirty-one other passengers, most from other lands.

When the ship sailed within sight of Cleopatra's marble palace, Adhaniá stood stiff and dry-eyed, watching her beloved Alexandria fade into the mist. Even the beacon from the great lighthouse on Pharus Island gave off a weak light that barely strained through the thick fog. After a while Adhaniá could see nothing but the damp, dreary fog.

Egypt disappeared from her sight completely.

Other passengers strolled the deck, but none approached or spoke to the mysterious woman swathed in green with the fierce-looking Bedouin guard at her side.

Adhaniá missed talking to her best friend; Heikki had been her companion for many years, but the distance between them was widening. She could not seem to recapture what they had once shared. Sometimes she caught his gaze and realized Heikki knew it as well.

So much had changed for her. She had left childhood behind in Egypt and was stepping into a world unknown to her.

* * *

The first three days were cloudy, with only an occasional glimpse of the sun. But the weather worsened when a storm struck on the fourth day. The ship rolled and heaved while waves swept across the deck, forcing the passengers to remain below to ride out the storm.

In her cramped quarters, Adhaniá was miserable. Poor Makana was so ill she was rolling on the small bunk, moaning as if she were dying. It was Adhaniá who played handmaiden to her servant. She held the jar for Makana while she was sick and bathed her brow with cool water.

"We are going to die!" the poor girl lamented. "We will sink, and our bodies will be washed onto some distant shore or not be found at all."

Adhaniá was quickly losing what little patience she had with the servant. "Nonsense. The storm will pass, and we shall reach our destination, just as we are supposed to." In truth she was feeling a bit ill herself, but she did not mention it to the already hysterical Makana.

On the ninth day out, Adhaniá awoke to a calm sea. With relief, she quickly dressed herself and rushed on deck, where she found many other passengers enjoying the bright sunshine. Adhaniá wore her purple cape, with the hood hiding her face, but she still drew many curious glances as the passengers speculated on her identity.

Adhaniá chanced a glance at Heikki, who was looking ashen and uncomfortable. When she realized why, her laughter danced on the wind. "I should not find such delight in your discomfort, but I confess I do. You were ill during the storm, were you not?"

He did not answer, just looked embarrassed.

"You might take comfort in knowing that at times I felt a bit queasy myself."

When the ship groaned against a huge wave, Heikki

gripped the side of the railing. "I will be happy to reach dry land," he admitted.

A feeling of sympathy washed over her, but she could not resist taunting him as she once had. "Poor Heikki," she purred. "A desert dweller at sea in a storm."

"I didn't take to my bed during the storm," he remarked with force. "At all times I was guarding your door."

She felt a prickle of guilt. She had sworn to despise him for the rest of her life, but she could not. "I am sorry. Please sit down and rest yourself."

"Nay. Too many people are looking your way. It is the purple cape—they know you are a person of importance, and they might approach you if I relax my guard."

Her gaze traced the flight of a seabird across the blue sky, and a smile curved her lips. "No one will hear from me that you were seasick." She met his gaze. "You have my word."

Heikki stood stoic, almost as still as a statue, nothing moving but his dark gaze, which fell on her face. "Many people were ill in the storm. You were one of the few who did not suffer overmuch."

Adhaniá leaned her elbows on the railing and rested her chin on her palms. "I suppose every Badari at the games knows of my disgrace."

"Like grains of sand sifting through your fingers, this will all pass into nothingness."

"But to be sent to Rome—banished from my beloved Egypt—is almost more than I can bear," she said, shaking her head. "I have never had an ambition to see that warring country."

Later that afternoon a calm sea stretched out before them, and Adhaniá managed to persuade Makana to drink some fruit nectar, and later take small sips of ale. But the girl continued to moan and complain.

In the evening the two stood on deck and watched the sun drop like a golden ball into the sea. Adhaniá stared at the waves that washed against the ship, her heart giving a sudden lurch because a thought hit her that she had not considered. With every passing moment, she grew ever closer to Rome and to Marcellus.

She closed her eyes, wondering if he sometimes thought of her.

Nay. She had just been a brief diversion, and he probably didn't even remember her name.

CHAPTER TWELVE ✗

Marcellus walked down the Senate steps beside Marc Antony. The site where the Senate was meeting was only temporary quarters while the old building was being reconstructed.

"I didn't expect to see you here today, my friend," Antony said, straightening his toga. "You have the look of a man who is about to ask a boon of me."

Marcellus smiled. "You are beginning to read me too well. There *is* something I would ask, and you have the power to grant it."

Antony was amused. "Ask, and I'll decide."

"The sails of the ship bringing Lord Ramtat's sister were sighted today."

"And how would you know that?"

Marcellus felt a bit embarrassed, but he plunged ahead. "She sails on the *Parnethous,* and I've had a man watching for it to arrive."

Antony stopped in midstep. "Why would you do that?"

"I would like to be among the escort that takes her to the villa where Queen Cleopatra resides."

Antony smiled, and then laughed. "Perhaps I should head the detail myself if this woman is beautiful enough to catch your attention."

Marcellus himself didn't understand why he couldn't forget Lady Adhaniá, or why he carried her veil beneath his breastplate next to his heart. He had fought against his desire for her—had even seen other women when he returned to Rome, but they had not satisfied his need. He glanced up at the afternoon sky. "If you decide to be her escort, take me with you."

Antony looked thoughtful for a moment. "Queen Cleopatra may have already chosen an escort for the lady."

"I have considered that. Caesar might be persuaded to send a Roman escort to honor her brother, who fought beside him."

Antony shook his head and smiled. "You have put some thought into this."

The admission came hard. "I must see her."

"I have never seen you so desperate over a woman. I warn you, you tread dangerous ground."

"I've also considered that."

"I will approach Caesar about it, young architect. But remember, this puts you in my debt."

Since the storm had blown the *Parnethous* off course, the ship had been at sea thirty-six days when the captain informed the passengers that their destination was within sight and they would disembark by midafternoon.

Adhaniá strained her eyes, looking toward the shoreline. Instead of the huge, sprawling city she had expected, she saw what looked like a small fishing village.

Adhaniá had dressed with care, donning the heavy robe of the Bedouin and placing an equally heavy covering over her head. "Surely that cannot be Rome," she exclaimed to Heikki, who stood at her side.

"Nay, it is not. The captain has arranged to put us ashore at that village, where we can more easily make the journey downriver to the villa Queen Cleopatra occupies."

The air was hot and damp, and she lifted the weight of her hair off her neck, wishing she could remove the stifling veil so she might find some relief from the oppressive heat.

"I would imagine Apollodorus has already informed Queen Cleopatra of your arrival. The queen will no doubt send someone to be your escort."

Adhaniá imagined Apollodorus had also informed the queen about her disgraceful actions. She was determined to conduct herself in a manner that would reflect well on her and Ramtat, so perhaps, in time, everyone would forget what she had done.

Makana was leaning heavily against the railing, her head bent low, keening softly.

Adhaniá's fury exploded. Makana had no knowledge of dressing hair or preparing Adhaniá's clothing—so what good was she? She made a quick decision.

"Makana, your constant wailing has worn away my patience; therefore, I shall send you back to Egypt."

The woman's face whitened. "Mistress, how can I make amends? If you send me home in disgrace, my father will not speak to me, and I will be shamed before the whole tribe."

"You should have thought of that before now. I will not have you in the presence of our queen. You are no credit to yourself, and your behavior casts disparagement on the Badari tribe."

The woman cried out and clung to Adhaniá's robe. "Please, mistress. Have mercy!"

The woman's sobs drew attention, and Adhaniá stepped away from her. "Hush. Do you want everyone to know of your complaints? You asked to go home and I am granting your wish."

"Forgive me, mistress," Makana cried. "I can't help missing my mother. I didn't want to come with you, but neither do I want to return home in shame," she whimpered.

Adhaniá knew only too well what it felt like to be in disgrace. Though Makana had served her ill, the poor girl was in misery. "Heikki will write my brother and explain to him that you fell ill on the voyage and I decided to send you home. When you reach our village, you can tell them what you will." She looked at Heikki. "Make arrangements immediately for Makana to be on the *Parnethous*'s return voyage to Egypt. Then write instructions to my mother that Makana is to be escorted to the Bedouin camp as soon as she reaches Alexandria."

Heikki was well aware of the servant's dissatisfactory behavior. She had complained and cried all the way across the desert and now across the sea. It had irritated him, and he wondered how Adhaniá had tolerated Makana as long as she had. He nodded. "I will speak to the captain at once and make out the scrolls for Sheik El-Badari and Lady Larania."

The wretch dropped to her knees and tried to kiss Adhaniá's hand, but she jerked it away just in time. "Thank you, mistress." She blinked owlishly. "You are kindness itself."

"Leave me."

"But suppose there is another storm like the one on the voyage here?"

Adhaniá was having difficulty holding her temper. "If that be the case, you will be ill again, only this time I will not be there to tend you. Go now from my sight."

The young woman looked doubtful for a moment before

hurrying across the deck, as if she feared her mistress might change her mind.

Adhaniá stared after her with her most censorious glare. To arrive at Queen Cleopatra's residence without a personal servant would be one more disgrace to add to all the others. Her back stiffened. This time it was not her fault—Ramtat had chosen her servant unwisely.

Heikki soon returned to her side, and they both watched as the sails were lowered and the ship drifted closer to the shoreline. He watched Adhaniá out of the corner of his eye—she had found a new independence. Lately there had been a glow about her that enhanced her beauty. He wondered if Adhaniá was aware that their relationship had changed: No longer were they the carefree companions they had once been—he had become the servant, she the mistress—just as his father had predicted.

Adhaniá listened to the sound of the oars slapping against the water. "Thus far, I am unimpressed by what I see. Do you know the name of that village?"

"I am told it is Ostia."

" 'Tis little more than mud huts and dirt roads." She gazed in every direction, disappointed. "Are we not to see Rome?"

"It would appear not at this time. That river you see in the distance is the Tiber. I am told Queen Cleopatra dwells outside Rome at Caesar's villa, which is located on its banks."

She drew in a deep breath. "What is that unusual fragrance that clings to the air? It is unknown to me, but I do not find it unpleasant. Do you know what it can be?"

Heikki had already asked the same question of the boatman. "I was informed the aroma comes from those trees you see in the woods." He pointed in the distance. "They are called pine trees. Notice their odd shape, and the leaves are long and splintery."

"Everything is different here—the trees, the river—even the sky does not seem as blue."

"So it would seem," Heikki said, watching the gangplank swing into place.

It appeared they were the only ones to disembark, and they drew curious stares from the other passengers. Dockworkers swarmed forward, hastily loading amphorae of olive oil and wine aboard the *Parnethous*.

Adhaniá's first step onto dry land was jarring. Pausing, she drew in a breath; the wonderful pine scent was much more pronounced on shore. She stepped around a heavy crate while her gaze ran along the docks, so different from those in Egypt. Alexandria was a patchwork of civilization with ships from every nation crowding the waterfront. Tradesmen from all over the world flocked to the magnificent city to sell their wares.

"Look you there," Heikki said, indicating a curtained litter. Six strong bearers wearing the amulets of Queen Cleopatra stood nearby. "You shall ride in comfort today."

Then Heikki froze, his eyes darkening as he nodded toward the distance with a contemptuous snarl on his lips. "Roman soldiers. No doubt your welcoming committee and escorts. I'd hoped Apollodorus would send our own Egyptian guards."

Adhaniá nervously drew her veil across her face, her heart beating faster as she stared at the soldiers through a thin layer of gauze. They were at too great a distance to distinguish their faces, but she found herself hoping Marcellus would be among them.

Her heartbeat stopped—one of the Romans was a head taller than the others, and she knew at once it was Marcellus. Unexpected joy sang through her heart. She watched him dismount, his scarlet cape flourishing about him. He was expressionless as he approached her with a steady tread. He looked magnificent in his uniform. His breastplate was of bronze, molded to fit his upper torso, and embossed with the emblem of the imperial eagle. Leather strips tipped with bronze fell to his knees, while his tall sandal boots were strapped about his muscled legs.

When he stopped before her, he unhooked his red-plumed helm and tucked it under his arm. Bowing his head, he spoke: "Lady Adhaniá, welcome to my country. I have been given the honor of escorting you to Queen Cleopatra."

His formal greeting was a disappointment. He merely seemed to be a man who had been given a mission. Her hands shook, and she clasped them behind her so he wouldn't notice. When she started to speak, she found her throat had suddenly gone dry. At last she managed to utter, "I am grateful to you, Tribune Valerius. Can you tell me how long it will be until we reach our destination?"

His answer was clipped, and his gaze moved away from her to watch as her personal belongings were loaded onto a donkey-drawn cart. "Within two hours, I should think." He nodded behind him. "I have brought an extra horse, should you wish to ride to the villa."

Heikki had been directing the placement of Adhaniá's trunks and now appeared beside her. His frown showed how little he trusted the Roman. "My lady will travel in the litter, but I will be happy to use the horse to ride beside her."

Marcellus nodded. "As you like."

Adhaniá hid her disappointment. Heikki was right, of course; she should not arrive at the villa on horseback. It would be unseemly.

When she was seated in the litter, Adhaniá heard Tribune Valerius's deep voice as he gave directions to the servant who would be transporting her belongings to the villa. How different he was from the man who had asked for her veil. She saw only a high-ranking officer, self-assured and doing his duty. She imagined Apollodorus had suggested Marcellus as her escort since they were already acquainted.

She studied him through the thin curtain. His dark hair was clipped short in the Roman fashion. His jaw was square and seemed to be carved of granite. Then he glanced her way, and his eyes held the same warm glow she remembered. She watched him slide his helmet into place, and her heart was gladdened just to look upon him again.

"Are you comfortable, Lady Adhaniá?" he asked solicitously.

"Aye," she managed to say past the thickening in her throat. "Very much so. Thank you, Tribune Marcellus Valerius."

Adhaniá watched Marcellus swing onto his horse and take a position on the left side of the litter, while Heikki rode at her right.

What was happening to her?

Why was she suddenly so happy to be in this strange land?

As the procession moved away from the docks, Marcellus took his position at the head of the column, and she could no longer see him. She sighed and gazed across the river, where she glimpsed the tops of sprawling buildings and huge colonnades.

Rome, she thought with trepidation.

Marcellus, she thought with yearning.

Several hours passed before they reached their destination. When they passed beneath the arched entry to Caesar's huge villa, Heikki dismounted and helped Adhaniá from the litter.

"Thank you, Tribune," he said dismissively. "I will see Lady Adhaniá inside."

Already servants were rushing forward to see to her needs. She had only a quick glance at Marcellus before he nodded, spun his horse around and rode away in the gathering dusk.

Adhaniá felt suddenly empty inside, as if the light had gone out of the sun and a cold wind blew off the Tiber.

CHAPTER THIRTEEN ✗

The hour was late, and only a pale crescent moon strained through tattered clouds, casting the streets of Rome in darkness. Even so, Senator Quadatus stealthily crept between darkened corridors, using every means available to pass unnoticed. Hearing voices just ahead, he quickly ducked into a dark alleyway, stepping into unidentifiable puddles. The stench permeating the air made him gag. Waiting impatiently until two men passed, Quadatus hurried out of the alley in the direction of his home.

He trembled with excitement, and at the same time shuddered with fear. Tonight, Senator Cassius had taken him into his confidence and revealed a plan that would rock Rome to its foundations.

Unaccustomed to moving with such haste, he was sweating and puffing, having trouble catching his breath. When he reached the street where he lived, he dashed forward, seeking the safety of his home. For some time he had been aware that Cassius was meeting with others, and he'd suspected they were hatching a plan to strip Caesar of his power—but never had he thought they would go so far as to take the dictator's life!

He gasped, bending to catch his breath. He had been flattered that the elder statesman had asked him to his home tonight. But now, he felt only fear and dread.

He pounded on his front door, where a yawning servant admitted him. He stood for a moment, still having difficulty catching his breath. He had never considered himself a coward, but tonight's dealings introduced him to real terror. One wrong move, or an ill-spoken word at the wrong time or place, and Cassius would have his throat slit.

"Are you ill?"

Quadatus turned to his wife. She was still beautiful to him, and he still desired her as much as he had that first moment he'd laid eyes on her. He ached for her, even knowing her heart would never belong to him. He wished he could confide in her, explain his hopes and fears, but she must never know the secrets he had discussed with Cassius tonight.

Sarania would undoubtedly betray him if she could.

Quadatus looked into beautiful, frigid eyes and found no warmth there for him.

"Is something the matter?" Sarania asked again. "You seem out of breath and pale."

"Nay. Everything is as it should be. Everything I desire is about to be mine."

Sarania shook her head as if she cared naught. She stepped away from him, seeming to cringe at the thought of his touching her. "I was just on my way to retire for the night."

"Shall I go with you?"

She shrugged with indifference. "As you like."

He grasped her wrist and pulled her to him, tracing a finger across her lower lip. "Don't forget, one word from me and your son is a dead man. Knowing this, should you not give me what I want more willingly?"

Her head fell back, and Quadatus saw the naked fear in her eyes. "If I were not such a coward, I would have long ago driven a dagger through your black heart rather than submit to you."

His smile showed no warmth. "My dear, be kind to yourself," he taunted. "It takes a certain malevolence to take a life. You do not have that in you." He placed his lips near her ear. "Lest you forget, I do possess that ability."

She wiped her damp eyes on the back of her hand. "It does not take evil—it takes courage. Something I lack."

He followed her toward the bedchamber and grasped her arm, spinning her around to face him. Kicking the door shut, he thrust her onto the bed. "I have need of you tonight."

She stifled her cry and relented, allowing him to do with her whatever he wanted. She would do whatever it took to keep Marcellus alive. She felt only disgust as he put his hands on her breasts, and she felt sick as he rammed himself into her body. Every time he took her, it felt like rape. But Sarania closed her eyes and reminded herself that it was only her body he was using—he could not touch that place she kept as a shrine to her dead husband.

"Look at me!" Quadatus ordered.

Sarania showed him eyes that held no emotion and a body that was limp and unfeeling. When he finished with her, he shoved her away.

"Try to find more delight in what I do to you or I can make it very unpleasant for you."

"If you want to delight someone, fill your bed with servant girls who might welcome their master's touch."

He stared down at her. "Have a care," he warned. "You tread on dangerous ground."

She sat up and stared into his dark eyes. "If anything happens to my son, I will no longer have a reason to live. Though I am too much of a coward to harm you, I will have no trouble ending my own miserable existence."

"Perhaps I no longer care what you do."

"I pray to the gods every day that you will lose interest in me."

"You do not know of what you speak. I am about to become one of the most important men in Rome. Think you I will not be rewarded if I help Cassius eliminate Caesar?"

Her hand went to her throat. "You would not dare!"

Quadatus realized he'd said too much—if Sarania repeated his boast to anyone else, he would be a dead man.

"Think nothing of what I said. Wine tends to loosen my tongue."

She saw fear reflected in his eyes. "You were with Cassius tonight—is that what the two of you discussed?"

He took her chin and raised it to him. "Forget what I said; I was merely boasting."

She jerked her head away from him, knowing he had spoken true, but that she must dissemble so he would not be wary of her. "I have already guessed you had too much wine," she replied wisely, then shrugged. "I take no account of what you say when you have drunk overmuch."

He managed to smile. "Aye, that was all it was."

Sarania rolled over in bed, pretending to be sleepy. She listened to his fading footsteps and heard the door close behind him as he left her chamber.

She had to find a way to warn Marcellus. By the gods, Cassius and his followers were treasonous and ambitious, and they must be stopped.

What must she do?

No one would believe her.

Once again, she must get word to Marcellus.

But how?

Tears dampened her face. Her son would be the last one to believe anything she said.

Sarania muffled her cries against her folded arms. She must keep watch on Quadatus without him becoming suspicious.

CHAPTER FOURTEEN ✗

Lapidus took a sip of wine, rolled it around on his tongue and gave Cassius a satisfied smile. "Everything is beginning to come together. Our numbers are growing. When we gain enough followers, we can topple Caesar. At the moment everyone is cautious, and most of the senators believe Caesar is godlike."

"It will not be easy to win others to our side and keep everything secret. Someone may talk," Cassius said with concern.

The two senators studied each other for a moment, and then Lapidus said, "Your guest tonight, Quadatus, is an ambitious man. I could read the greed in his eyes from my hiding place. I say line his palm with silver and he will be your man."

"Perhaps," Cassius agreed. "But he is a senator of little import."

"True. But he might be able to bring others of his kind to our side."

Cassius frowned, dipping his hands into rose water and drying them on a clean linen cloth. "He is a strutting peacock. I consider it an embarrassment to even be seen in his company. Did you hear him ask me to introduce him to Caesar? The man has gall, if nothing else."

Cassius watched Lapidus's eyes brighten with a cunning gleam. "If one needs a person to rut around in pig swill, one must seek a swine. I can assure you in this instance Quadatus will serve us well enough."

"How so?"

"He is the stepfather of Tribune Marcellus Valerius, architect to Caesar and friend to Marc Antony."

"From what I've heard of the tribune, he cares little for his stepfather. And who can blame him—Marcellus has an impressive bloodline; Quadatus has no bloodline at all—at least, none he can claim."

"Marc Antony will always be loyal to Caesar. Brutus? He is not yet ripe to pluck. But we might persuade him later on if enough of the others join us."

Cassius frowned and took a sip of wine, wiping his mouth on the back of his hand. "We must explore every avenue."

"If you want my opinion, I believe Quadatus will be loyal to whomever can profit him the most. If someone else stroked his ego, he would betray you without thought."

"And who would take his word against mine?"

For all his assurances, Lapidus still had doubts. "I see your point. Perhaps you are right."

"We must proceed cautiously until the time is right." Cassius smashed his fist into the palm of his hand. "Then we shall strike!"

Queen Cleopatra stood on the terrace of Caesar's villa overlooking the Tiber River. Although Caesar owned several homes, he'd told her this was his favorite. And it was large enough to accommodate her entourage. Not only that, it was conveniently located outside Rome, which was a filthy, overcrowded city.

Gazing down at the wild, untamed Tiber River, she thought how different it was from the Nile, which was so important to Egyptians, whose entire existence depended on its life-giving bounty.

Cleopatra heard a slight sound behind her and turned to smile when Caesar slid his arms around her waist, pulling her against his body.

"I have imagined you standing here so many times. I am content with you in my world."

She dropped her head back against his shoulder, the golden beads entwined in her ebony hair clinking together. "You speak pretty words, but they will not heal the hurt I experienced last night."

"That was my fault." He turned her to face him. "I should never have invited you to my house in Rome. I am sorry for the cutting remarks Calpurnia and Octavian made in your hearing. If I had intervened, it would only have made matters worse for you. You do understand that?"

"Your wife and nephew buried their knives deeply in my heart. I thought I was going to a feast in my honor, when in fact, I was the main course."

This proud young queen made Caesar burn as if he was on fire. She had taken her place in his heart and he had little room for anyone but her. "I never thought you could be hurt by cruel words. Have I not seen you take on a chamber filled with your squabbling governors and reduce them all to quivering flesh?"

"That was in my world—last night I was in yours."

"You brought out the protectiveness in me, and yet, I could do no more than accept their words—your hurt became mine. But you must understand Rome. Here, if you are not a true Roman, you are a barbarian. You can only be one or the other. Citizens of Rome are not allowed to marry barbarians."

Cleopatra gave him her most queenly stare.

"It's something I intend to change," Caesar assured her.

"You already have a wife."

"Before returning to Rome, I had not seen Calpurnia for seven years. While she is barren, you have already given me a son."

"I might not have accepted your invitation to come to Rome had I known your citizens would resent me. Perhaps they need to be reminded that it is my Egyptian grain that fills their soldiers' bellies as they march off to war."

He sighed. "It is a debt incurred by your father that you must honor."

She would like to have asked if Romans knew the meaning of honor, but she wisely kept silent. Caesar was honorable, and he was the only Roman who mattered to her. Instead she would talk about what was really bothering her. "Marc Antony told me he fears trouble for you among some of the senators."

"He has said as much to me. He is like a clucking hen seeing plots around every corner."

"He is your loyal friend and wants to protect you."

Caesar lifted her face, watching her eyes as he asked, "What do you think of my watchdog?"

"I think Antony is a handsome man, and he thinks so, too. He swaggers too much, and he drinks too much."

"Most women find him irresistible."

"I find him necessary to your safety—if he is as loyal as you claim he is, listen to his counsel."

Caesar dropped a kiss on her forehead. "You listen to his warnings. I have an appointment. I need to cool some of the hotheads in the Senate who debate me at every turn and hold on much too tightly to the purse strings."

Cleopatra wanted to hold on to him, but she could not. "Beware," she warned.

He smiled and turned away, his purple cape swirling out behind him. When his footsteps faded, she glanced back at the twisting river that meandered around a bend and disappeared in the distance.

"Apollodorus."

The Sicilian came to her, bowing low, as if he had expected her summons. "Most gracious majesty."

Her golden sandals were noiseless as she paced the marble floors. "Has Lord Ramtat's sister been comfortably settled in her chamber?"

"I have been told she has."

From her vantage point Cleopatra watched Caesar's departure. "I have not seen her since she was a child. I have heard she has grown into a beauty."

"She turns heads."

"Tell me everything you know about her."

He nodded. "She is brave and intelligent, but she does not always use good judgment."

Cleopatra listened as he related the incidents he had witnessed in the Bedouin camp, a slow smile growing on her face. "I believe I will want her to take instructions from my dancers. She could prove valuable to me, since she speaks Latin. We can put her in any great house, and she can report back to me."

"Lord Ramtat would not like his sister to be put in such a situation," Apollodorus warned.

"My brave General Ramtat has often risked his life for me. Why should I not expect his sister to do the same?"

"As always, it will be as you say."

"Find Marc Antony at once and ask him to attend me. I need ears and eyes so I can protect Caesar."

The sun had already lightened the eastern sky by the time Marc Antony came to Cleopatra. He stood near the door, waiting to be announced. He had been fascinated by her since first he saw her, and had become even more so with each subsequent meeting. To him, her beauty rivaled the sun, and her wit and intelligence were superior to those of any woman he knew. To his chagrin, Cleopatra had never looked at him as a man—she saw only Caesar.

"Antony," she said, blessing him with her most gracious smile. "Thank you for coming so promptly." She clapped her hands, and everyone scurried from the room with the exception of Apollodorus, who remained at her side.

"You have only to command me and I shall obey."

She smiled once more, her green eyes gazing into the depths of his brown ones searchingly. She motioned him to a cushion and had Apollodorus pour wine for him.

"I am told you are to be trusted. I am further informed that you are Caesar's loyal friend."

"Until my death."

"Listen while I tell you what I have in mind. Tell me if you think it is possible for me to put one of my spies among Caesar's enemies."

He look startled for a moment and then bent his head, listening to her speak. When her plan was laid before him, he nodded. "And this young woman, Lord Ramtat's sister, will she agree?"

"From what I know of her, she is daring and rash—and more than that, she speaks several languages. She is exactly the kind of woman we need. And her loyalty to me is unquestionable."

"It could possibly work."

His voice had the ring of sincerity, and Cleopatra saw something in his eyes she did not understand—was it admiration or trickery? "We will need someone you trust to be our go-between."

He stared at her for a long moment. "I know just the man to help us in this endeavor."

"Do you trust him?"

"I have every reason to trust him. I believe he would die in Caesar's service."

"Then tell him our plan as soon as possible." Cleopatra's heart was troubled as she stared at him. "I feel we are running out of time."

"Then we must strike quickly."

"Arrange it!"

CHAPTER FIFTEEN ✣

Marc Antony felt a pang of doubt as he watched Marcellus approach across the mosaic floor. There were so many tangled webs in Rome, so many false friends—dare he trust this young architect? Aye, he must. There was no one else for this task. Caesar's very life might depend on what was decided today.

Marcellus forcefully slapped his clutched fist against his shoulder in a salute. "Hail, Antony."

Antony motioned him forward. "Be seated. We must talk."

Marcellus dropped down on a cushioned stool and curiously regarded the great man. "I came as quickly as I could. Your messenger said it was urgent."

Antony wasted no time on pleasantries. "If you will recall when I arranged for you to be Lady Adhaniá's escort, I said you would owe me a favor."

Marcellus smiled. "Indeed, I do recall. Name what you will and it is yours."

"You indicated before that you don't trust Senator Quadatus."

Marcellus was taken by surprise. "My stepfather? I trust

him not at all. In fact, less than anyone I know." He sat forward, frowning. "Why?"

"I have been doing some investigating, following up on the message your mother gave you. I have reason to believe there is a growing plot against Caesar, and Senator Quadatus is somehow involved."

Marcellus thought for a moment as he digested that bit of information. "Alone, Quadatus is not powerful enough to reach Caesar—he would need the help of very powerful allies. I have heard he has, of late, become friendly with Cassius. If anything would make me suspicious of him, it would be such an odd pairing."

"Quadatus will be the weak link between Cassius and his conspirators, and if we concentrate on him, we might be able to break him."

Marcellus took a moment to look about, to make sure no one was near. "What do you suggest?"

"If this is to work, you will have to make friends with your stepfather. Would that be a problem for you?"

"I am willing to do anything you ask of me—but if I suddenly become friendly with him, he will be suspicious."

"We must contrive a way to draw him in without arousing his mistrust. Some days ago, Queen Cleopatra informed me she has a plan to protect Caesar. To put the plan in place, we need your help."

"You have only to tell me what you expect of me."

Antony stroked his chin. "This plan wobbles on the edge of a blade, and we could all be cut to bits if we fail."

Marcellus frowned. "Tell me the plan."

"Invite Senator Quadatus for an evening of entertainment," Antony said. Knowing how Marcellus felt about Lady Adhaniá, he decided not to tell him about her part in the plan just yet. "I will be at your home the night you entertain the man. And so will a certain little dancing girl who is connected with the queen's household—she speaks several languages, but Quadatus will not know this."

Marcellus searched the older man's face. "Do you recall that I told you my stepfather asked me to invite him to my home on a night when you would be there?"

"Aye. I do recall that."

"I thought it odd at the time. But if what you suspect is right, and he is spying for Cassius, I'm sure he will attend to further his own ambitions."

"I will leave it up to you to get him to your house."

Marcellus looked steadily at Antony. "You should know I detest the man, and I have reason to believe he might have had something to do with my father's death."

Antony leaned back thoughtfully, not in the least shocked by Marcellus's declaration—he had heard the same gossip himself. "All the more reason for you to bring him down. I believe if we can cast our net wide enough, we might catch a traitor or two."

Adhaniá had been with the queen's household for three weeks, and in all that time, she had not seen Cleopatra. She had been given a luxurious apartment, and Cleopatra had sent her own handmaiden with her greetings and a message that she wanted Adhaniá to practice with her dancers daily—which was a puzzlement since it was dancing that had caused her trouble in the first place.

In the cool of the evening Adhaniá walked in Caesar's garden, feeling homesick. Other than dancing each day, she spent the rest of her time in boredom. She wished for the hundredth time she could go back and change the past. Since she had sent the wretched Makana back to Egypt, she had no one to attend her, and no one to talk to in her loneliness.

If only she were allowed to visit with Heikki, she would

have him to talk to—but that was impossible in the queen's household. He had been posted as a guard outside her apartment, and there he must remain.

Adhaniá heard soft footsteps on the pathway and turned to see one of the queen's own handmaidens walking toward her. The queen only surrounded herself with beautiful people, and this handmaiden was no exception. Her skin was black as ebony, her eyes large and dark. Her hair fell to her hips, and she moved gracefully.

"Lady Adhaniá, Queen Cleopatra has asked that you come to her at once. If you will follow me, I will take you to her."

Adhaniá nodded, her hurried footsteps matching the handmaiden's. At last she would see the queen. Perhaps her majesty was angered that she'd come in place of Danaë. Hope grew in her heart—perhaps the queen wanted to send her back to Egypt.

Caesar's villa was very grand, with marble floors and walls. They passed through three fountain rooms before arriving at the queen's private apartment.

On entering the room, Adhaniá dropped to her knees and lowered her head, waiting to be noticed.

"Come forward," a sultry voice instructed her.

Adhaniá stood but did not raise her gaze to the queen's face. She decided she would guard every word she spoke so she would not shame her brother yet again.

"The last time I saw you, Adhaniá, you were quite young. I knew then you would grow into a beautiful woman, and you have."

Adhaniá could feel her face redden—how did one respond to a compliment from the queen of Egypt? "Thank you, majesty."

"Your brother was one of my best generals before he met Danaë and decided to retire from my service so he could spend his days with her. Is it not so?"

"I have heard that said, majesty."

"You must also know that you and I share a sister in Danaë."

"Yes, majesty." She stared at the floor. "And I know that Danaë saved your life."

"You may raise your head," Cleopatra said in amusement. "It is quite safe to look upon me."

Adhaniá was not prepared to see a small woman who was bedecked in yellow silk, with a simple golden crown on her dark head. She found it difficult to speak as she looked into amazing green eyes very much like Danaë's.

"You see something strange?" Cleopatra questioned.

"It's only . . . you look like Danaë."

"And so I should since we share the same father." She patted the stool beside her. "Come and sit with me. Talk to me—I would have news of Egypt."

Adhaniá knew the queen must have carriers going daily between Egypt and Rome. She could not think why she wanted to talk to her. "What would you like to know?"

"I am told you speak and write several languages. Which ones are those?"

Adhaniá tried to speak, cleared her throat and tried again. "Egyptian, Latin, Greek and, of course, Badarian."

"How good is your Latin?"

"I . . . am proficient." She didn't want to sound as if she was boasting, so she hurriedly explained, "I had a strict teacher who would rap my knuckles if I mispronounced a word."

Cleopatra leaned forward and examined the young girl carefully. "Tell me, Adhaniá, what would you be willing to do for your queen?"

Adhaniá was taken completely by surprise. "I would consider it my duty to do whatever you asked of me."

"I will tell you what I want, and we shall see if you are still so willing to do your duty."

"I am your loyal subject," she replied with sincerity.

Cleopatra clasped Adhaniá's chin, and the gold bracelets on her wrist jingled. "What I require of you may go against your mother's teachings." She smiled. "But I have heard you are a very daring young woman."

"The reason my brother sent me to Rome was to overcome my rash behavior. Ramtat is sorely displeased with me. But I would not have you displeased. Ask what you will of me and I will do it with a happy heart."

Cleopatra gazed at Apollodorus, who had just walked into the chamber. "You were right about her—she is delightful." Her eyes took on a faraway look. " 'Tis a pity I must use your innocence, Adhaniá."

Adhaniá swallowed hard, afraid of what the queen might want of her. "Am I allowed to ask what service I am to perform for you, majesty?"

Cleopatra's eyes took on a shrewd look. "I would see how well you dance."

Adhaniá's mouth flew open, and she stared at the queen. "I beg your pardon, majesty, but dancing is the very reason I was banished from Egypt."

Cleopatra's voice hardened. "But now you are in Rome, under my care. I desire you to dance and serve Egypt." Her voice softened. "Have I not instructed you to practice with my dancers?"

"Aye, majesty."

"I am told you do quite well, and I have need of your skills."

"I will do whatever you command."

"Then you shall dance."

Adhaniá now spent most of her days practicing new dances under the watchful eyes of Cleopatra's own dancers. The twelve women were the best Egypt had to offer, and their movements were like poetry, any one of them beautiful enough to draw and hold a man's attention.

After a few days of training, Adhaniá was asked by the head dancer to show the others some of the Bedouin dances. After Adhaniá had finished a traditional dance with many hip movements, the other dancers were delighted. But when she performed the Dance of Flames, they swarmed around her, begging to be taught the steps.

One morning when Adhaniá was practicing, her body aching from the rigorous movements, the doors were thrown open and Queen Cleopatra herself entered the chamber. Adhaniá immediately fell to her knees, along with the other dancers, and she waited for Cleopatra to speak.

"Adhaniá," the queen stated, touching her bowed head. "You may stand."

Adhaniá rose but kept her head lowered.

"Look at me."

She raised her head. "Most gracious majesty?"

"I am told you possess a unique talent. I will see you dance with the flaming torch."

Adhaniá nervously licked her lips. "Yes, majesty."

She feared she might miss a step or drop the torch. But to her relief she performed the intricate dance faultlessly, twirling the fiery torch, tossing it over her head and deftly catching it. When the dance ended, she looked at the queen, fearing she might be displeased.

"Leave us," Cleopatra said to the others, and she waited until everyone had scurried out of the room. "Come closer and sit on the stool near me. We will talk."

Adhaniá quickly complied. It was difficult to be in the presence of such greatness and not tremble. She clutched her hands in her lap and met the queen's eyes.

"Your dance is exciting and unusual, and one I would think no Roman has ever witnessed. Perhaps your steps are not as skilled as those of my dancers, but if you were in a room dancing with them, all eyes would eventually turn to you. You are beautiful . . . you do know that, do you not?"

"I have never given the matter much thought, majesty."

Cleopatra took Adhaniá's chin and raised her face. "You have the kind of beauty that will draw men's lust."

Adhaniá's mouth flew open in horror. "I promise you, majesty, I would never do such a thing!"

"Not even if I asked it of you?"

She quickly dropped her head in fear. "I . . . I will always obey you."

"Aye. I believe you will. You will wear more clothing than my dancers so you need not worry about modesty." She smiled thoughtfully. "I am ready to place you where you can be my ears and eyes. There are those who plot against Caesar, and I must know their plans."

Adhaniá was stunned and could think of no answer. "I will serve you faithfully," she said at last.

"I have a warning for you, and you must take it to heart. No one is to know that you understand Latin or any other language except the Bedouin tongue. That way you can use your ears in my service."

"Yes, majesty."

"I am sending you to the villa of Tribune Marcellus Valerius. I do not know how long you will remain there, but hear this: He will have my instructions, and you will do as he says, as long as it is in my service. There may be those who will attempt to trick you and find out what you know—do not let them! Can you do this for me?"

Adhaniá attempted to hide how deeply the queen's

words had affected her. She nervously moistened her lips as happiness burst through her. To see the tribune again had been her fervent hope. "I must confess to you, majesty, Tribune Valerius knows I speak Latin. He was at the Bedouin encampment with Apollodorus. And he was on the ship with me as far as Alexandria. He also escorted me to this villa."

"I am aware of this. Apollodorus has assured me that the Roman tribune will have a care for your safety. I am bestowing upon you as a gift, for your loyalty to me, a handmaiden. Layla has been trained by my personal handmaidens, and she will serve you well."

"Thank you, Majesty."

"You must do whatever is necessary to overhear the conversations of the guests at Tribune Valerius's villa. You will be told the names of the ones we suspect, but there may be others."

Adhaniá could do no more than nod.

"Even now my sewing women are making your costumes. You shall leave in two days' time."

"I shall be ready."

The queen smiled. "I regret that I must use you in this way. But Caesar's life may well depend on what you learn. I will protect him, no matter the cost."

With a swish of silk, Cleopatra departed, leaving Adhaniá stunned. For a long moment she pondered their conversation, trying to make sense of it. She did not quite comprehend how she could be of help to the queen by dancing.

But the thought of seeing Marcellus again sent her heart pounding.

Then she thought of Ramtat. He would certainly not approve of what the queen required of her. But had he not commanded her to obey the queen in all things? And so she would.

It was but a short time later, as Adhaniá was walking in the garden, staring at the river, that the handmaiden Cleopatra had given her arrived. Heikki was standing guard nearby.

Adhaniá thought Layla had the gentlest eyes she'd ever seen. She was not Egyptian; her hair was coppery red and her eyes a soft gray. She was shorter than Adhaniá, and over her light-colored skin she had a scattering of freckles across her nose. She was a lovely young woman and could not be much older than Adhaniá.

Layla bowed deeply. "It is my pleasure to serve you, mistress."

Adhaniá smiled. "Rise, Layla, and tell me about yourself."

Layla stood with her hands demurely clasped before her. "I have no memory of ever living anywhere but in the palace in Alexandria, where my mother was a kitchen slave. I aided her there when I was younger. Two years ago, I came to the attention of the queen's steward and was placed under the care of the queen's handmaidens. They trained me daily, but I have served no one until now."

"Do you speak any languages other than Egyptian?"

"I was trained in Latin, mistress, as are all handmaidens since the time Caesar came to Alexandria."

Adhaniá thought of the unsuitable Makana, who had made her life miserable until she was sent back to Egypt. "I welcome you, Layla. I need a friend as well as someone who can dress my hair and see that I am properly attired."

Layla smiled shyly. "I am happy to serve you, mistress."

Heikki stared at the young woman in awe: The sun slanted into the garden and fell upon her hair, streaking it with fire. He wished he could touch the glowing strands and look closer at her face. For the first time in Heikki's life, he found a female other than Adhaniá wondrous to look upon.

CHAPTER SIXTEEN ✗

Marcellus had been awakened in the early morning hours when a messenger from Caesar summoned him to the dictator's home in Rome. For over an hour he'd been pacing impatiently in the long chamber, awaiting Caesar's pleasure. General Rufio, head of Caesar's Sixth Legion, appeared at the door and bade Marcellus to follow him. On entering the chamber where Caesar was seated at a desk, Rufio took a stance behind him.

Caesar kept Marcellus waiting while he examined the scroll in front of him. At last he shoved it aside and nodded for Marcellus to be seated. Caesar studied the tribune for a long moment before he spoke. "I am pleased with the work you have done on my aqueduct. It would seem you've inherited your father's talent."

"I thank you, Caesar. But, in truth, I do not have half his gift."

"Antony thinks you do. He chose you to work on the aqueduct while I was out of the country—as you may know, I empowered him to speak with my voice, and I heartily approve of his choice."

"I am humbled by your praise," Marcellus said, in truth feeling uncomfortable with the great man's compliment.

Caesar thumbed through the parchment before him. "I have here your report on the project, and on the temple you built in Argines. Your work on the aqueduct was finished two months early and saved me coinage, and I have never seen a more beautiful temple outside of Egypt. How do you account for that?"

"Much of the credit for the aqueduct goes to a former Greek slave, Damianon, who carried out my instructions without fault."

"Aye, aye, I see it all here in the report. But it was you who found the graft, and you who recognized merit in the Greek and empowered him to work on your projects. Those are the qualities I look for in a true leader. I commend you on a job well done. But let us speak of the temple—that was your work and your design, was it not?"

Marcellus bowed his head. "The temple was my design. But I must insist on sharing your praise for the aqueduct with Damianon."

"Duly noted." Caesar rubbed the back of his neck wearily. "I knew your father well; he was an honorable man."

"I have always been proud to be his son."

Caesar watched Marcellus closely as he said, "The same cannot be said of your stepfather."

Marcellus thought carefully before answering. They lived in dangerous times—one carelessly spoken remark could have far-reaching and disastrous consequences. He was not sure if the dictator was testing his loyalty, but Marcellus decided to sidestep the issue. "Some would say that's the way of it."

"And you," Caesar pressed, "what would you say?"

"I would say my mother plainly finds something in the man to admire."

"You tell us nothing," General Rufio stated sourly.

Caesar smiled broadly and stood, preparing to leave. "Oh, I think he has told me what I wanted to know. I know exactly where Marcellus Valerius stands with regard to Senator Quadatus." He paused in the arched doorway and turned his hawkish gaze on Marcellus. "I am sorry, you will no longer be known as architect Tribune Valerius."

Marcellus was confused. He frowned, coming to his feet. "Have I displeased you in some way, Caesar?"

"The opposite is true. Marc Antony sings your praises, and I have seen for myself that you are a credit to your father's house. Henceforth, you shall bear the title of Master Architect of Rome."

In stunned silence, Marcellus stared after Caesar as the dictator walked away with his hands clasped behind him.

General Rufio clapped Marcellus on the back. "Congratulations! You have just become a member of an elite group—one of Caesar's trusted circle. I hope you stand ready to serve him well."

Marcellus frowned. "I am, and have always been, Caesar's man."

CHAPTER
SEVENTEEN ✗

Adhaniá was approached by the queen's head handmaiden. "Your costumes have been packed and sent on ahead to Tribune Valerius's villa. The litter awaits you."

Adhaniá felt her stomach tighten with fear. "Are there any last-minute instructions?" She had hoped the queen would change her mind and forsake the daring plan.

"Her majesty says only that she has put her faith in you, and she hopes it has not been misplaced."

Hardly comforting words, Adhaniá thought as she gathered her courage. "Tell her majesty I shall not disappoint her."

Heikki stood stiffly beside one of the two litters that would transport the dancers. When Adhaniá appeared with her handmaiden, he helped them into the litter and motioned the queen's bearers forward. When he had touched Layla's hand, he felt his heart skip a beat. Confusion registered in his mind; he was unsure what was happening to him.

★ ★ ★

Adhaniá felt numb. She turned to stare out through the thin curtains, hoping she would not fail the queen. Her mother would be scandalized if she knew Adhaniá was to dance for men with the hope of prying secrets from them. But scandal and Adhaniá were becoming close friends. She was committed to Cleopatra, and she would do what she was told.

When they reached the river, the litter was carried aboard a barge that would ferry them across the Tiber. There were many people onboard, so she and the other dancers remained in their litters.

On the other side, the bearers moved at a good pace through the streets of Rome. She had been curious about the city that held sway over most of the world. At first all she saw were a few huts and hovels where foul odors dominated the air. She covered her nose, noticing the raw sewage puddled in the street. But when they reached stone roadways, the stench lessened and the streets were wider.

Adhaniá noticed there were no great avenues or boulevards like the ones in Alexandria. Rome's streets were narrow and twisting and seemed to meander with little sense of purpose.

Her Alexandria had been planned and laid out by the Great Alexander himself—there seemed to have been no plan to the construction of Rome. The buildings were close together, and it was difficult to see where one ended and the other began, especially since they had all been made of the same material. She was surprised to see no carts or wheeled conveyances, so she pulled the curtain aside and spoke to Heikki.

"Do you know why there are only people on horseback and in litters?"

"Aye. I was told that wheeled transports are banned during the daylight hours because their noise is too great and the streets are not wide enough to accommodate them."

"But surely they must have need of wagons and carts, if only to haul produce and goods to the marketplaces."

"The transports come at night. I am told the noise often keeps people who live near the marketplaces awake."

She dropped the curtain back into place and leaned against the soft cushions. The Romans might have conquered most of their neighbors, and even countries across the great sea, but it seemed to Adhaniá that they had neglected their own cities, if Rome was any indication.

She could now see some fine columns and tall buildings in the distance, but they still could not compare with Alexandria. That great city was built of marble, while Rome was mostly brick and mortar.

When they reached what Heikki informed her was the Forum Trajan, she was more impressed. There were clusters of shops and well-appointed homes. From the huge columned temples located on the square, it was obvious that the Romans had copied Greek architecture. One tall statue seemed to stare across the forum, while smaller ones were clustered along the roadways.

"It seems," she said to Heikki, "Rome has taken the best of those they conquered and made it their own."

"I have heard that said." He laughed. "But you will never get a Roman to admit it."

"I do know Caesar takes credit for his new calendar when, in truth, he borrowed most of it from an Egyptian mathematician, Sosigenes. I believe Caesar calls the calendar the Julian year, after his own house."

Heikki was happy Adhaniá was no longer angry with him, and he was pleased to tell her what he had learned about Rome. "We are entering what is known as the patrician part of the city, where the wealthy estates are located. We will soon be nearing Tribune Valerius's villa."

Shortly thereafter, they passed beneath an ornate arched gateway with walls that enclosed the huge estate. There were tall trees and the aroma of many varieties of flowers. She could hear the musical sound of fountains splashing in the distance. The two wide, arched doors opened and three servants rushed forward to greet Adhaniá and the other dancers.

Dusk had fallen, layering the land in different shades of gold. In the shadows the color was muted, while the treetops were splashed with red and appeared to be on fire. The huge villa itself shimmered as if it were sprinkled with crushed gold.

Heikki offered his hand to Adhaniá and helped her stand. She was relieved Marcellus was not there to greet her because she would have been embarrassed to face him. It was cooler when she stepped into the atrium. The floors were cream and yellow mosaic, and the room was wide and spacious, with trees and flowers growing around an ornamental pool. The walls had wondrous mosaics portraying the Great Alexander and his victory at Issus. Although Alexander had been Greek, Adhaniá had always thought of him as an Egyptian hero. Was not his well-preserved body displayed in Alexandria for all to see?

Adhaniá was impressed with Marcellus's villa. It was the home of an architect, tastefully decorated, and subtly displaying its owner's wealth. An unexpected thrill went through her at the thought of being so near him.

She blushed, reminding herself that he would again see her dance. What would he think of her now?

The housekeeper spoke to the dancers, but Adhaniá shook her head, pretending not to understand anything she said. Already her deceit was put into play.

"I am sorry," Heikki said in his halting Latin, "the dancers do not understand your language. You may speak to them through me." So saying, Heikki turned to Adhaniá and pretended to relate the message to her. What he really said was a warning that Adhaniá must keep up her pretense even in front of the servants.

Adhaniá smiled and nodded.

Soon she would have to face the master of this house, and she longed for, and feared, that moment.

CHAPTER EIGHTEEN ⚸

The litter that carried Quadatus passed quickly down the nighttime streets, the torchbearers running to stay even, their flames casting flickering shadows along the roadway. Quadatus straightened his fine white toga and stared down at the golden rings he wore on three of his fingers.

He smiled smugly.

He had won!

For whatever reason, his stepson had changed his mind, and he had received the coveted invitation to dine at Marcellus's home. Quadatus had heard murmurings in the Senate earlier that Marc Antony himself would be present at the affair. If Quadatus played it smart, he might well advance his career. He would flatter Antony . . . play up to him. He had not felt this good in a very long time.

The litter bearers slowed their pace when they approached the grand home of his stepson. He thought of all the years he had coveted the Valerius holdings. He still did. Marcellus had powerful friends, but then, so did Quadatus, if he could count Cassius as his friend.

The huge grounds were ablaze in torchlight. With a satisfied smile, Quadatus walked up the wide steps, speaking to several important senators as he advanced. He was met by his stepson and smiled at him.

"It is a pleasure to be here, Marcellus."

Marcellus nodded. "It is a visit long overdue. I trust you left my mother in good health."

"She is in fine spirits."

It was all Marcellus could do to make polite conversation with the man he suspected of murdering his father. "Let us go in," he said, stepping aside so his guest could precede him.

As they entered the marble and mosaic chamber, Quadatus stared in awe at the high ceiling depicting scenes of Diana the Huntress. "Magnificent," he said, turning around so he could take in the entire mosaic. "I have always admired this room."

A frown creased Marcellus's forehead. "Have you? I am told my mother chose the scene when my father built this house for her."

Quadatus's mood darkened, and Marcellus was wise enough to change the subject. "I believe you will like the entertainment tonight. Queen Cleopatra herself furnished the dancers."

Quadatus's jaw dropped. "If that be the case, they must be fine dancers indeed."

Marcellus watched Quadatus's face glow as he recognized several important men among the guests. Couches had been placed beside low tables, and already refreshments were being served by silent servants. Marcellus felt distaste rise in his throat like bitter wine. Just having this man in his house was an abomination. He forced a smile when what he really wanted to do was toss Quadatus out the front door.

There was a shadow of suspicion lurking in Quadatus's dark eyes. "Tell me, Marcellus, what made you change your mind about inviting me to your gathering? You were so against it when last we spoke."

"You can thank my mother. I reconsidered for her sake. After I had time to think about it, I realized it meant a great deal to her. And Marc Antony mentioned to me that he would like to meet with you socially."

The older man's eyes were gleaming with delight, and he looked like a snake about to strike. "I'm grateful, although I had not expected such an honor."

"I do not honor you—I merely placate my mother."

"Will Caesar be here tonight?" his stepfather asked cunningly, ignoring Marcellus's remark.

"He was not invited," Marcellus practically snarled, attempting to restrain his temper. Before the evening was over Quadatus's ego would convince him that he had won his way into the inner circle on his own merit. But whatever else Quadatus might be, he was certainly no fool. Marcellus would be forced to play a game with the man if Quadatus was to be of use to Antony.

At the moment Quadatus was looking around, smiling. Marcellus directed him toward Antony, just as the two of them had planned beforehand.

Quadatus stiffened as Marc Antony walked toward them, and Marcullus noted that the man could hardly contain his glee. "Antony, may I present my stepfather, Senator Quadatus?"

No one could playact better than Antony when it suited him. Tonight Quadatus was the prey and Antony the hunter. "Good Quadatus, I have often seen you from a distance, but we have not met, have we?"

"Indeed, we have spoken on occasion but have not been formally introduced."

"Marcellus," Antony stated loudly, so his voice carried to

the others in the room, "I hope I am among the first to congratulate you on your promotion to Master Architect of Rome."

"What is this?" his stepfather asked. "I was not aware of such a promotion. Why was your mother not told?"

Marc Antony shook his head. "It has not been formally announced yet. Come, let us not dwell on anything but amusement tonight. Do what you must, Marcellus, to liven up this dull gathering. All the others have talked about is politics and war. I came to be entertained. I believe we have a surprise this evening."

"I'm afraid I've already spoiled the surprise," Marcellus said contritely. "I told Quadatus that the Queen of Egypt has sent her personal dancing girls to perform for us."

Antony placed his arm around Quadatus's shoulders and led him to the couch he was to occupy. "You will sit with me, and we shall discuss the merits of the dancers. You will be my honored guest tonight."

Quadatus beamed, and his hands shook as they approached a table laden with food and wine. There was wild fowl stuffed with mushrooms and spices, fish smothered with olives and garlic, honey and spice cakes, bowls of dates, nuts and ripe olives. "I have rarely seen such a feast," he remarked, practically licking his lips. "And it will be an honor for me to join you, Great Antony."

Marcellus couldn't help smiling at Antony's tactics. He would ply Quadatus with wine and try to pry secrets from the man under the guise of friendship. And no one could ferret out secrets better than Marc Antony.

Adhaniá's hands shook as Layla fastened a gold bracelet about her upper arm. Her black hair had been threaded with golden beads, and her hands and feet dyed with henna.

She stared into the beaten silver mirror, hardly recognizing herself. The two other dancers were to wear bright yellow costumes, but Adhaniá's was as white as a vestal virgin's gown.

Even though she had practiced dancing for weeks, she still feared she would make a mistake. Tonight she would face a room full of strangers, all except for Marcellus. Cleopatra had said to follow his instructions, so he must know she would be one of the dancers. Adhaniá focused on her image in the mirror after Layla outlined her eyes in kohl.

Turning away, she closed her eyes, gathering her courage. What she did tonight was for the queen, and she must not fail. She concentrated on duty and her love of Egypt, hoping to chase the shadows of fear from her mind.

Marcellus took a glass of wine and nursed it along, taking small sips and refusing refills. He wanted to keep a clear head tonight so he could watch Antony set a trap for his stepfather. Marcellus shared a couch with General Rufio, and they were near enough to overhear Antony and Quadatus's conversation.

Suddenly a lone flute player appeared, sinking to his knees, his haunting notes catching everyone's attention. Another musician entered, sank to his knees and strummed a lyre, stilling the roar of conversation. Two dancers bounded into the room, their transparent yellow costumes revealing more than they hid. Their hips moved invitingly, their arms weaving and reaching toward the men. Their exotic beauty was unquestionable, and all eyes were upon them. Many remarked on which one they thought was the more comely.

Marcellus heard Antony's voice raised above the din. "Trust Queen Cleopatra to bring such beauties with her from Egypt. I visited their dressing chamber earlier in hopes of speaking to them, but none of them understood one word of Latin. I am told they speak some barbaric Bedouin dialect." He smiled and poked Quadatus in the ribs with his elbow. "But they do not need to talk, do they? Have you ever seen prettier females?" He poured more wine into Quadatus's nearly empty chalice. "Admit it—they are incomparable."

Marcellus's attention was drawn back to the flautist when a drummer joined the group, his heavy drumbeats reverberating through the air.

Suddenly a new dancer leaped into the room, her movements so graceful she stunned those who watched her. Her white costume was not see-through like the dancers in yellow, and she was the only one who wore a veil.

The other dancers wove their hands upward and moved their hips, inching closer to the men, while the dancer in white circled the room, elegantly arching her neck.

Marcellus sat forward, aware that the other men had done the same. A lone flautist played a plaintive tune, and the drummer thrummed a slow beat. The dancer in white slowly swirled her hips, her dark eyes meeting every gaze except Marcellus's.

He felt a tightening in his chest. He had seen those eyes before. There could not be two women with the same melted-gold–colored eyes.

The dancers in yellow were flirtatious, arousing the men with their exotic movements, but Marcellus could not tear his gaze from the dancer in white, who clearly avoided looking at him. He observed the modest way she swayed her hips, as if to draw as little attention to herself as possible.

The drumbeat echoed in his head, and he took a sip of wine to cool the ache inside him. He felt her movements in every beat of his heart. He had dreamed of this woman for weeks . . . knew what it felt like to hold her in his arms, and he still carried her veil close to his heart.

It was Adhaniá!

His cheering guests were yelling praises for the scantily

GET UP TO
4 FREE BOOKS!

You can have the best romance delivered to your door for less than what you'd pay in a bookstore or online. Sign up for one of our book clubs today, and we'll send you **FREE* BOOKS** just for trying it out...**with no obligation to buy, ever!**

HISTORICAL ROMANCE BOOK CLUB

Travel from the Scottish Highlands to the American West, the decadent ballrooms of Regency England to Viking ships. Your shipments will include authors such as CONNIE MASON, CASSIE EDWARDS, LYNSAY SANDS, LEIGH GREENWOOD, and many, many more.

LOVE SPELL BOOK CLUB

Bring a little magic into your life with the romances of Love Spell—fun contemporaries, paranormals, time-travels, futuristics, and more. Your shipments will include authors such as KATIE MACALISTER, SUSAN GRANT, NINA BANGS, SANDRA HILL, and more.

As a book club member you also receive the following special benefits:

- **30% OFF all orders through our website & telecenter!**
  (Plus, you still get 1 book FREE for every 5 books you buy!)
- **Exclusive access to special discounts!**
- **Convenient home delivery and 10 days to return any books you don't want to keep.**

There is no minimum number of books to buy, and you may cancel membership at any time. See back to sign up!

YES! ☐

Sign me up for the **Historical Romance Book Club** and send my TWO FREE BOOKS! If I choose to stay in the club, I will pay only $8.50* each month, a savings of $5.48!

YES! ☐

Sign me up for the **Love Spell Book Club** and send my TWO FREE BOOKS! If I choose to stay in the club, I will pay only $8.50* each month, a savings of $5.48!

NAME: _____

ADDRESS: _____

_____

TELEPHONE: _____

E-MAIL: _____

☐ **I WANT TO PAY BY CREDIT CARD.**

☐   ☐   ☐

ACCOUNT #: _____

EXPIRATION DATE: _____

SIGNATURE: _____

Send this card along with $2.00 shipping & handling for each club you wish to join, to:

**Romance Book Clubs
1 Mechanic Street
Norwalk, CT 06850-3431**

Or fax (must include credit card information!) to: 610.995.9274. You can also sign up online at www.dorchesterpub.com.

*Plus $2.00 for shipping. Offer open to residents of the U.S. and Canada only. Canadian residents please call 1.800.481.9191 for pricing information.

If under 18, a parent or guardian must sign. Terms, prices and conditions subject to change. Subscription subject to acceptance. Dorchester Publishing reserves the right to reject any order or cancel any subscription.

dressed women who were reaching out to them with entic-
ing movements. Quadatus, in a drunken state, pulled one of
the women down beside him and tried to fondle her breasts.
But she merely smiled and pushed Quadatus away, dancing
out of his reach.

Marcellus's attention went back to Adhaniá, and he
watched her lower her veil. The sight of her face brought
gasps from his guests. Marcellus had only glimpsed that face
one night onboard a boat and only in shadow. He reached
deep for a clear breath as he stared at luscious lips that
parted seductively, twisting knots in his stomach and heating
his blood.

Adhaniá finally met his gaze, and he knew she was holding on to her courage by a thin thread.

Anger suddenly flared inside him because Adhaniá had
been chosen to join the entertainers. He intently examined
each woman's face and sudden realization hit him. With
new understanding, he stared into the amber eyes of
Cleopatra's spy.

Adhaniá!

The other dancers struck a pose and dropped to their
knees while Adhaniá whirled, dipped and turned—her costume fanning out gracefully around her, showing no more
skin than her shapely ankles.

The others in the chamber didn't notice the fear in Adhaniá's eyes, but Marcellus did. His guests seemed to be concentrating more on the dancers in yellow costumes, no
doubt because they showed more skin and were more daring
in their movements.

Fools, he thought, shaking his head in disgust—they were
missing the greatest treasure of all. Adhaniá brushed past
him, her gown touching his hand.

The music slowed, and the other dancers moved forward.
One came close to Marcellus, and it was obvious she was

flirting with him. But he paid her scant attention. He was staring into Adhaniá's tear-bright eyes.

He shook his head to clear it. She tugged at his heart, and he wanted to protect her from the other men's leering gazes.

But he was no better than they because he could not control the reaction of his body to her swiveling hips. She had entrapped him, and he could not look away.

CHAPTER NINETEEN 🦎

Adhaniá caught Marcellus's steady gaze, and she no longer felt like crying. Somehow he brought her a calmness that helped her get through the dance. He gave her courage when she needed it most.

Apollodorus had informed Adhaniá that the man of suspicion would be seated next to Marc Antony, and one of the dancers had described Antony to her. If she was supposed to make the man interested in her, she had failed miserably. His attention vacillated between each of the other girls, and he never seemed to focus on her.

To her relief, the dance had finally ended.

The men called out to the women, urging them closer. As they had been advised to do, the Egyptian dancers approached. Marc Antony motioned Adhaniá to him. She forced a smile and did as he bid.

"This little jewel is a favorite with Cleopatra," he informed Quadatus. "Is she not a rare beauty?"

The man's bleary red eyes swept over Adhaniá with interest. "She's wearing too many clothes," he said, grasping at her arm and pulling her toward him.

Marcellus's anger flared when he saw his stepfather's hands on Adhaniá. "This one is for me," Marcellus told Antony with a look that dared him to deny it.

Antony glared at his young friend, reminding him of his duty. "Nay. She will entertain me and Quadatus."

Marcellus took a steadying breath and realized his emotions were showing. "I beg pardon," he said stiffly, settling back on his couch with General Rufio.

Antony seated Adhaniá between himself and Quadatus. "Pretty little thing, but she does not speak a word of Latin. As I told you, she only speaks some babbling language of the Bedouin tribes in the Egyptian desert."

Quadatus ran his hand down Adhaniá's arm, and she showed no outer sign of the revulsion she felt.

"Would it be possible for this pretty dove to grace my bed tonight?"

Antony took Adhaniá's hand in his, giving her a guarded look. "Not this one. I am told the other two are trained in the ways of pleasing a man, but as I said, this one is Queen Cleopatra's favorite, and her purity is her trademark. To go too far with her is to die."

Quadatus pulled her back into his arms, reluctant to let her go. His mouth touched her neck, and he was panting when he whispered in her ear so no one else could hear, "You do not understand my words, little beauty, but soon I will have money and power, and perhaps I can entice you to share it with me."

Adhaniá moved out of the senator's arms, forcing a smile. Her gaze locked with Antony's, and she gave a quick nod. Understanding flashed between the two of them, and Adhaniá knew she could trust him.

"As I said, Quadatus, this one is not for you. Not yet anyway."

Quadatus took another drink of wine, looking peevish

and sloshing some on his tunic. "Then let the others come to me. I want no queen's favorite. I have grown too accustomed to my head to lose it."

Antony nodded to Marcellus, and he stepped forward, taking Adhaniá's hand. "You will come with me."

She was aware that the other dancers were climbing on the couches, and she hid her face. "Where are you taking me?" she whispered.

"Away from this drunkenness." He was angry with Antony for allowing Quadatus to touch Adhaniá. "The stench of wine is too heavy in this room tonight. We will walk in the garden and breathe fresh air."

"But I should not leave. The queen—" She looked back toward the other women. "What should I do?"

Her innocent question went right to Marcellus's heart. "You should never have been allowed to become a part of this deception."

She was suddenly alert. "I do not know what you mean."

There was a bite to his tone. "It seems you are growing accustomed to dancing for men who lust after you."

She pulled back, jerking her hand free. "You have no right to say such things to me. I do not obey you, Roman. I serve my queen."

"Adhaniá, I didn't know you were to be one of the dancers. I don't like you being used in this way."

"Did no one tell you I was the spy? Did you not recognize me at first glance?"

"I did not. Not until I saw your eyes." When they stepped out into the garden, he clasped her shoulders and turned her to face him. "Do you know what danger you face?"

"There is nothing I can say to you." She moved away from him. "I believe I should return to the others."

His mood was dark. "Did you want that pawing drunk to touch you?"

She rubbed her hand over her throat. "I want to wash every part of my body where that man touched. I did not like his hands on me."

"And I don't want him to touch you again."

She gazed up at the crescent moon, wishing more than ever that she was safely back in Egypt. Drawing a deep breath, she said, "I will do as my queen commands."

"You are not the one to drag secrets from a man. You are too innocent in the ways of the world. I don't know why you were chosen."

A shadow passed over the moon, giving her courage to speak because he could not see her clearly. "I was chosen because I can speak Latin and the others cannot. The house of Tausrat has always been in the service of the royal family. I will do as I am bid."

He touched her hair because he could not help himself, and the exotic scent she always wore invaded his senses. "I want you to keep your innocence."

"It isn't your choice."

He moved closer to her. "If I could have one wish, it would be that you could remain with me tonight." He drew her closer, his mouth very near hers. "But only fools wish for the impossible."

Adhaniá trembled at the thought of lying with him, having him hold and touch her. More than anything she wanted to lay her head on his shoulder and have him keep her safe. "We both know that cannot be."

He raised her head, bringing her closer to him, his mouth briefly brushing against hers, and he felt her quiver. With this exceptional beauty in his arms, Marcellus had no mind of his own. He craved what he could not have—he wanted to touch her and make her his. He felt her melt against him when his mouth brushed across her lashes, gently moving back to her mouth. "You know you want to stay with me."

His wine-scented breath touched her mouth and she went weak. Adhaniá reminded herself that she was there for a reason, and she must not fail in her duty. "You grow too bold, Roman," she told him, hoping he did not hear the tremor in her voice, for indeed she did want to stay with him. "My dance was not for you, nor are my favors. You forget we are united in a common cause."

Behind them a man cleared his throat, and Marcellus released Adhaniá and turned to see a tall man dressed in Egyptian fashion.

It was Apollodorus.

Marcellus straightened, looking into dark, menacing eyes.

"I am here to take her back to the queen." The Sicilian held out his hand to Adhaniá. "You must come with me now. Her glorious majesty will be expecting you."

With a mixture of relief and a sudden pang of disappointment, Adhaniá stepped away from Marcellus and turned to the Sicilian. "I am ready, Apollodorus."

"Your queen has chosen an innocent to toss to the wolves," Marcellus stated with anger.

"Egypt's affairs are not dictated by you, Roman."

Marcellus watched Apollodorus lead Adhaniá across the garden toward a side door. He was angry, and he would tell Antony just what he thought of the plan he'd hatched with the Egyptian queen.

"Wait," Adhaniá said, pulling away from Apollodorus and hurrying back to Marcellus. "Senator Quadatus whispered something in my ear that might be of interest to you." She shuddered. "He said he would soon come into wealth and power, and that I might want to share it with him."

Marcellus frowned. "Then he discovered you speak our language."

"Nay. He said he knew I could not understand his words."

Marcellus watched her walk away beside the tall Sicilian. He'd had no faith in the plan, but it seemed it was beginning to work.

He felt sick inside—Adhaniá had already proved useful. They would use her again.

For reasons Quadatus did not understand, he was being solicited by two different factions of powerful men. Marc Antony was the more powerful of the two, but Cassius had his own merits. Quadatus smiled to himself, deciding to play the game from both ends—his loyalty would go with whichever side offered him the most. For the moment the dancing girl in his arms was smiling at him, her skin smelled of some exotic spice and his head was reeling.

Marcellus had returned, and he clapped his hands. "The entertainment is at an end. Leave us, ladies."

There were moans of disappointment, and some of the men begged Marcellus to let the women stay. But he refused to relent.

"Did you invite me here only to have my greatest wish snatched away?" Antony asked, still playing his part.

"Maybe I just wanted to whet your appetite," Marcellus replied with bared teeth.

"Do not let the fun end now," his stepfather said, slurring his words. "It is yet hours before the sun rises."

Marcellus felt revolted by his mother's husband, but his voice was smooth when he said, "Queen Cleopatra herself told me I could have use of her dancers any time I wanted. If you would like, I will ask the queen if you can invite the Egyptian dancers to one of your gatherings." Marcellus watched Quadatus carefully, noting the eagerness on the man's face. "Would that please you, Stepfather?"

"I may be drunk, but the one thing I am not is a fool. Why would the queen of Egypt do such a favor for me?"

"She wouldn't. She would do it for me."

"And the reason . . ."

"Rome has not taken the queen to its heart. The truth of the matter is that she is trying to woo our senators. Her reasoning is if more people see and understand Egyptian customs, they might be more willing to accept her."

Antony smiled at Marcellus, sending him a silent message of approval. "I couldn't have said it better myself."

Quadatus nodded. "I find that sound reasoning. If I were to have a banquet, say a week from now, would it be possible to have the dancers perform for me? I have been thinking of the little dancer in white—she is hard to forget. I would like to have her perform for my guests."

"What do you think, Antony—could you ask the queen for a favor?" Marcellus queried, his anger smoldering just below the surface.

Antony smothered a laugh, thinking Marcellus was a quick thinker. "I shall speak to her myself on your stepfather's behalf. I believe she may well agree."

Quadatus's eyes gleamed with expectation as he took another drink of wine, sloshing more on his already stained toga. "This is excellent wine."

"It's from my own vineyards," Marcellus said, staring at Antony over the drunkard's head. "I'll send you a case."

Quadatus's eyes gleamed even more. His stepson had entertained him gloriously tonight, and one of the most influential men in Rome had befriended him. He glanced around the room at other important senators, men in Caesar's camp. He had no notion what Marcellus and Antony wanted of him, but he would enjoy their favor until he found out.

"Hail, Marcellus," he said, slurring his words.

General Rufio cried, "Hail Marcellus's wine!"

CHAPTER TWENTY ✣

For two days a heavy mist hung low over the land, shrouding the countryside in its grip, testing Marcellus's patience. He'd had no word from Antony, and he waited for some word from his stepfather. He found the whispering innuendos and plots against Caesar troubling.

When the message finally came from Quadatus, it was late in the afternoon. Marcellus immediately went to Antony, where a servant led him to a bath chamber. The room was huge, the walls exquisitely crafted with a mosaic of mounted Romans soldiers in full battle armor. Antony was stretched out on a table with a towel draped over his lower body while three scantily dressed females massaged him with fragrant oils.

"Quadatus is holding a banquet in three days' time and begs to be allowed to show off Queen Cleopatra's dancers."

Antony grinned, wrapped the towel around him and sat on the edge of the table. "Then we have him! After what he confided to your little Egyptian, we know he is plotting with Cassius and the others."

"That is not the way I see it. I've been thinking and have

come to the conclusion that Quadatus is too unimportant for us to waste time with."

Antony, with his usual astuteness, said, "Something is bothering you, and it's not Quadatus. Care to tell me what it is?" he asked, knowing full well it was the Egyptian beauty.

"Many things." He stood and began to pace. "For the most part, I don't like the notion of sacrificing an innocent young woman in a plan that may or may not uncover plots and stratagems."

Antony threw back his head and laughed. "I knew it would be difficult for you to accept Lady Adhaniá as our spy. Hence, I kept her identity a secret from you until the end." He slid off the table and reached for a tunic. "You already know the seriousness of these plots. And if Lady Adhaniá can help in any way, Queen Cleopatra will use her." His gaze hardened. "I can't have you acting like a jealous lover when she's performing her duty. Since Quadatus has already confided in her, she is the obvious one to pull secrets from him. However, I suspect your stepfather was too drunk to remember what he said to her the night of your banquet."

"She can't possibly know the danger to herself, should she be discovered as a spy. I have heard that Cassius openly opposes Queen Cleopatra, and he is gathering followers who are in opposition to anything Egyptian. I'd say that puts Adhaniá in danger."

"Come with me," Antony said, slipping his feet into a pair of sandals and strolling toward the door. "It's time I explained to you what we know, and it's time you met Queen Cleopatra."

The villa where Cleopatra resided was surrounded by fountains, gardens and a huge artificial lake. The wide beaten-brass doors swung open, and a man wearing the slave bracelet of the queen bowed low as Antony and Marcellus entered.

"Inform Queen Cleopatra I request an audience with her as soon as possible," Antony told the slave.

They were quickly ushered into a small informal chamber, and Antony began pacing the room.

"My hope," Marcellus stated, standing as if at attention, "is that we are not chasing shadows. Can you tell me why we are doing this?"

"Because," a woman said, coming through the high arched doorway in a swirl of green silk, "to do nothing is to admit defeat, and I refuse to hand over victory to those who would harm Caesar."

Marcellus knew he was in the presence of the queen of Egypt. She swept across the room, her movements like poetry. She wore a Grecian gown, and a simple gold circle crowned her dark head. She was smaller in stature than Marcellus had expected, but she was majestic, and no one would mistake her for an ordinary woman.

Antony bowed low, and Marcellus followed his lead.

"Rise." Her voice held the forcefulness of command. "Tell me all that has transpired."

The queen had a disarming manner that put one at ease, but Marcellus suspected such a persona was misleading—her unusual green eyes sparkled with life and intelligence. She had not outlived those who plotted against her without shrewdness and daring.

"Majesty," Antony said, catching her eye, "may I present Tribune Marcellus Valerius?"

The queen nodded the merest bit, then turned her attention back to Antony. "I hope you have come to tell me we can proceed with my plan."

"I believe so, majesty." Antony nodded to Marcellus. "But our friend here has doubts about using Lady Adhaniá as our spy."

Cleopatra swung around to Marcellus. "Why should that be?"

He met her gaze. "Quadatus is evil and debased, and she is innocent in the ways of the world."

"Adhaniá is a citizen of Egypt who speaks and writes four languages." There was a sharp edge to Cleopatra's voice. "She has been educated far beyond what most of your pale Roman women are taught. Adhaniá is brave and daring and has a striking beauty that has already tempted secrets out of this man." She drew in her breath, looking weary. "It is my opinion that she is well suited to her task. Neither of you are my subjects and are free to withdraw from this plan. However, Adhaniá *is* my subject, and she *will* do as she is told."

"I have sworn a vow to keep Caesar safe from harm," Antony stated with feeling. "I concur with your plan."

They both looked at Marcellus.

"I would gladly place myself between Caesar and harm, but I don't agree with using Lady Adhaniá as a common dancer," Marcellus stated, unwilling to place her in peril, even for Caesar's sake.

"I am left with little choice." Cleopatra seemed to crumple right before their eyes. "My priestesses have warned me of Caesar's impending death, and I, myself, have seen his demise in a vision. We must not delay, for only this morning my priest of Isis predicted the deed will occur on the Ides of Martius, by calculation of Caesar's new Julian calendar." She put a trembling hand to her forehead and brushed an ebony strand of hair from her face. "I am told Caesar will be drenched in blood on that day. Since we are approaching the month of Februarius, we have not much time to stop the men who plot his death." She opened her hands in a helpless gesture. "But I am a guest in your country and limited in what I can do."

The queen had the power to inspire, and Marcellus felt

some of her passion for protecting Caesar. "You can depend on me to aid you, majesty," he said earnestly. "But must we use this young woman?"

"Yes, I must." She turned the full power of her green eyes on Marcellus. "I believe you when you say you would readily put your life at risk to save Caesar, so I will tell you my new plan." She sat down on a stool, but the two men remained standing. "Tribune Valerius," she said with a winsome smile, "since you are so worried about Lady Adhaniá, I have decided to place her under your protection. Would that ease your concerns?"

Marcellus was so stunned he could think of no reply, so he merely bowed.

"None would protect her with the same steadfastness as Tribune Valerius," Antony answered for Marcellus.

Adhaniá was practicing her dance steps, and since the day was swelteringly hot, she was dressed only in a thin, pleated tunic that fell just above her knees, belted with a green linen belt. She wore her long ebony hair loose, and it fell down past her shoulders, almost to her waist.

"Pardon, mistress," one of Cleopatra's handmaidens said, bowing. "The queen has asked that I bring you to her at once."

"Will I have time to dress?"

"She said at once."

Adhaniá grabbed up her sari wrap and draped it about herself. Her bare feet were noiseless as she rushed across mosaic floors beside the servant.

On entering the chamber where the queen waited, she stopped short at the sight of Antony and Marcellus. Clutching her thin wrap about her, she went to her knees, her head bent. "Majesty."

"Rise up, Lady Adhaniá. We have matters to discuss."

Adhaniá was well aware that the two Romans were staring at her—if only she had been allowed time to change her robe, she would not feel at such a disadvantage.

"You know Marc Antony and Tribune Valerius. They are here because I have formed a new plan that will involve you."

"What must I do, majesty?"

"I called you here to let it be known that I am honoring Tribune Valerius for his loyalty to Caesar by bestowing a gift on him."

Adhaniá met Marcellus's gaze but said nothing as she waited for the queen to name the honor.

"That gift is you, Adhaniá."

The young woman's hand went to her throat, and she shook her head. "Majesty, surely—"

"Do not interrupt." The queen's eyes were fathomless pools of green. "The gift is, of course, a deception." Her voice softened. "Surely you must know I would never give you to another. But the Romans who hear of this will believe it is true—and I will make certain the word is spread."

Adhaniá dropped her head, wondering once again what Ramtat would do if he knew what was happening to her here in Rome. She wanted so badly to implore the queen to send her back to Egypt. She overcame her fear enough to answer the queen. "I will do as you command, majesty."

Marcellus had seen the horror revealed in Adhaniá's eyes, and he had watched as she conquered her fear. "May I ask what your majesty means by this gesture?" he inquired.

Cleopatra nodded. "If circumstances were not so dire, I would not implement such a reckless plan. But we have no time. We must strike quickly and with lethal force."

The queen looked at each person in the room and motioned for Adhaniá, who was still kneeling, to come and sit beside her. "I would not use you so if it were not important. I will give you a choice: You can withdraw and no one will cast blame on you, or you can do all I ask of you. Tell me, Lady Adhaniá, which will it be?"

Adhaniá swallowed a lump. "Your majesty knows I will do what is expected of me."

"Then you shall be taken to Tribune Valerius's home, where you will remain until this matter is concluded."

Feeling Marcellus's gaze on her, Adhaniá lowered her head and could do no more than nod.

"You will take your handmaiden, Layla, with you, and your man, Heikki, will be your guard, so you will feel safe. I dare not send any of my own guards lest it look suspicious." She turned her gaze to Marcellus. "I will expect you to see to her safety at all times. And beyond that, Caesar must not learn what we do to protect him. For if he knew, I fear he would object."

Marcellus was still stunned. "Of course, Lady Adhaniá's safety will be my foremost concern."

"Go. Make preparations to receive my little dancer on the morrow," Cleopatra told Marcellus. Then in a dismissive gesture, she waved her hand. "Leave me now. I have much to consider. Report to me anything that appears suspicious."

Both men had been dismissed, and they backed toward the door. As they left, Marcellus could hardly contain his anger. "Lady Adhaniá was frightened. Could you not see that?"

Antony nodded. "Perhaps. But she will do what is expected of her all the same. And so must we."

"It is easy for you and me to go along with this plan—we are sworn to protect Caesar—but she is an Egyptian who is being forced by her queen to participate in a dangerous venture to protect a Roman."

"Queen Cleopatra will use you, me and anyone else to save Caesar. Did you not see how much she loves him?"

Marcellus shook his head. "If Lady Adhaniá's brother were here, he would not allow this to happen to his sister."

Antony stared into the distance. "Most probably not. And I have little doubt when Lord Ramtat hears what has happened, he will be angry. But he is not here. It rests in your hands to see that no harm comes to her. Can I depend on you to do that?"

Marcellus's jaw tightened. "As I stated before, you can be sure Lady Adhaniá will be my first concern."

CHAPTER
TWENTY-ONE ✗

Once more Adhaniá was in Marcellus's home. Only this time, she would be staying until her appointed task was completed. She had little faith in her ability to charm secrets out of Senator Quadatus, and she feared the queen would be disappointed in her.

As Layla began unpacking the trunks with a deftness the wretch Makana had lacked, Adhaniá paced restlessly about the room, unconsciously examining each item. The chamber was beautifully arranged—the bed was huge, and there were three couches, plush and inviting. There were tables crafted of cedar from Lebanon, and a mural of Greek women holding hands and dancing. Through a wide doorway she saw a garden she had yet to explore.

She wandered into the private water closet and was amazed at the grandeur: A fountain, carved with five sea nymphs, spilled water into the huge bath.

Returning to the bedchamber, Adhaniá spoke to Layla, "I believe I shall rest now. Should I fall asleep, wake me within an hour."

Layla nodded, placing a bowl of fruit and cheese on one

of the low tables. "Heikki is just outside your door, mistress, so you can rest in peace. No one will get past him. But should you need either of us, you have only to call, and we will hear."

Adhaniá watched Layla withdraw into the connecting chamber before she eased her weary body onto the bed and lay back, burrowing deeply into the softness of the cushions. Unbidden, thoughts of Marcellus swamped her mind. He fascinated her, and he made her quake with longing.

She closed her eyes, thinking Marcellus personified many different men: first she had seen him in the robe of a Bedouin; then, on the boat to Alexandria, he'd worn a fine toga; now he would play her host. But the day she'd seen him in a Roman uniform was the day she realized the chasm that yawned between them, and that their worlds could never meet.

With that thought in mind, she rolled to her stomach and slowly drifted to sleep.

In the cool of the evening, Adhaniá stepped out into the garden, pausing to take in the sweet aroma that wafted through the air. She took the path that led toward an ornamental pool and stopped to sit on the edge, seeing fish dart among the blooming lily pads. Dipping her hand into the water, she watched the water ripple across the pond, thinking about Marcellus. She did not know how long she remained there lost in thought, but suddenly the reflection of a man shimmered in the water.

As if her thinking about him had conjured him up, Marcellus had appeared.

Turning to him, she noticed he wore a plain white toga that fell to his knees and sandals that laced up his muscled calves. Looking into his intense brown eyes caused color to creep up her cheeks. "I am glad to see you. I have been wanting to congratulate you on your promotion to master architect. You are very young to have reached such a high rank."

" 'Tis no more than a title."

"An exalted one. I am told there is only one master architect in all of Rome, and you are he."

He noticed her hair fell down her back like an ebony waterfall. "I like your hair this way," he said, sitting beside her.

Suddenly unable to look into his penetrating brown eyes, she lowered her head to stare at her clasped hands. "You must know it was not my choice to be here. I feel as if I was forced on you. I doubt my queen gave you much say in the matter either."

Marcellus smiled. "I could have refused. Unlike you, I answer only to Rome. Queen Cleopatra fears for Caesar's life, as do I. That's the only reason I agreed to help her."

His gaze went back to her hair, and he noticed the way the sun reflected off the ebony color, making it appear blue-black. "In truth," he said, dragging his gaze away from her, "I like having you in my home. Usually I come home to an empty house. Today, I knew you would be here."

"You have many slaves."

"Slaves, aye," he said, his dark eyes filled with mirth. "But what would I say that would be of interest to them, and with what wisdom would they answer?" His gaze fell on her dainty hand resting next to his leg. "I hope you have been made comfortable."

"Your housekeeper has tended me very well."

He could not resist taking her hand in his. Even though he spent most of his time under the sun, her skin was still darker than his, a honey-gold color. She did not pull her hand away when he measured it against his. "So small . . . and, yet, you may now hold the weight of Rome in your grasp."

"I beg you not to put too much importance on my

capabilities—it frightens me," she admitted, and when he released her hand, she was sorry she had spoken of her fear. "It's just that . . . I do not know what I can do to help my queen."

"How could you know?" There was an angry edge to his voice. "You have been drawn into an intrigue you cannot possibly understand."

"Is not one obligated to obey one's sovereign?"

"What would your brother say if he knew about the position in which you find yourself? I have no sister, but if I did, I would not want her involved in such a dangerous venture."

"I don't know," she answered honestly. "I believe Ramtat would be angry. But as he served the queen in many dangerous conflicts, so must I."

"You have been asked to sacrifice yourself for Caesar—not your queen."

"Caesar is a friend to my brother, but more than that, he is the father of our future king, the queen's child, Ptolemy Caesarion. It will be an honor if I can aid him in any way. But what am I to do?"

"None of us is sure of what we do. But make no mistake, there are those who would do Caesar harm if they got the chance."

"Your own stepfather."

"Aye. Him most of all. But he has not the power, or the courage, of Cassius and Lapidus, who are the greatest threats."

"I have a limited knowledge of Roman politics, so I do not understand why they would want to kill a man who has done so much for their country."

"There are those who are ambitious . . . jealous. Caesar did not get where he is without making enemies along the way."

She leaned forward so that her hair swirled across her face, and he reached out to brush it aside. His hand drifted through strands that rippled through his fingers. "You look so young in this simple white shift and with nothing lining your eyes." He drew his hand back. "I can hardly believe you are real and not a fantasy I conjured up in my dreams."

She frowned. "No man has ever said the things to me that you say. Is it the Roman way to compliment a woman you hardly know?"

He laughed so hard, he couldn't answer for a moment. "I don't believe it is solely a Roman trait, but rather that of any male overcome by the beauty of a woman such as yourself." His voice deepened. "Has no man told you how beautiful you are?"

"They would not dare for fear of my brother." She shook her head. "I lived a very different life at the Bedouin camp—no man would think to pay me such a compliment. And you should not either. My brother would not approve."

Marcellus hid his grin. "I beg your pardon. My heart ran away with my head. It was unwise for me to speak so."

She met his gaze, and her lips curved into a smile. She shook her head, sending her hair spilling across her shoulders. "May we speak of other matters?"

He moved away from her. "Of course. Tell me, are all the women in Egypt as well educated as you?"

"I know not. But I can tell you that my brother believes that a woman must reach her potential, whatever that might be. I found it easy to absorb other languages. Sometimes I find myself thinking in Greek. Since arriving in Rome, I often find myself thinking in Latin."

He arched his brow. "And what else did you find easy to learn?"

"You will think me vain if I tell you."

Dusk was falling, and the servants had just lit the torches in the garden. The flickering light fell on her face, and Marcellus felt a catch in his throat. "I promise I will not."

"I am well versed in mathematics, science and philosophy. My aunt taught me the healing herbs, and I like that subject very well. I have some skill with the sword and the bow, and my horsemanship is adequate."

He laughed and held up his hands in surrender. "No, you're not vain. Your horsemanship is more than just adequate, as is your skill with the bow. You did win the Golden Arrow. I believe if I had been your brother, I would have awarded it to you."

She ducked her head. "I brought shame upon Ramtat that day. If I could relive the past, I would not be here."

"And that would be a pity, else I might never have seen you again. I am glad you came to Rome."

Marcellus knelt in front of her and tilted her face. "You are the most extraordinary woman I have ever known. Yet you are so young."

As their eyes met, Adhaniá had to stop herself from leaning toward him. She savored the touch of his fingers against her skin. "This last year I became old enough to be considered a woman," she informed him.

His mouth moved closer to hers. "A very desirable woman." His head dipped, and as his mouth slowly brushed against hers, he heard her gasp.

Adhaniá's lips trembled and then parted beneath his. Of their own accord, her arms slid around his shoulders.

Marcellus had not meant for this to happen—she was under his protection—it was wrong. But he could not stop kissing her; her lips were so soft, and he was intoxicated by her nearness. He gripped her shoulders and brought her closer, crushing her breasts against him. He hungered, he trembled, but when his body swelled with need, he released her.

Standing, he quickly stepped away from her. "I ask your forgiveness. I am your host, not your ravisher."

She was trembling and turned from him to dip her fingers in the water while she studied his reflection behind her. "It will not happen again."

"Certainly not." He gave her a quick bow. "I will wish you a good evening, Lady Adhaniá."

Adhaniá watched him move away, wishing he would stay. There was something between them she did not understand, but it was strong and powerful. She remained at the pool until encroaching shadows crept across the garden. She marveled at how such a simple thing like the touching of lips could make her heart beat so fast.

Aching with an unfamiliar feeling, she abandoned the garden and sought her bedchamber.

The soft bed soothed her, and she found comfort just knowing Heikki was outside her door. Otherwise she might have given in to her urge to seek out Marcellus and beg him to press his mouth against hers once more.

It seemed the banishment from her homeland had done nothing to curb her wild spirit.

CHAPTER
TWENTY-TWO ✗

Adhaniá had been residing in Marcellus's home for five days, and so far she had not been asked to dance. Still she practiced each morning so she would be ready when the time came. In the afternoons she often walked in the garden in the hope that Marcellus would come to her there—but he did not.

On the sixth day, Adhaniá felt as if she was living on the edge of a volcano, waiting for something to happen. She paced the floor in boredom and then made a decision: She would go into the city and visit some of the shops. When she approached Heikki with her request, he was against it at first, but she finally convinced him when she promised to stay at his side and keep her face covered at all times.

The streets were crowded with humanity, and sometimes Heikki had to push people aside to make room for Adhaniá to walk. She stepped carefully across a broken stone in the street, noticing that many bricks were worn from years of passing feet.

She stopped at a shop and bought several ribbons in colors she'd never before seen. She bought a delicately woven shawl for her mother and a carved wooden horse for her nephew, Julian. She and Heikki ate a honey cake and sipped a cup of delicious nectar.

For the moment she had forgotten about her troubles and was actually enjoying herself. Heikki was more like the friend she had grown up with, and she had decided to forgive him all. It was midafternoon; the heat and the smell of unwashed bodies was overpowering.

"I am ready to leave," she told Heikki.

They were making their way across the Forum when a young boy ran up to Adhaniá, his grimy face streaked with tears, his small hands clutching at her robe.

"Please, mistress, help me! They will take me to the slave market if they catch me."

Adhaniá gazed across the street, where two Roman guards were dashing in and out of small shops, searching the face of every child they met. Without hesitation, she shoved the youngster behind her and gave Heikki a look that dared him to object. She felt the child trembling against her, and her heart went out to the frightened boy.

Without thinking, she spoke to the child in Latin. "Do not move," she warned him. "They are farther down the street, but remain hidden until they have gone around the corner."

As soon as the guards were out of sight, Adhaniá turned to the boy and went down on her knees. "Why were they after you?"

He lowered his tear-streaked face. "I was hungry. I took only a small loaf of bread."

His clothing was in tatters, and it was difficult to tell the color of his hair, which hung down his back in tangles. Hunger had ravaged his poor body: The skin was stretched tightly across his small face, and his eyes were bright sapphire blue. "Do you live nearby?" she asked.

He shook his head. "I live in the catacombs. I sneak into the caves at night because the older ones will send me back to the streets if they catch me." He took a step away from her. "I'll just be going now."

"Wait!" She reached out to him and drew him closer, attempting to wipe some of the grime from his face with her silken scarf. "You are to come with me. A child as young as you should not have to live in a cave and steal bread to eat."

Heikki looked on disapprovingly. "He can't come with us."

"I thank you, mistress, but no," the child said with feeling. "I'd rather live out my life in the catacombs than become a slave."

She smiled. "You would not be a slave. Perhaps I need a friend. I am a stranger in your city and yearn for someone to talk to."

He smiled, showing a missing tooth. "Excuse me, mistress, if I don't believe you—you're too pretty to be lonely."

"And you speak pretty words for a street urchin."

Heikki shook his head. "You can't trust these beggars—they will steal from you the first chance they get and disappear before you can catch them."

The child moved around Adhaniá and kicked Heikki in the knee, then dodged back behind her. "I would never take from a friend. And I am not a thief."

Heikki reached for him, but the child dodged his grasp. "You took a loaf of bread, little *thief*."

"Enough," Adhaniá said, holding up her hand. "We have to leave this place at once or the guards may return, searching for this child." She looked into the boy's shimmering blue eyes. "I leave it to you—decide if you come with me or go on your way."

He hesitated, undecided, and then nodded. "I guess I could go with you. I have nothing else to do today. But if I don't like it with you, or if you try to put a slave collar on me, I'll not stay."

Adhaniá took the grimy little hand in hers. "No one is going to put a slave collar on you." She gazed into eyes that had seen too much and looked years wiser than they should at his young age. She saw mistrust, and she saw hope. "Let us leave this place at once."

With Heikki looking on in disfavor and grumbling under his breath, the three of them hurried down the street.

When they reached the litter, Adhaniá pushed the child inside. When she was settled beside him, she inquired, "Can I trust you?"

"You can trust me until my debt to you is paid. Until then, I am yours to command, beautiful lady. After that, I make no promises."

The litter was lifted, and the bearers started off at a steady pace, with Heikki moving beside them. Adhaniá tried not to react to the stench that clung to the small child. "This is my promise to you: No one will hurt you, and you will never again have to scavenge for food."

The child looked doubtful but said nothing.

When they arrived at the villa, Heikki helped Adhaniá out of the litter while the boy dodged out the other side.

Before Adhaniá could decide what to do with the child, she saw Marcellus stalking toward her, his red cape fanning out behind him and his sandal boots crunching on the rock walkway.

"Heikki," Adhaniá said quickly, seeing Marcellus's angry expression, "take the boy to my chamber, see that he is bathed and have Layla find something suitable for him to wear."

Heikki, his arms loaded with her purchases, grumbled as he herded the urchin away. With dread in her heart, Adhaniá turned to Marcellus, whose dark eyes were narrowed with displeasure.

Before she could speak, he gripped her arm. "Where have you been?"

"I—"

"Who was that child?"

She resented his dictatorial tone. "I do not have to account to you for my actions, and the child is my . . . friend."

"I know exactly what happened—the little thief approached you with a tale of woe and drew you in. You should know there are hundreds of abandoned children on the streets of Rome. Their way of surviving is to steal what they can. Don't think kindness will change him."

"I trust this boy." She tilted her chin upward. "And no matter what you say, he stays with me."

"As you wish—you have been warned. You will find, much to your sorrow, that I am right about him."

She started to walk away, but he stepped in front of her. "When I came home and found you gone, and no one knew where you were, I thought someone—I feared—"

"Did you suspect I had run away?" She stepped around him with the intention of going to her chambers.

"No. I didn't think you had left of your own accord. But no matter," he said softly. "You have correspondence from Egypt. Apollodorus delivered it in person—he was displeased to find you were not here, and I could not tell him where you were. I must send word to him at once that you are safely home or the queen's guards will be swarming throughout Rome in search of you."

She halted in midstride. Once again she had caused a disturbance because of her actions. "I am sorry to have caused you trouble."

"I was concerned," he admitted.

"Is the message from my brother?"

"It bears Lord Ramtat's seal."

She took the parchment from him and moved to a bench beneath a shade tree. Breaking the seal, she began to read:

> *Dearest sister, we miss your laughter and your brightness in our lives. It seems so long ago that you left us. Be assured our mother is well. A mere two weeks after you left, we took up residence in Alexandria to await the birth of our child. I know you will share our joy when the baby is born. Take the best care of yourself, and I hope to bring you home soon.*

She glanced up at Marcellus, who seemed to be waiting patiently for her to finish reading. "Ramtat says he hopes to bring me home soon."

"That must please you."

She glanced back at the message:

> *You will remember we discussed the matter of your marriage before you left. I have been giving it much thought, and I have someone in mind for you. He is a highborn gentleman and a mere five years older than yourself. You will remember Lord Tayman's son, Barasat. There are still details to work out, and I have not yet approached him with the offer. We will speak of this when you return home. Your loving brother, Ramtat*

Adhaniá raised her head, her eyes swimming with tears. Marcellus took a step toward her. "Is something amiss?"

She stood and paced down the path and back again. "The worst! When will my brother stop punishing me? Have I not done enough penance for my crime?"

"Can I help in any way?"

"Not unless you can convince my brother that I do not want to marry someone he has chosen for me." Angrily, she brushed her tears away, furious with herself for allowing

Marcellus to see her cry. "It is of little matter at the moment. I do not even remember the man he speaks of. How can I wed a stranger?"

Marcellus felt Adhaniá slipping away from him. The wind had shifted, and he felt the spray from the fountain on his face. He had always known he would have to let her go—he could never have her for his wife since she was not a Roman. And he couldn't have her any other way. She was a highborn lady who could only be taken by a husband in a marriage bed.

He stared into eyes that were the color of wild honey. He could tell by the paleness of her skin she was feeling sick. He would move the earth to help her, but he could not gainsay her brother's command. Feeling as if a fist were tightening in his chest, he spoke to her of another matter. "I have received word from my stepfather. He has heard of the queen's gift to me and wonders if you could entertain at his banquet tomorrow night. I have already sent him word that you will attend."

He watched her eyes widen, and he knew she was frightened.

She clasped her hands. "This is what we have been waiting for."

"It is."

"So, it has begun," she said with regret in her voice. "I will make myself ready."

He stepped toward her. "If it were within my power to choose, I would not have you do this. My stepfather is vile, and you must be on your guard against him at all times. Don't trust anything he says, but keep your ears open in the service of your queen."

"Will not your mother be present?"

"Nay. She never attends his banquets. As before, there will be only men to watch you dance."

Adhaniá shuddered. "I will give them what they want,"

she said bitterly. Her hand shook when she untangled a lock of hair that had fallen across her cheek. Then she glanced up hopefully. "Will you be there?"

"I have not been invited, and if there are conspirators present, they would not speak freely in front of me. But have no fear, you will be well protected at all times."

She could feel his dark gaze, and it was as if he were silently asking her something. "I will only feel safe if Heikki is with me."

"Of course."

Adhaniá suddenly remembered his warmth when he had held her in his arms. Now he appeared detached and cold.

In truth Marcellus felt neither cold nor distant; he was trying to control his need for her. "Be on your guard against trickery when you meet Cassius. He will be suspicious of you at first. Know that he will test you in some way—be ready for anything."

"I will be vigilant."

He bowed. "Sleep well tonight, for tomorrow will be a long day for you."

When Adhaniá entered her chamber, her footsteps lagged with weariness. She was developing deep feelings for Marcellus, and he was the one man she must not love.

Love?

Surely not love.

She had little time to consider her feelings for him because her little urchin came running toward her with Layla chasing after him.

"She's not going to make me get in that bath," he cried, grabbing Adhaniá's waist and clinging to her when Layla tried to pry his fingers loose.

Adhaniá extracted herself from the boy's grip and sat

down on the couch, patting the cushion beside her. "Let us talk about this. You do need a bath—why do you refuse?"

"Do I have to tell you?"

"I wish you would. I am about to confide in you about a matter that could mean life or death for me."

His blue eyes grew big and round. "You are?"

"Aye."

"You tell me first," he said suspiciously.

"Very well. Though I cannot tell you all my reasons, I must have your promise to tell no one outside this room that I speak and understand Latin."

Adhaniá watched him shake his head in confusion. "How could that be a matter of life or death? You're in Rome; everybody speaks Latin."

"You must trust me—I am serious. Will you keep my secret?"

Adhaniá watched him consider as if he were trying to understand why she would want to hide her knowledge. "Even if someone threatens to tear out my tongue, I will keep your secret."

She smiled at his dramatics. "Now, will you tell me your name?"

He nodded slowly, almost reluctantly. "My name is part of my secret. It is Thalia, but I am called another name on the streets."

She frowned, not understanding. "Thalia is Greek for blooming, or perhaps . . . butterfly. Unless I am mistaken, it is a female name."

"That's the other part of my secret. I *am* female."

Astonished, Adhaniá examined the child's delicate features with a new understanding. "Why would you pass yourself off as a boy?"

" 'Tis not safe for a girl on the streets of Rome. I pretend to be a boy, and I've even learned to fight like one."

Adhaniá's heart melted as she took the frail hand in hers. "You no longer have to hide or fight—you are safe with me, Thalia." She stood, shoving the child toward Layla. "Go with her and she will see to your bath." Adhaniá raised her gaze to the handmaiden. "See that my little friend is fed and properly dressed. She will sleep on the couch in my chamber tonight."

When Thalia came to her later, Adhaniá would not have recognized her. The child's face had been scrubbed clean. Her features were dainty, her blue eyes almost too big for such a tiny face and she had a deep dimple in her chin. Most startling of all was the golden color of her hair.

"You are lovely, Thalia."

The child held out the skirt of her blue gown and spun around, smiling. "I never thought to wear anything so fine as this. Do I get to keep it?"

Adhaniá smiled, catching some of the little imp's laughter. "You may indeed keep it, and you shall have more besides. I give you my word that you will never again be forced to disguise who you are. Will you trust me?"

The child hesitated for a moment. "I have only had faith in one other person in my life, but I do believe you."

Adhaniá smiled and touched the pale cheek. "I will make certain you never have cause to distrust me."

"There is something I don't understand."

"And what might that be?"

"You are not Roman. You speak with an accent, and your skin is a different color . . . more golden."

"I am Egyptian, Thalia. Have you ever heard of Egypt?"

"I know the queen is here in Rome."

"And I am of her household."

Thalia thought about that and nodded.

★   ★   ★

Night shadows passed through Adhaniá's dreams, tugging at her mind. She tossed her head back and forth, caught in the agony of her nightmare. A sudden gust of wind caught at the tall pine tree outside her door—the branches scraped against the roof like hands grasping for her. She twisted and turned, trying to escape.

"Marcellus," she cried, "help me!" The sound of her own voice woke her, and she lay in the darkened room, taking deep breaths and trying to calm herself.

Thalia came to her from her bed on the couch. "Mistress, are you ill? Has something frightened you?"

"'Tis merely a bad dream. I am sorry I woke you. Go back to sleep."

Adhaniá knew she was playing a perilous game and danger walked beside her. It was a long time before she fell back to sleep.

In a chamber across the courtyard, Marcellus had fallen asleep with architectural plans for a library he was building spread on the bed around him. The oil lamp had burned low and then gone out completely, casting the room in darkness.

In his dream, he walked through the garden, his steps hurried. Adhaniá would be waiting for him near the fountain. When she saw him, she ran into his outstretched arms, and he held her close, his body shaking with need. His mouth found and devoured hers, and she whimpered with the same longing he was experiencing.

Adhaniá—his Adhaniá. He would die for the touch of her body pressed against his.

He would die if he dared touch her.

Marcellus's eyes snapped open, and he jerked up in bed, shaking with desire. What had Adhaniá done to him? He ached with a longing that gave him no peace. He had to stop thinking about her.

He slid off the bed and walked outside. Adhaniá's chamber was just across the garden from his, and he wanted to go to her. Instead, he went back inside, re-lit the lantern and gathered his drawings.

Work was the best balm for a troubled mind.

CHAPTER
TWENTY-THREE ⚮

Heikki offered his hand to Adhaniá and helped her into the litter, but not before she caught sight of another guard who wore a hooded cloak. At first she wondered who the man might be, and why he felt the need to hide his face. Then she smiled, knowing who he was. Queen Cleopatra must have sent Apollodorus to guard her.

Adhaniá was nervous about dancing for the Romans tonight, but having Apollodorus with her lessened her apprehension.

The streets were dark and strangely quiet in the part of the city they passed through. Adhaniá smiled at Layla, who seemed nervous and unsettled. Waving her hand airily, she told her, "Try not to worry; we are well guarded."

"I know we are, mistress. But everything is so strange in Rome. Do you not find it so?"

"I suppose I do. Tonight is certainly out of the ordinary for me," Adhaniá admitted, glancing at the flickering torchlight that cast strange patterns on the filmy curtains.

"Is it very difficult, the Dance of the Flames?"

"That is not my real concern; the dance is easy. I was just

thinking what my brother would say if he knew I was dancing before a roomful of Romans."

Layla nodded. "Mistress, may the gods give wings to your feet tonight."

"And calm my fears," Adhaniá muttered.

When they arrived at Senator Quadatus's home, torch-bearing servants led the way to the back door, and Adhaniá was shown to a chamber while her two guards stood just outside. After Layla had helped her into the costume, she pulled a cloak about her. Now that the moment had come, Adhaniá's hands shook, and her knees felt weak.

She feared there was little hope she would uncover anything these Romans were planning.

Adhaniá nervously stepped into a corridor with Heikki on one side of her and Layla on the other. She avoided looking at the hooded man who walked behind her—if it was Apollodorus, he would not want her to draw attention to him. When they passed a curtained area, Adhaniá caught a glimpse of a woman who ducked into the shadows so quickly, she wondered if she had only imagined it. For a moment she wondered if it had been Marcellus's mother.

Heikki looked at her worriedly and spoke to her in Bedouin, the only language they would speak tonight. "Are you ready for what you must do?"

"As much as I will ever be," she answered in the same language.

She felt the mosaic tile cool beneath her bare feet and shivered. "When I am ready to enter the room, you must be prepared to hand me the torch, Heikki."

"This I already know."

In her nervousness, she stumbled, and the cloaked man reached out to steady her. She lowered her head, going through the dance steps in her mind. Her entourage halted in the shadow of the arched doorway, and Adhaniá peered inside the large banquet chamber. Plump couches stood beside low tables abounding in food and wine flasks. The men were eating and drinking with relish, and she heard several lewd remarks that made her blush.

"Which are the men I am supposed to single out, Heikki?" she asked quickly.

He turned back to the hooded man, whispered to him, then nodded toward the fat man guzzling his wine. "Senator Quadatus you already know. The man beside him is Senator Cassius."

Cassius lifted a cluster of grapes and tore one off with his teeth. He watched Quadatus shuttle from couch to couch, strutting like a peacock. The man was baseborn, at least on his mother's side—he had only won a seat in the Senate by his prowess at war. Granted, Quadatus had fought well in battle, but his manners were crass. He had married well when he chose his second wife, who came from a patrician family of the highest rank. Most people, including Cassius, wondered why a highborn lady had married such a man. He detested Quadatus, but he needed someone unscrupulous, a man who would do anything to further his ambitions. That man was Quadatus.

His suspicions were running rampant, fed by the fact that Tribune Valerius had suddenly taken an interest in his stepfather. "Tell me—why is your stepson not here tonight?"

Quadatus dropped down on the couch and reached for a leg of mutton. "Rome, the city that rules the world, now turns its hands to building bridges and libraries. Thanks to Caesar, my stepson heads those projects and has no time for frivolity, or so he told me," Quadatus spat, envy poisoning his words.

"There is no doubt Marcellus is Caesar's man," Cassius reminded him.

"No doubt at all. Even Queen Cleopatra favors him. She gave him a valuable dancing girl as his slave."

"You implied Marc Antony has treated you like a personal friend."

"No one could have been more surprised than I." Quadatus took a bite of the meat and chewed for a moment. "I tell you, Antony likes me."

Danger signals stabbed in Cassius's brain. "He allowed you to call him 'Antony'?" Cassius knew Marc Antony well, and Quadatus was not the kind of man he would befriend unless he had a reason—Antony always had a reason for what he did. Sweat popped out on Cassius's forehead, and he swiped it away with a damp hand. If Antony was suspicious, or if he had heard any rumblings of plots against Caesar, he would strike before Cassius had time to flee Rome.

"When you were with them, did either of them try to question you—did Antony?"

"Nay. I would have known if they were setting a trap for me." Quadatus grinned and took another bite of the meat, the grease gathering in the crevices about his mouth. "You will see how my stepson honors me this very night. He has loaned me a gift beyond price."

"You have hinted as much. But the last time I noticed, Marcullus had no liking for you. How is it he has so readily embraced you now?"

"It's his mother's influence. I did right in choosing Sarania for my wife."

Cassius was not so sure. Time was against him and his fellow conspirators. Tonight he must decide whether to draw Quadatus into their circle. "Whatever can it be that has you so excited this evening?"

"My stepson loaned me his Egyptian dancer!"

"Ah, a dancer. They are plentiful as gnats on a goat—why should this one be exceptional?"

Quadatus licked his lips just thinking about her. "I'll wager you haven't seen the likes of this one. When you watch her dance, you will agree no other can compare with her."

Cassius's eyes narrowed. "Has it occurred to you that your stepson may have sent her as a spy? Can you trust anyone who is connected with Queen Cleopatra?"

"Bah, you worry like an old woman. She is just what she seems—a beautiful dancer who will entertain us for the night. I am told she is from some Bedouin tribe in Egypt and speaks only her native tongue."

"Let her dance so I can judge for myself. I trust no one who stands close to either Caesar or Marc Antony. And even less someone connected to that Egyptian harlot."

"I despise my stepson, but why do you mistrust his motives?"

"Fool, there must be a solid reason for Caesar to reward Marcellus, and that gives me reason to be suspicious."

"Marcellus was born into a family of privilege and wealth, and that, in itself, is reward enough," Quadatus said bitterly, "but I have no reason to mistrust him."

Adhaniá stood poised at the entrance as the flute players began to play, and the man playing the lyre plucked the strings. When the drummer joined the other musicians, it caught everyone's attention, and Adhaniá burst into the room with a torch in her hand.

As before, her costume was modest. But what the men didn't know was that her robes were layered, and she wore three, each more revealing than the last. The first costume was white with gold bells sewn about the hem that tinkled when she moved. The second was a soft blue, and the last was vermillion, reminding her of a desert sunset. It was the most revealing.

When she whirled about the room, the hues blended in flashes of color.

*   *   *

In the shadow of the corridor Marcellus stood beside Heikki, a gray linen hood hiding his features. "She did not recognize you," Heikki said, watching Adhaniá dance.

"Nor should she know. I am responsible for her safety and would not have allowed her to come into this house of vipers without my protection."

Heikki glared at the tribune with dislike. "It is I who am her protector, not you!"

"Whether you like it or not, your queen made me responsible for Lady Adhaniá. If you were her protector at the Bedouin camp, you did not do so well—did you?"

The two men glared at one another, and then Marcellus said, "We are not here to trade insults. We both want to keep Adhaniá safe."

Heikki nodded. "I don't like those men looking at her with lust. The Dance of the Flames is meant to heat a man's blood, and it has only begun. See how she tosses the torch and catches it without burning her hands—it is an art few dancers can master."

Heikki was right about the dance heating a man's blood. Marcellus watched her whirl while fluidly removing her outer costume and tossing it away. The pale blue gown shimmered against her skin and cupped her breasts, outlining them for all to see. He felt fire in his loins as Adhaniá swayed and enticed with her impassioned movements. He detested his stepfather's lascivious gaze, which swept across Adhaniá's soft curves.

Marcellus leaned against the wall and closed his eyes, trying to blank out the sight of her. How she tormented him!

He had been too long without a woman.

He did not want any woman but her.

Adhaniá heard the men react to her dance with shouts of encouragement. She tossed the flaming torch into the air, every line of her body elegantly poised. Without missing a beat, she caught the torch and swung it around her head. One hand gracefully arched upward while she twirled the torch with the other one. Her hips moved in time with the drumbeat, and she edged closer to the men seated on the couches. A thin pink veil covered the lower part of her face, showing only her eyes outlined with kohl. Her dark lashes swept across her golden eyes seductively. The golden beads that fell across her forehead made a tinkling sound with every move she made.

As the music built to a frenzy, she whirled, gracefully removing the blue costume and tossing it aside. Now she wore the thin vermillion costume. Her stomach was bare, and when she moved her hips, her long, shapely legs were visible through the filmy material. With the last haunting sound of the flute, she gave a great leap into the air, tossing the torch to the drummer, who aptly caught it and extinguished the flame.

Adhaniá immediately bowed and went to her knees, then touched her forehead to the floor.

The chamber was silent.

She raised her head, thinking the Romans had not enjoyed her dance because they showed no reaction, when, in truth, they were transfixed. One man stood up drunkenly, reeling in her direction, before Quadatus intercepted him.

"Sit down, Bartatus, she is not for you."

"Never have I seen such beauty of motion," the drunk said, reluctant to sit. "I want only to touch her. Surely she will not object to that."

Adhaniá cringed inside at other crude remarks, but she acted as if she understood nothing that was being said. She rose gracefully to her feet and flourished her hands in an elegant movement.

"Did I not say you would like her?" Quadatus gave Cassius a satisfied smirk. "These natives from Egypt dance like no other women."

"I would pay five hundred *danarii* for such a woman," Cassius admitted. "Were it possible to own her, I would give even more."

Quadatus was glad he had at last provided something for Cassius to admire. "I don't believe my stepson will part with her, since she was a gift from Queen Cleopatra."

"I would speak to her," Cassius said, his eyes narrowing. "Have her come to me."

"Come here, girl," Quadatus called to Adhaniá. "I would visit with you."

Adhaniá took a hesitating step, then shrugged her shoulders as if she had not understood what he wanted. Cassius's face was wet with sweat, and since he was a huge man, his toga had bunched at his waist in a wet circle. She saw lust in the depths of his eyes. She had been warned that she would be tested and must not be fooled.

Cassius motioned to her. "Come here, little dancer. I have some news to impart to you."

Cautiously, Adhaniá approached the couch where the two senators waited. She glanced from one to the other, deliberately acting as if she were confused.

"Look how her skin shimmers like gold, and her eyes are most unusual," Quadatus remarked. He touched Adhaniá's hair, and she forced herself to stand there emotionlessly. "This dancer is a jewel beyond price."

Heikki stepped forward with murder in his eyes, but Marcellus pulled him back. "I like it no less than you do," he said, wishing he could rip out his stepfather's throat. "This is why she is here. Adhaniá knows what she's doing."

"Do you understand me, woman?" Cassius asked, watching Adhaniá closely. "Do you speak Latin?"

She said something back to him in a language he did not understand.

"You can see," Quadatus said, "it is just as I told you—she speaks the gibberish of some desert tribe. Do you speak Egyptian, girl?" Quadatus asked, saying the few words he knew in Egyptian.

Again Adhaniá answered in the Bedouin dialect.

There was a satisfied smile on Heikki's face, and he leaned back and whispered to Marcellus, "She just told your stepfather he has the manners of a swine, and she said Senator Cassius smells of camel dung."

Marcellus was not amused. He wanted to take her away from this house. He pulled his hood forward and leaned against the wall, ready to rescue Adhaniá if one of the men went too far.

Cassius stared at the dancer for a long moment, then reached out and seized her arm. "I believe she understands everything we say." He drew her closer to him so he could watch her face. "I have just heard the saddest bit of news," he said, touching her shoulder and dragging his finger across the arch of her neck. "'Tis tragic, really. Have you heard that Queen Cleopatra met her death today? I learned about it just before I arrived."

Adhaniá felt a stabbing pain in her heart, and she could not catch her breath. She felt tears gathering behind her eyes, but she neither allowed them to fall nor allowed her expression to change. She shrugged her shoulders, pretending indifference and even managed to look puzzled.

Cassius continued to watch her. After a long silence, he shook his head. "No one is that good an actress—she did not understand a word I said. A woman from Egypt such as she would wail and cry if she thought her queen was dead." He turned to Quadatus. "You do know the Egyptians look upon their queen as some kind of incarnate deity?"

Quadatus gripped her chin and stared into her eyes as if he could read the truth there. "She did not even blink when you told her about the death of her beloved queen. I am convinced she does not understand Latin. Elsewise, she would not be so calm."

"I believe you."

Quadatus looked amazed. "Did Queen Cleopatra really die?" He was unmindful that the girl had pulled away from him.

"Fool, I will tell you later." Cassius took Adhaniá's hand and led her to the couch. "Little dancer, you will sit beside me."

Adhaniá managed to maintain her puzzled expression, and Cassius laughed delightedly. "Can you imagine owning this beauty, who could never complain because she does not know the words."

"It's more than probable Marcellus has already enjoyed her," Quadatus grumbled. "I feel certain she shares his bed each night, for who could resist such a tempting morsel?" He touched her arched neck and allowed his hand to drift down and across her breast. "What I wouldn't give to take her to my bed."

Adhaniá wanted to strike the hateful man—she wanted to shove his hand away, but she merely smiled, reached for a grape and popped it into her mouth, the twisting movement taking her breast away from his hand.

Heikki could stand no more—he marched forward, glaring at the men. Grasping Adhaniá's hand and helping her to stand, he said in halting Latin, "She will leave now."

"It is yet early. Allow her to linger a little longer," Cassius said, gripping her arm.

Adhaniá brushed the fat senator's hand away and said to Heikki in Bedouin, "Get me away from here. I cannot abide their hands on me." To the men, she smiled sweetly, posed her hands together and bowed toward them.

"Do not worry," she heard Quadatus remark. "I will ask my stepson to send her to us another night."

Cassius sat forward, his gaze following the swaying hips of the beauty. "I want her to dance for me again. Arrange it for this same night next week."

Quadatus's eyes gleamed with triumph. Perhaps it was time to get his stepson out of the way once and for all. Then Sarania would inherit all of Marcellus's property, including the little dancing girl. "I shall see what I can do."

Adhaniá ran out of the room and down the corridor, not stopping until she was outside. Glancing around to see if anyone was nearby, she took a deep breath and fought against tears. Burying her face in her hands, she whispered to Heikki, "Tell me quickly—is the queen dead?"

He shook his head. "Nay, she is not."

Adhaniá's cape was draped across Marcellus's arm, and he gently placed it about her shoulders. "Your queen is not dead. It was merely Cassius's way of testing you. I know not how you endured the news as well as you did. Queen Cleopatra would be proud of you."

Adhaniá spun around to face Marcellus. "You! You are not Apollodorus."

"Shh," he cautioned quietly, reminding her that others might be watching. He placed his hand on her arm . . . his gaze soft, his hand gentle, almost caressing. "Did you think I would not be here with you? Would I allow such a jewel to go unguarded?"

"Take me home," she said, climbing into the litter beside Layla.

Marcellus drew the curtains. "I'm sorry you had to endure this humiliation tonight."

She felt her cheeks burn—Marcellus had witnessed the Dance of the Flames, and she wished he had not. She buried her face in the silken cushion and closed her eyes in shame. It was over, and she had heard nothing worthy of reporting to the queen.

But she knew in her heart she would be required to return the following week—how would she endure it?

CHAPTER
TWENTY-FOUR ✗

It was in the early morning hours just before dawn when the storm struck with such suddenness, it woke Adhaniá from an exhausted sleep. She hurried to the arched doorway to watch thunder and lightning chase each other across the night sky, illuminating the garden in bright flashes.

Adhaniá was now fully awake and realized there would be no more sleep for her tonight. She glanced at the couch where little Thalia slept peacefully, unaffected by the violent storm.

With her mind on what had happened earlier in the evening, she shuddered. It had been degrading when Senator Cassius stroked her with his disgusting touch. Disregarding the rain, she moved quietly out of her bedchamber so she would not awaken Thalia.

Adhaniá glanced longingly across the courtyard to a wide arched doorway—a servant had informed her when she'd first arrived that Marcellus's bedchamber was across the garden from hers. She was drawn to him in a way that kept her off balance. If only her mother were with her, Larania could explain the confusion and longing that battled inside her.

She yearned for the sight of Marcellus and the touch of his hand on hers. When she awoke each morning, he was her first thought, and when she sought her bed at night, her last thoughts were of him. Her attachment to Marcellus had nothing to do with his handsomeness. He was as honorable and as determined in his duty to Rome as she was to Egypt. She wanted to be with him every waking hour, but that was not possible. If Ramtat had already decided on a husband for her, and if he persisted in the match, she was bound by honor to marry whomever her brother had chosen. It was the Badari way.

A sudden gust of wind shredded scarlet blooms off lily plants near a fountain, scattering them across the stone walkway, reminding her of blood. Rain pelted down in heavy drops, and Adhaniá gathered her cloak about her with the intention of returning to her bedchamber. But she paused, straining her eyes against the darkness. A shadowy figure detached itself from the hedge at the far end of the garden. At first she thought it might be one of the servants, but when a flash of lightning played across the figure of a man, she watched him pull back into the shadows in an attempt to hide himself.

An intruder!

Adhaniá quickly ducked behind the fountain, waiting for the man to make his next move.

Should I cry out for help?

Who would hear above the noise of the storm?

When the trespasser finally did emerge from the darkness, she watched him inch forward, guessing his destination. He was heading straight for Marcullus's bedchamber. There was no time to seek help. If the intruder was going to be stopped, she would have to do it herself.

Her heart slammed against her chest when the man disappeared inside, and she ran across the garden with no thought of her own safety. When she stepped inside the darkened bedchamber, she waited for the next flash of lighting so she could locate the intruder.

Adhaniá gasped, and her blood turned to ice—lightning flashed across a shiny blade that was raised and ready to strike Marcellus while he slept. Without pausing to think, she rushed at the intruder, grabbed his arm, and a violent struggle ensued. She was determined to keep a firm grasp on the arm that held the dagger. With all her strength, she attempted to pull him away from Marcellus. Adhaniá was strong, but the intruder was stronger.

"No! You will not do this," she cried.

The man turned his fury on Adhaniá—the blade pierced the fleshy part of her arm, then she felt it slide toward her neck. Her arms trembled with the effort she was expending. She cried out when he held the point of the blade against her throat.

Suddenly she was free, and someone knocked her to the floor. In the darkness, she heard a scuffle, and then a piercing cry, and a body landed on the floor next to her.

"Marcellus!" she whimpered, jerking back when she felt someone touch her.

"It is I," he said, kneeling beside her and holding her against him. She couldn't seem to stop trembling even though she was safe in Marcellus's arms.

"Did he hurt you?" she asked, turning her face to his bare chest, feeling his arms tighten about her.

Marcellus scooped her into his arms and placed her on his bed, leaving her long enough to strike a flint to light a lantern. In the flickering light, he bent to the man lying face up with a dagger in his chest. Removing the dagger, he studied the man's face. "He's dead."

Adhaniá shivered from cold, from fear, but mostly from relief—Marcellus was safe! It could very well have been he lying dead instead of the intruder.

* * *

Marcellus threw his cape over Adhaniá, then turned to the servants who had apparently heard the commotion and burst into the bedchamber. "Take the body away," he ordered.

The servants worked quickly—two carried the body out of the chamber while another cleaned the blood off the floor.

Marcellus paced the chamber, his gaze falling on Adhaniá. When he saw that blood had soaked through his cape, he called out to a servant, "Bring healing ointment and bandages." He went down on his knees beside Adhaniá so he could examine the wound more closely.

He frowned. "Why didn't you tell me he stabbed you? The wound is deep. Are you in pain?"

"In truth, I hardly feel anything at all."

"You are pale," he said, taking the tray from a servant and sending him out of the room with a nod of his head.

Adhaniá winced as he cleaned the wound. She bit her lip to keep from crying out when he poured an herbal concoction over the wound. Her face whitened, and she shivered from cold as well as pain.

He bandaged her arm, and when he was satisfied the bleeding had stopped, he stood. "You will need to remove your wet clothing. You can pull my cape about you for modesty's sake, and then I want to know exactly why I found you in my bedchamber wrestling with a man who was bent on killing me."

"You must turn around," she said, sliding off the bed, her teeth chattering.

He poured her a glass of wine and kept his back to her while she undressed. "May I turn now?"

"I am covered."

He swung around to her and was suddenly struck by what she had done for him. She looked so small and helpless in the cape that pooled at the floor around her feet. "Drink this," he said, handing her the wine. He waited until she took a few sips and saw that she was still trembling.

Adhaniá was surprised when Marcellus scooped her into his arms and seated himself on the bed, holding her in his lap. "I am only trying to warm you while you tell me what happened," he assured her when she attempted to move out of his arms.

She had been so frightened, and now her wound had started throbbing and aching. "I was in the garden, and I saw someone sneaking in this direction."

She was so slight; he wondered at her strength. "What were you doing in the garden on such a night?"

"The storm woke me."

"And we all know you go charging into the fray." He smiled down at her. "So you came to save my life."

She turned her face up to his. "I didn't stop to think. My brother says that is one of my failings."

Marcellus held her close while new and deep emotions swamped him. "When I awoke and saw you struggling with that man, I feared for you." He lightly touched her cheek. "You spilled your blood for me."

"I would have done the same for anyone."

"If the man's thrust had been truer, you would have more than a wound." He felt a sharp ache, thinking how she had risked her life to save his. "Little Bedouin princess, you have attached yourself to my life and have done me only good."

She pulled back and looked at him. "Who was that man? Why did he want to harm you?"

"His name was Haridas. He once worked for me as a stonemason."

"But why did he sneak into your house when everyone was sleeping?"

Marcellus closed his eyes and pressed her against his chest. "I know who sent him. I do not yet know why."

She pulled away and looked into his eyes. "Who sent him?"

He lifted the wine goblet to her lips, insisting she take another sip. "An enemy of Rome," he said in anger, his thoughts on his stepfather. "A man who allies himself with Caesar's enemies."

"What will you do?"

He took a deep breath. "Bide my time. Watch and see what my stepfather will do next."

"Your step—"

He placed his finger over her mouth. "You are hurt, cold and weary from your struggle. Try not to think about what happened here tonight. Think only that I owe you my life." He pressed the wine to her lips once more and watched her take a deep drink.

She curled up in his arms, and he felt her sigh.

"You have brought me luck, little dancer."

All her pent-up emotions shook her, and she was overcome with weariness. She yawned, saying, "By Badari practice, when someone saves a life, he is responsible for that person's well-being until death."

He smiled down at her, knowing the wine was taking effect; her eyes had already drifted shut. "Then I place my life into your care, my dearest heart."

Marcellus knew the moment she fell asleep, for she went limp against him. He touched his lips to hers, but she did not respond. A feeling of possessiveness took hold of him—she was his, and he dared anyone to say otherwise. Adhaniá had danced her heart out tonight, not for her native Egypt but for Rome. Rome owed her a debt.

Standing, he threw a coverlet over her for protection before he stepped out into the rain. He wanted to hold her, and to go on holding her for the rest of his life. But now was not the time.

There was a small lantern burning when he entered her

bedchamber to lay her on the bed. Suddenly someone tackled him about the legs, taking him by surprise.

"Leave her alone," the golden-haired child demanded, clamping her arms around his legs and tugging. "Get out of this room!"

He reached down and lifted the child, placing her away from him. "Who are you?"

"I'm Thalia, and I'm not going to let you hurt her."

He smiled as realization hit him. "You can't be the grimy urchin Adhaniá brought home with her. I thought you were a lad."

She doubled her little fists and glowered at him. "Don't think because I'm a girl I can't stop you. And why is her arm bandaged? Did you hurt her? You better not have!"

She was small and ethereal, but she faced him unafraid in her defense of Adhaniá. Marcellus pulled a lightweight coverlet over Adhaniá. "Rest easy, little one—the man who inflicted the wound on your mistress no longer lives." His hand drifted across Adhaniá's cheek as if he could not help touching her. "I am the last person who would do her harm."

"Is she unconscious?" Thalia asked, deciding to trust him, and going to the bed to glance down at Adhaniá.

"She is but asleep." He stepped back, watching Adhaniá breathing. "Her injury came from her attempt to save me from an assassin." He smiled down at the small girl, whose eyes were filled with concern. "I'm sure Lady Adhaniá will explain everything to you when she awakes."

He turned and walked out into the rain, his anger soaring and vengeance burning in his heart.

Oh, yes, he knew who the villain was in this night's work, and Quadatus would pay with his life!

The child placed her hand on Adhaniá's forehead to make certain she was not feverish. She was relieved to find her skin cool to the touch. Adhaniá was the first person ever to be kind to her, and Thalia would protect her friend with her own life.

There had been something sweet in the master's eyes when he'd stared down at Adhaniá. She had seen naked hunger in his expression, but there was no evil intent in him. She was a child who had seen the sordid side of life on the streets, and she would recognize evil when she saw it.

Thalia was determined to remain beside Adhaniá all night. The lantern flickered and went out, and the storm moved away, allowing moonlight to chase the darkness from the corners of the room.

Thalia had already guessed that Adhaniá was involved in some kind of intrigue that was dangerous.

"I will watch over you," she whispered softly. "You will come to no harm now that I am here."

CHAPTER
TWENTY-FIVE ✗

Marcellus was in full uniform when he dismounted and ascended the steps two at a time. He didn't bother knocking, but thrust the door open to encounter a startled servant.

"Take me to your master," he said in a deadly calm voice, watching the servant bow and scurry down the corridor. "Leave me now," he said as the man stopped at the closed door of his stepfather's bedchamber.

Again without ceremony, Marcellus thrust the door open to find Quadatus still in bed, a glass of wine in his hand and a big-breasted slave curled up beside him. Marcellus looked at the man in distaste. To his way of thinking, to take a slave to bed was little different from rape, since the slave had no say in the matter.

"Send her away. Perhaps she will go from your bed to dressing my mother's hair."

The pathetic woman slid out of bed and gripped a robe about her, hastening past Marcellus.

Marcellus could tell by Quadatus's startled expression that he had not expected to see him alive. It was all Marcellus could do to keep from running the man through with his sword. He was now certain Quadatus had sent the stonemason to his house last night. But he would play this game to the end—Quadatus's end.

"You sent a message you wanted to see me, Stepfather, yet you look surprised."

"I . . . er . . . he . . . you came so promptly. You look fit."

Marcellus's eyelids lowered. "I never had a better night's sleep in my life."

Quadatus's face lost its color, but his words were dipped in malice, "You look splendid bedecked in all your finery."

"I am in a bit of a hurry. After last night there is work to be done."

Quadatus's face paled even more. "Last night?"

"Yes," Marcellus said, smiling to himself as he toyed with his stepfather. "The storm blew down one of the cypress trees at the front of the villa, and it must be replaced."

His stepfather looked relieved. "Oh, to be sure, to be sure."

Marcellus was a patient man—he would bide his time and strike when the moment was right. For now, he would stay with Antony's plan, though he had little faith in its success. "I must hurry, so tell me quickly why you sent for me."

Quadatus had recovered enough to think more clearly. "Cassius was so taken by your little dancer, I was wondering if she might perform for us again six days hence?"

Marcellus was silent for so long, Quadatus thought he would refuse.

"If you like," he said at last. "I am glad she pleases you."

"I thank you," Quadatus replied. "Will you join us for dinner this evening? Your mother would be glad for your company."

"I have a meeting with my stonemason tonight—you know, the Greek who replaced Haridas."

"Uh, I don't know the Greek of whom you speak."

"I suppose not." Without another word, Marcellus stalked out of the bedchamber, knowing if he remained much longer he would throttle his stepfather.

He frowned when his mother approached from the shadows of a deep alcove.

"Marcellus, I would speak to you." She gazed behind her to see if Quadatus was within hearing. "But not here. May I come to your house this afternoon?"

Marcellus wondered if his mother knew that her husband had sent an assassin to his house the night before. "We have nothing to say to one another."

"What I have to tell you is of some import." When she saw he wasn't going to relent, she touched his arm. "Please. There is something—" She heard Quadatus's footsteps and forced a smile. "A lovely broach I have been admiring. Would you not purchase it for me? What could the price of such a small item mean to you?"

Marcellus frowned, removing her hand from his arm. "Is that all I am to you, Mother, a source of silver?" With a cold stare, he moved away from her and out the door.

Sarania watched her son leave, her heart aching because he had looked at her with such contempt. She was desperate to talk to him, but it would be difficult, since Quadatus had her watched at all times.

"What was that about?" Quadatus asked, grabbing Sarania's arm and spinning her to face him.

" 'Twas nothing of import. I merely asked Marcellus for a few pieces of silver, and he refused." She tried to make light of it. "Do you not think it strange that he should refuse, since he always gives me whatever I ask for?"

Quadatus pressed his thumbs against the throbbing pulse at her throat and applied pressure. He smiled as he watched her face redden, and applied more pressure until her eyes bulged and blood ran from her nose. As if coming out of a trance, he shoved her away and watched her fall to her knees, gagging and trying to catch her breath.

"Do not think you can fool me, Sarania. If I ever discover you are plotting against me, you will regret it."

She managed to gain her feet, but her legs would barely hold her weight. "I know nothing of plots." Her voice came out in a painful whisper. "And as for my son," she said, wiping blood from her nose, "he hardly knows I'm alive."

"Oh, aye, your son. He places himself high so he can look down on us all." He gripped her chin and squeezed until he saw pain in her eyes, then he released her, his mouth thinning. "After tonight Marcellus will no longer be a thorn in my side. He will bother no one." He laughed audaciously. "You wonder why I tell you this?" His low-pitched laughter reminded her of a snake's hiss. "It's because there is nothing you can do to stop me."

"He is my son!" she cried, reaching out to him. "I will do anything you want—please spare him!"

He stared at her, frowning. "After tonight, you will have no son. He goes to meet with his stonemason, but he will not arrive there alive."

Sarania shook her head in disbelief, tears trailing down her cheeks. "Why do you take delight in telling me this?"

"For all the nights you lay cold in my arms—for all the days you avoided my touch. Marcellus is a difficult man to kill, as I discovered last night."

"You . . . you tried . . ."

"I did. But as you saw, he survived." He stared into space. "I wonder what happened there?" His mind snapped back to her. "But no matter—tonight will do just as well."

"I will fight you."

He shoved her so hard, she went sprawling across the floor. "You can do nothing to me. And know this: I will set guards to watch every door and window, so don't attempt to leave."

"But why kill him?"

"Maybe because he reminds me of his father—or because you care about him. Or perhaps it is because you, being his only living relative, would inherit a great deal of money . . . and a certain dancing girl I have taken a fancy to."

Trembling, Sarania watched Quadatus turn away and disappear back into his bedchamber. He was a madman bent on destroying Marcellus. Somehow she had to get a message to her son to warn him of the danger.

But how?

Weakly, she staggered to her feet and braced herself against the wall for a moment, then went to her own bedchamber. Closing the door, she leaned against it until she could catch her breath. Her personal servant, Durra, came to her with concern. "You are ill, mistress?"

Durra had been given to Sarania as a wedding present from her father the day she had wed her first husband, and she was the only person Sarania could trust in this house. "I am ill, frightened and helpless." She dropped heavily onto the bed, clutching her throat, which still throbbed with pain. "I need you to do something for me."

Durra nodded. "Anything, mistress."

"My son faces a grave danger." She placed trembling hands over eyes that were blinded by tears. "You must go to Marcellus's home and seek out the dancer and beg for her help. Quadatus has set guards on all the doors, so you will have to leave by the secret passage."

None except Sarania and Durra knew of the passageway that had been laid out by Marcellus's father when he'd built this house. Sarania had never used it, and she had never told Quadatus about its existence. The exit was cleverly hidden in the statue of Jupiter that stood near the rear garden gate.

Sarania motioned her servant closer and said in a whisper, "This is what you must do . . ."

Marcellus had ridden away early in the morning hours, and no one seemed to know when he would return.

Adhaniá tried not to think about the horror of the night before. Trembling, she moved toward the ornamental pool and sat on the edge, allowing her hand to drift through the water. She had a feeling she would soon be returning to the queen's quarters. A sudden ache grew in her heart. She did not want to leave Marcellus. More surprising still, the thought of returning to Egypt and never seeing him again stabbed at her heart.

She was so deep in thought, she did not hear Thalia enter the garden. The child sat down beside her and stared into the pool. Thalia was lovely with her golden hair flying about her head in riotous curls. The child had only been with her for a couple of days and already the little imp had captured her heart. Already Thalia was not quite as gaunt and thin as she had been when Adhaniá first came upon her. Her cheeks had a rosy glow, and she seemed happy. One thing was certain: when Adhaniá left Rome, she would be taking Thalia with her.

"How do you like your new sandals?" Adhaniá asked, noticing the girl was staring at her feet and wiggling her toes.

"They are very fine, although they pinch my feet a bit." Thalia glanced worriedly at Adhaniá's bandaged arm. "How is your wound this morning, mistress?"

"It's a little sore, but it does not bother me overmuch."

"He loves you, you know."

Adhaniá looked at Thalia in confusion, wondering what she could mean. "If you speak of Heikki, I know he does. There was a time when we were like brother and sister." She sighed. "But that all changed when we came to Rome."

"I wasn't speaking of your guard," the child stated with feeling. "I mean the master. I saw how he looked at you when he carried you to bed last night."

Adhaniá took in a deep breath and let it out slowly. "Nay, you are wrong. I believe he likes and respects me—but love, never."

Footsteps sounded on the graveled path, and Layla appeared, looking about until she located Adhaniá. "Mistress, there is a servant who wishes to speak to you. She says it is urgent."

"Was she sent by Queen Cleopatra?"

"She says not, mistress. But she will not say who sent her and insists on speaking to you about a grave matter."

"Don't see her," Thalia warned. The child had learned caution on the streets of Rome. "After what happened to the master last night, you must be careful. I feel trouble when it raises its head, and this woman will be trouble."

"Did she appear dangerous to you, Layla?"

"She is but an elderly servant, mistress. I saw no harm in her. But she did seem desperate about something."

"Bring her to me."

The woman wore a well-stitched white mantle fastened at her shoulder with a silver broach. Her hair was mostly gray, and she walked as if it was an effort.

"Mistress," she said, going down on her knees before Adhaniá, "thank you for seeing me. My poor mistress is in need, and only you can help her." She looked at the child and then at the servant, unsure if she should speak in front of them.

Adhaniá nodded at Layla and Thalia. "Leave us."

Both looked doubtful, but they withdrew, and Adhaniá reached down, helped the poor woman rise and seated her on the bench. "You look ill. Can I get you something?"

"Nay, mistress. I am merely distressed for my sweet mistress."

Adhaniá bent down beside her. "Why don't you tell me who your mistress is, and why she sent you?"

"My mistress is Tribune Valerius's mother. She bade me come to you on a grave matter." The servant looked doubtful for a moment. "You are the Egyptian dancer, are you not? I was told you could not speak Latin."

If someone had sent the woman to spy on her, she was already caught, so there was no reason to deny she knew Latin. "I am from Egypt, and as you see, I do speak your language. If you are a friend, I beg you tell no one I understand your language; if you are a foe, it is already too late."

"I am not your foe, mistress, and neither is Tribune Valerius's mother. She sent me to warn you that there is a plot to kill her son tonight."

Adhaniá stood, recalling the night before, when Marcellus was almost killed. "When? How?"

"My mistress bids me to tell you her son plans to go into the city tonight. If he leaves this house, he will not survive the night—he will be riding into a trap. Please believe this!"

Adhaniá began pacing. "I do believe you, for what mother would want to see her son come to harm?"

Durra met her gaze. "My mistress knows her son well, and she feared that if she told him about the planned attack, he would not believe her."

"Tell me what I should do," Adhaniá said.

Durra looked so relieved she grasped Adhaniá's hand, then, realizing she'd been too familiar, she pulled away. "Dear, gracious lady, my mistress begs you to keep him here." She looked embarrassed for a moment, and then said, "You are a dancer, so you must know many ways to entice a man. Surely you can make him want to stay with you tonight."

In truth, Adhaniá did not have the knowledge to entrap a man. She frowned, pacing to the fountain and back. "Is your mistress certain it will be tonight?"

"She is."

"If they do not succeed tonight, they will only try another time." She shook her head. "And another."

"Perhaps after tonight you could warn him about the intended assassination, and he can go after the offender, catching him off guard."

Although Adhaniá had already guessed Marcellus's stepfather was behind the plot, she did not say so. "Does Marcellus know who is sending the assassins?"

"He knows."

Adhaniá's mind was whirling, and she was frightened. "Inform Marcellus's mother that I shall do what I can to keep him safe tonight. But I am not sure he will stay for me."

The servant bowed. "All rests in your hands, mistress. My lady feels you are the only one who can save her son."

CHAPTER TWENTY-SIX ☙

Adhaniá stood stock-still. Panic stole her breath and welled inside her. Dropping her head in her hands, she blushed as she imagined what she must do to keep Marcellus with her until dawn.

It didn't matter what it took; she would humble herself, beg on her knees, anything to keep him from danger.

But what if he didn't want her?

She had no experience in offering herself to a man.

No matter the outcome, she must make herself ready. Marcellus might return at any time, and she had to go to him before he left again. Her footsteps felt heavy as she moved down the path to her bedchamber, where Layla and Thalia waited for her. Neither asked what the servant had wanted of her, although she could see they were both curious.

Kicking off her sandals, she moved toward the bath. "Layla, help me prepare for tonight. Lay out the sheer white costume."

"Mistress, will you dance tonight?"

"I believe I shall."

Adhaniá removed her clothing and descended the three

steps into the bath. A puzzled Layla poured oil of lotus into the water while Thalia sat on the edge, dangling her feet into the pool, tossing an apple into the air and artfully catching it.

Glancing at Layla and feeling bewildered and overwhelmed, Adhaniá said hesitantly, "I need . . . you must give me . . . instructions. Tell me what you know about seducing a man."

Layla stared at her as if she'd lost her mind. "Pardon, mistress?"

"What man?" Thalia asked suspiciously, finally asking the question that was plaguing both her and Layla. "What did that serving woman want of you? I told you not to trust her."

"Her warning was dire. She told me that if Marcullus keeps his appointment tonight, he will be set upon by assassins. To keep him with me until dawn, I must know how to please a man."

"Hit him over the head," Thalia suggested, taking a bite of the apple. "If he's unconscious, he can't go anywhere. If you are too squeamish to do it, I'll do it for you."

"Hush, child," Layla scolded. When Thalia started to object, Layla held up a hand to silence her. "What you suggest is grave indeed, mistress, especially for a woman of your innocence. Although there are those who think you are merely a dancer, you are a highborn lady of Egypt."

"What you say is true, but I must make sure Marcellus does not leave this house tonight. I will need to tempt him so he will want to remain with me all night."

"You may not know how you affect men, mistress. I have seen you dance and heard my queen say you are a natural temptress. Perhaps all you will need to do is dance for Tribune Valerius."

"Nay, Layla. You know in your heart I will need to go beyond dancing."

Layla glanced at Thalia, who was splashing her feet in the

water and pretending she was not listening to their conversation, when in truth she heard every word. "Since that may be the case, mistress, I will share with you what I know." She nodded at Thalia. "What I have to say is not for young ears."

Adhaniá smiled at the child. "Leave us."

"But I could help—I know how to trick people into doing what I want," Thalia said, setting her chin obstinately.

"Go now."

The girl drew her feet out of the water and stomped away, leaving Adhaniá frowning after her. Then she turned her attention to Layla. "Now tell me everything . . ."

Marcellus had just come from his bath, barefoot and wearing only his tunic. Tonight he was meeting the Greek, Damianon, whom he had wisely made his assistant. The man's work habits were beyond anything Marcellus had expected. When he had given the Greek his freedom, he'd thought the man might leave—but instead, Damianon had become indispensable. The meeting tonight was to discuss plans for a library Caesar wanted dedicated to the god Mars, from whom he believed he was descended.

"Will you wear armor tonight, master?" Planus asked, brushing the plume on Marcellus's helm.

Marcellus was thinking about Adhaniá—he had been all day. He had not properly thanked her for saving his life the night before and was considering walking across the garden to her chamber. After last night, his feelings had undergone a dramatic change. Try as he might, he could not get her out of his mind, and he did not trust himself near her.

Planus stood beside his master patiently waiting, holding the new breastplate. "Master?"

Marcellus's mind snapped back to the present. "Nay. I will wear—"

He was interrupted by a soft rap on the door and waited

for Planus to see who it was. When he heard Adhaniá's voice, he bade his manservant to admit her and to leave them alone.

Adhaniá stepped into the chamber with trepidation. If her mission failed, she would have to tell Marcellus about his mother's warning, and that could be just as hazardous as letting him go not knowing what to expect.

But now that she stood before him, his hair still damp from the bath and his tall form clad only in a tunic, she considered leaving because her mouth went dry. She wanted to reach out and twirl a wet strand of hair around her finger.

He noticed she was nervous and wanted to put her at ease. "Excuse my manner of dress," he apologized. "I have just come from my bath."

Her gaze flickered over him and her chest tightened. "I should not have come."

"Stay. I haven't properly thanked you for saving my life last night. And I wanted to inquire if your wound is healing."

Adhaniá shook her head, unable to breathe. He filled the room—he filled her heart.

She wanted to run.

She wanted to stay.

"There is no reason for you to thank me, and the wound hardly troubles me at all. I have come to you on a very different matter."

Marcellus smiled lazily down at her, and it was almost her undoing. He couldn't possibly know the power behind his smile, or perhaps he did.

"What can I do for you—name it and it is yours."

"You will think me vain and foolish if I tell you." She gathered her cloak about her. "I should leave." Everything Layla had so carefully explained to her went right out of her head.

"I never met a young woman with less vanity than you have, and nothing you do will seem foolish to me." He clasped his hands on both sides of her face and forced her to look into his eyes. "Tell me."

"It's just this new dance I have been practicing." The lie did not come easily to her lips.

But was this not for a noble cause?

"I would like your opinion and was wondering if you would let me show you the dance."

Folding his arms over his broad chest, he said, "Ordinarily I would be delighted to watch you dance. But it will have to wait until tomorrow," he said regretfully. "I have an appointment I must keep."

Adhaniá took a step toward him and gave him her most pleading smile—the one that had always worked on Heikki when she wanted her way about something. "It is but a short dance."

She watched his gaze darken and sweep across her face. Heat rose in her cheeks, and she wondered if she could go through with her plan. When his gaze fastened on her eyes, she saw barely concealed yearning and puzzlement. Adhaniá was sure he did not believe she was there to dance.

His resistance crumbled as he touched her hair, and his fingers drifted through the strands as if he could not stop himself. For the moment he was distracted, but could she hold his interest for an entire evening? Most probably Marcellus was drawn to women who were wiser in the ways of luring a man.

With her heart in her mouth, she touched his arm. "As I said . . .'tis but a short dance." Adhaniá was shaking inside. She wished she could remember what Layla had told her to do.

Unexpectedly he smiled and dropped down onto a couch, nodding. "You have my attention. Entertain me."

She tried to hide her shyness but was not completely successful because she could feel a blush climbing her face. "You understand the dance would be better if I had music?"

"I understand."

At the moment he was merely humoring her. She would need to put sensuality into her dance if she hoped to entice him. Slowly, she unfastened her cloak and tossed it aside. Marcellus deftly caught it and brought it against his face, closing his eyes. "Dance for me, little Egyptian." His voice thickened as he stared at her in a costume that revealed more than it hid. "Dance only for me."

Taking a stance with legs spread and her hands sweeping upward, she moved her hips in small circles, then reached toward him as if she was inviting him to join her. When she saw him staring at her breasts, she became bolder in her movements. He had asked her to dance for him alone, and that was just what she was doing.

She lost her embarrassment and thought only of him. She imagined his hands touching her, his mouth dominating hers. She moved closer to him, wetting her lips and tossing her hair so it swirled about her head like an ebony fan. Closer and closer she moved to him, swirling, twirling, using her body to entrap him. For in truth, she knew of no other way to make him want to stay with her. When she swept her right arm upward she felt the pain of her wound, but it did not deter her.

At first Marcellus smiled at Adhaniá's antics, wondering what she was doing. But when he noticed her costume was no more than a thin veil of fabric, and she wore nothing underneath, her wild, exotic beauty captured him and held him entranced. He swallowed tightly, angry with her—angry with himself. He knew he should turn away, but his eyes focused on the dark nipples that were visible beneath the sheer costume.

He could neither move nor speak.

Images flashed through his mind of her body wrapped around his, and he hardened with need. He wondered what it would feel like to have her beneath him, and he swelled painfully. Her golden skin shimmered in the soft, flickering light—her legs were long and beautifully shaped, and he imagined them locked about his waist. Her midriff was bare, and he wanted to press his lips against her navel.

If he could only clear his head, he would insist she leave immediately. But his mind was anything but clear. Realizing where this was leading him, he rose slowly.

Whether she was there by design or had innocently sought his advice on her dance, he had to stop her. "Adhaniá—" His voice was deep with feeling. "I believe you should cease. I have seen enough. You will not perform this dance for anyone—ever!"

Marcullus watched her eyes widen with alarm, and he wondered at the cause. "I don't know what you were thinking to come here like this. But never do it again." He grabbed up her cloak and covered her. "Never."

"But—"

Holding on to his sanity by only a thin thread, he grasped her shoulders and propelled her toward the door.

Swallowing, she quickly twisted her body toward him and threw her arms around his neck, pressing her mouth against his.

He was startled at first, then Marcullus shaped his mouth against hers. With an impatient growl, he jerked her against him, crushing her breasts against his hard chest, his hands moving to the curve of her waist, his mouth grinding against hers. She smelled of the desert, mysterious and exotic, intoxicating his senses. He had never craved a woman as he craved her.

He pulled back to look at Adhaniá and saw passion shining in her golden eyes. "Do you know what you are doing to me?" he demanded.

"I want to be with you."

He traced a finger across the swell of her breast and felt her deep intake of breath. "I don't think you know what the consequences will be if I continue."

"Oh, but I do."

He was undone. Bending, he kissed her swollen nipple through the thinness of her costume.

A sweetness built in the pit of Adhaniá's stomach and spread throughout her body.

He stepped back as reason returned. "I shall not be the one to rob you of your innocence. You should leave." Yet he still held her to him.

Adhaniá feigned a hurt expression. "You don't want me?"

His jaw hardened like granite. "More than you can possibly imagine. That's the very reason you must leave."

In desperation, she leaned toward him and gently blew against his lips. That simple act caused Marcellus to draw in a thick breath and emit an agonized groan.

He lifted her in his arms, taking care not to hurt her wounded arm. His mouth hovering just above hers, he could think of nothing but burying himself in her sweet warmth. "I am just a man, and you have pushed me too far." His voice deepened. "If you want to leave, say so now."

Adhaniá's voice came out in a breathy whisper, and a feeling of awareness cut through her like a knife. "I want to remain."

Marcellus's eyes drifted shut, and sweet yearning stabbed at him like a dagger while want and need poured though him like hot honey that had been heated by the desert sun.

"If you were mine to keep . . ."

"Tonight I am."

* * *

Adhaniá felt every breath Marcellus took and every move he made as he laid her on his bed and slid up the length of her body. He was fire, melting the very heart of her. She felt his hands tremble when they slid down her thighs.

"This is wrong," he admitted. "But I am not inclined to let you leave now."

With a cry, she drew his dark head down to her. "Pretend I am yours to keep, and you are mine."

She saw him swallow deeply.

"I will have you," he growled, as her silken hair sifted through his fingers. He adjusted his position so the swell of his body rested between her inviting thighs.

Marcellus knew how to touch her in places that made her catch her breath. His mouth moved along the column of her neck, and she arched her back, murmuring with pleasure as his mouth moved to the valley between her breasts.

Daringly, as if she were driven by an age-old instinct, she touched her tongue to his lips, and he grabbed her so swiftly it took her by surprise.

"Don't do that again." But even as he warned her, his gaze dropped to her lips, and he lowered his head. "You push me too far, little temptress."

Marcellus took her face in his hands, tilting it upward. "You are my torment, and perhaps my redemption."

He removed his tunic; beneath it he wore only a loincloth. Her gauze costume proved no problem for him to remove. Her teeth nibbled at his mouth, and he shook, trembling and groaning with need.

They were naked in each other's arms, and Adhaniá's virginal body was quaking.

Marcellus eased between her legs and lowered himself against her.

Adhaniá's eyes widened with surprise when he slid just inside her. Moaning his name, she closed her eyes.

He was more tender with her than he had ever been with a woman, always aware of the wound on her arm. And she could not know as he did—their mating was a moment of perfection. The gods had created her for him, and he would need her as long as he lived.

Marcellus buried himself deep in her warmth, watching her eyes widen. She tossed her head as he eased farther inside her.

Then she did something unexpected—she arched her lower body to meet his movements, and he thrust deep and hard, her warmth closing around him. He trembled with the effort to keep from giving her his entire length. Adhaniá had come to him pure—now she was pure no more—she was his.

When she whispered his name, his mouth closed over hers, and they were both lost to reason.

Adhaniá was swamped by many new emotions. Spasm after spasm shook her, and Marcellus tenderly held her in his arms. She groped for his hand, not knowing what was happening to her when he quaked and spilled his seed into her.

"Beloved," he whispered, breathing against her ear. "What's happening between us is not natural."

When she emerged from the beautiful fog he had created for her, she looked at him questioningly. "Not natural?"

"What I mean to say—" He seemed to grope for words. "It is that we are perfect for one another. You instinctively knew how to react to me, and I knew your body as if it was meant for me."

"I never want to leave you," she cried after her body had trembled once more.

He laid his face against her breasts and whispered, "But you will leave me."

She had experienced for the first time why a man was built differently from a woman. She ran her hand over his chest, the hair tickling her palm. Her fingers explored further—his arms were muscled. She laced her fingers with his and noticed how much longer they were than hers.

He lifted her hand and kissed each finger one at a time, and she thought she would melt.

"You hold me entranced," he told her. "Almost from our first meeting, I somehow knew our futures would intertwine."

"How can that be?"

"I know not. Call it fate."

She slid her body along his, glorying in the feel of him. "Perhaps it was fate," she said, tossing her head and gazing into his intense eyes. "I wish this night would never end."

Marcellus touched his mouth against her ear, and she shivered. "I have the same wish. But there will be an ending for us."

Her eyes widened. "As you said, fate brought us together, but what will tear us apart?"

"The dawning of the sun . . . your brother . . . Rome."

"Then let us make the most of what we have." She reached for him, and he took her in his arms, moaning her name.

For a long time, Marcellus held Adhaniá in his arms, and neither of them spoke. The lantern flickered and went out, and still he held her. When she turned to face him, he made love to her again, this time lingeringly, and with even more tenderness.

Even as Adhaniá's body reacted to his lovemaking, she rejoiced for another reason—she had kept him from danger. At one point, he left the bed and spoke to someone outside the door.

When he came back to her, she cuddled in his arms. "What was that about?"

"I sent poor Planus to tell the Greek I would be unable to meet with him tonight."

Adhaniá raised herself on her elbow and brushed his hair off his forehead. "I am glad you stayed with me."

He laughed and pulled her on top of him, his hand running across her back and hips. "I would die a thousand deaths to feel again what I felt with you tonight."

She laid her head against his chest, listening to the steady beat of his heart. "I do not think it would take such a sacrifice from you." She smiled, boldly allowing her hand to go lower, and she touched the swell of him.

Frantically, he took her again, and frantically, she gave herself to him.

Afterward, they held each other. "Tell me," he said, touching his mouth to her earlobe. "Why did you really come to me tonight?"

"There are more reasons than one—but I shall only tell you one." She dared not tell him the most important reason was to save his life. "I know I shall be leaving soon, and I did not want to go without having known your body."

It hurt her to say it.

It hurt him to hear it.

His body stilled. "Do you speak of returning to Queen Cleopatra?"

"We know her summons will not be long in coming."

He closed his eyes. "To let you go will be like tearing away my own flesh."

She sighed, turning her lips against his neck and feeling the pulse beat there. "Would that I never had to leave you."

He flipped her over onto her back, and this time he was not gentle as he drove into her body. She met his thrusts with her own, wishing this night would never end.

Adhaniá fell asleep in his arms, and night turned to dawn. She rose quietly from his bed and pulled on her robe, moving silently toward the garden. She paused to glance back at him and watched him sleep for a long moment. He had breathed life into her soul, he had given her joy and she had saved his life—at least for one more night.

CHAPTER
TWENTY-SEVEN 🦎

Marcellus opened his eyes, stretched and smiled while joy poured through his heart. He rolled to his side, expecting to see Adhaniá beside him. But she was not there.

His first inclination was to dress and go after her, to bring her back, but he reconsidered. If he saw her again, he'd want to take her back to bed, and that would not be wise. They both had a lot of thinking to do after last night.

Even now he wanted her.

He could never have enough of her. He felt guilty because she was probably sore today. He had taken her virginal body too many times.

"Sweet Adhaniá," he said, closing his eyes and inhaling the intoxicating scent of jasmine blossom that still lingered in the air. "You will soon belong to me alone."

He rolled to a sitting position, allowing his mind to dwell on what had happened between him and Adhaniá. She had satisfied a need in him no other woman had touched. He loved her in the deepest depths of his heart.

Standing up, he stared down at the rumpled bed where he had made love to the one woman for him. Glancing at the ceiling, he frowned. He would have trouble claiming her for his wife. But he would fight for her if he had to.

"Planus," he called, heading for the bath, though he was loath to wash the smell of Adhaniá from his skin, "lay out my armor."

He needed to see Antony at once.

The day was long and seemed to drag on forever for Adhaniá. Her body felt different, she felt more alive—and she ached to be in Marcellus's arms again.

Time was running out for them both, and last night was all they would ever have. Ramtat would never allow her to marry Marcellus. And even though he had bedded her, Marcellus might not want her as his wife.

What man would not take what was so willingly offered?

Adhaniá lingered near the ornamental pool, which had become her favorite place in Marcellus's garden. She had been told he'd ridden away early in the morning. And now she waited in hope that he would come to her tonight.

She lingered in the garden, refusing to eat. Both Layla and Thalia watched her with concern. Neither of them had asked about her night with Marcellus, and she had told them nothing. Her feelings for him were private, and she would keep them locked away in her heart.

By early afternoon Marcellus still had not returned, and Adhaniá worried that something might have happened to him. She tried not to think about the assassins who had been sent to kill him the night before. Surely they would not attack in daylight. Should she have told him about the plot before she'd left his bed?

Just as Adhaniá had decided to return to the house, she heard Layla talking to someone, and she frowned when she saw the servant who had come to her the day before. She tried to breathe but couldn't. Had the woman come to tell her Marcellus was dead?

"You failed to tell me your name yesterday," Adhaniá said, searching the woman's eyes. *Oh, please,* she thought, *do not bring me ill tidings.*

"I am called Durra, mistress. And I have come again at my mistress's bidding."

Adhaniá breathed easier. If Marcellus were dead, the woman would have told her right away. "You may inform your mistress, Durra, that her son did not leave the house last night. He is safe."

Durra bowed to Adhaniá. "My mistress asks me to thank you, and to tell you how grateful she is for your help." Durra bit her lip as if she were hesitant to go on. At last her earnest gaze met Adhaniá's. "My mistress seeks your help once more on a matter too important to delay. She begs you to meet with her and hear what she has to say."

"Can you not tell me?"

"My mistress said I could reveal this much to you: She has heard of a plot against Caesar's life."

There was sincerity in the woman's eyes, and Adhaniá believed her as she had the day before. "How can I be expected to stop this evil? Surely your mistress can find someone more able than I to carry the warning to Caesar."

"My mistress is being watched." The woman dabbed at tears that swamped her eyes. "She is risking her life to meet you. Please do not turn away from her."

Adhaniá felt as if a heavy hand had landed on her shoulders. "Where does she wish the meeting to take place?"

"By the fountain at Trajan Forum. It will have to be later this afternoon. She will tell you everything at that time."

"Why so late in the day? Is this some kind of trick?"

"Nay, oh, nay! My mistress is always under prying eyes.

The master has spies watching everything she does, and she fears him. I beseech you to help her!"

Adhaniá understood the woman's fear of Senator Quadatus. Just the thought of him filled her with dread. "I will find a way to slip out without being seen," she said, knowing if Heikki found out about the meeting, he would prevent her from going. "How shall I recognize your mistress?"

"She will linger near the large fountain. Look for a woman wearing a white-hooded cloak and this silver broach I have on."

"You may tell your mistress I will be there if I can get away."

It was late afternoon when Layla dressed Adhaniá in one of her own linen gowns and placed her own woolen cloak about her mistress's shoulders.

"I beg you to reconsider. I do not think it is wise for you to venture out alone on the streets of Rome, mistress. Do not forbid me to accompany you."

"She won't be alone," Thalia said. "She will be with me."

Adhaniá could not help smiling at the brash child. "Do not be concerned for me, Layla." She nodded at Thalia. "As you see, I have a capable guide." Momentarily, she felt fear, and wished she would have Heikki's strong sword arm at her side. "Should Tribune Valerius return, go to him at once and explain where I have gone and that I am meeting his mother at Trajan Forum."

Since the Forum was no great distance away, Adhaniá decided she could get away more easily if she did not call for the litter. Just as the sun was sinking low in the western sky, she and Thalia slipped out the open gate, hoping no one would notice them leaving.

The child was ever watchful for trouble, and since she

knew the city so well, she took Adhaniá by back streets and dank alleyways until the Forum was in sight.

Thalia pulled Adhaniá into the shadowed archway of a bakery, and then led her out the back door, explaining that it would confuse anyone who might be following them.

At last they entered the Forum plaza. Since it was so late, few people strolled about. Adhaniá noticed there were several temples around the square and a platform where the populace could gather to hear speeches. The woman at the vegetable market was packing away her produce for the day, and many shops were already closed.

"We should wait here against the wall until we locate the woman," Thalia suggested. "You will not want to draw attention to yourself."

Adhaniá nodded in agreement. Minutes passed with the slowness of hours as she searched for Marcellus's mother near the fountain.

"That must be her," she told Thalia, spotting a woman in a white cloak who was nervously surveying those about her.

When Adhaniá would have rushed forward, Thalia tugged her back into the shadows. "Mistress, there might be those who watch. Allow me to approach her first."

A short time later, Adhaniá was horrified when she watched the little scamp artfully dash around a flower cart and, without missing a step, snatch a cluster of bright yellow flowers. Then, as casually as if she were strolling for pleasure, Thalia sauntered away with her stolen bounty.

"Mistress," Thalia said, bowing graciously to the woman with the white cloak, "flowers to brighten your bedchamber?"

Sarania shook her head. "Nay. I have no need of flowers today." Her gaze swept across the faces of those who passed her. "Another day perhaps."

Thalia was persistent. "I believe you will want *these* flowers, mistress," she said, spying the silver broach. "My mistress has come to speak to you. Follow us into the alleyway, where it will be safer. Walk some distance behind us."

Sarania absently took the flowers. She licked her lips nervously and nodded, pulling her hood lower across her forehead, watching which way the child headed. When she saw Adhaniá, she moved in her direction.

Thalia led them down a shadowed alley that twisted and turned in such a way that Adhaniá was not sure she could find her way back.

At last, when they reached a cluster of vacant buildings, Thalia halted. "We should be away from prying eyes here."

Adhaniá waited for Marcellus's mother to approach. When Sarania pushed back her hood, Adhaniá understood why Marcellus was so handsome—his mother was a beautiful woman with smooth skin and the same luminous brown eyes as her son.

"I saw you the night you danced for my husband and his guests. Although we have not been properly introduced, I have come to trust you," Sarania said, glancing nervously behind her. "How can I ever thank you for saving Marcellus's life last night?"

Adhaniá wondered if the woman could guess what she had done to keep Marcellus with her. "There is no need to thank me. I would not want to see anything happen to Tribune Valerius."

"Once again I must infringe upon your time and ask for your help. There is nowhere else I can turn, and no one else I can trust."

"I am not yet certain I can trust you," Adhaniá remarked candidly. "You are married to a man who tried to have Tribune Valerius slain, yet you did warn me in time to save him."

Sarania's hand went to her throat, and she grew pale.

"There is more to the sad story than either you or my son can guess, but now is not the time to mention it."

"Tell me why you asked me here. Your servant said it had to do with Caesar."

Sarania looked crestfallen. "I wish I could have told my son . . . but he . . . Marcellus—" She shook her head. "He did not want to talk to me. And he would not believe anything I said." She held out her hand to Adhaniá. "You must believe me, or Caesar will be assassinated tomorrow morning!"

Adhaniá gasped. "Surely you are mistaken?"

"I wish I were. Take what I tell you as the truth. My husband, Cassius, Brutus and others will do the deed the moment Caesar reaches the Senate. Believe me—it is the truth. You must warn Marcellus and make him believe *you*."

Adhaniá heard voices and watched as a man walked toward them. He did not seem threatening until he was joined by two others. They were too far away to see clearly in the shadows of the alley.

"Let us turn our faces away," Marcellus's mother advised. "Let them pass us by, and I will tell you all I know."

Adhaniá's heart was beating with fear as she began to understand the danger involved in this secret meeting. She watched several other men join forces with the first three. Her gaze met Thalia's, and she saw the child edging farther back into the shadows.

"Nay—oh, nay!" Sarania cried. "They are my husband's guards! They must have followed me here!"

"Run," Adhaniá cried, pushing Thalia toward the gaping door of the vacant building. "Hide yourself until they leave—save yourself."

"I will stay with you," the girl protested, taking up a protective position beside Adhaniá.

"I order you to leave—hurry, they are almost upon us!

You are my only hope of rescue. I fear I have been betrayed by this woman."

Only at Adhaniá's pleading did Thalia melt into the shadows, where she lingered nearby so she could watch what happened.

With disappointment Adhaniá faced Sarania, whom she now believed had lured her to the Forum on false pretenses. "I was too quick to trust," she stated furiously. "How could you do this to—"

Now the men were almost upon them, and Sarania stepped protectively in front of Adhaniá. "I only stopped to ask this woman for directions. I am ready to return home with you now," she told the captain of Quadatus's guards. "She knows nothing about me, or who I am."

The leader was tall and broad, with thick lips that settled in a smirk. "Think you I do not know the dancer? I was told to take you both."

"Nay," Sarania said, dropping the flowers she was still clutching and pushing the man. "You will not take her. Run!" she commanded Adhaniá. "Save yourself!"

But they both knew it was impossible to escape. Two men forced Adhaniá's hands behind her back and bound them tightly, while another forced Sarania forward. Neither of the women protested because there was no one to come to their aid.

They were both led none too gently back down the alley toward the Forum. Adhaniá twisted to glance over her shoulder, glad the guards had not seen Thalia.

"Please let her go," Sarania pleaded. "She has done nothing wrong."

"Not another word from you!" a harsh voice warned.

Night shadows encroached, and shopkeepers were locking up. Sitting atop an ox cart was a menacing-looking man with a long scar down his cheek. He jumped down from the seat and opened the small door at the back of the cart. Adhaniá twisted, trying to escape when she realized they would be locking her inside.

"It'll go easier with you if you don't struggle," the scar-faced guard warned her.

Adhaniá twisted and turned, unwilling to give up so easily. The man doubled his fist and struck her hard across the jaw, and darkness closed in around her.

When Adhaniá slowly opened her eyes, she felt blinding pain. For a moment she wondered where she was, and why her jaw hurt.

With realization came panic.

She could tell by the swaying movements she was inside the ox cart. When she tried to sit up, it was too difficult because her wrists were bound behind her. At last, she managed to brace her shoulders against the cart, and it helped her to remain upright. She had no way of knowing how long she had been unconscious. She heard mounted guards riding on both sides of the cart.

She had to think, to plan. Inching her body toward the door, she kicked against it with all her strength, but it held fast. She would not be escaping in that direction.

Where could they be taking her?

She heard the sound of running water. It could be a stream, could be a river. Could be the Tiber River. Leaning back, she tried to think—there was something important she needed to remember.

Caesar!

Marcellus's mother had not betrayed her—she had been telling the truth, or the guards would not have taken her prisoner. She dreaded to think what it had cost the woman to meet her at the Forum. They were two women who loved the same man. Both of them now had information that would shake Rome to its very foundations, and neither of them was in a position to help Caesar.

Wearily she leaned back, her head swaying with the groaning of the ox cart. She would not abandon hope. She would wait and watch for the right moment to escape.

But even if she could escape, where would she go?

Despair settled heavily on her shoulders, and she was frightened. She thought of Marcellus and held his image in her mind, hoping it would help lessen her fear. It didn't.

The wheels bumped over the road, and Adhaniá tried to brace her back against the splintered wood. Caesar's life might depend on what she did tonight.

"Oh, Marcellus," she whispered, "I am so frightened. Please come and find me."

CHAPTER
TWENTY-EIGHT ✄

Antony sat behind his desk facing Marcellus. "I can see you have something on your mind—why don't you just say what it is?"

Marcellus lifted his brow. "So you can read minds."

"You are transparent at the moment, and you're making me dizzy, pacing the floor, sitting down and then getting up and pacing some more."

"I want permission to marry," Marcellus blurted out in agitation. "I want permission to marry Lady Adhaniá."

Antony frowned and shook his head. "Permission denied. You know the law; such a union is forbidden. You are a high-ranking Roman officer—Lady Adhaniá is Egyptian."

"She is from a prominent family, and a princess in her own right."

"Nonetheless, she's not Roman."

"You could intercede for me with Caesar. He will listen to you, and he has the power to overrule the law."

"Don't you think if it were possible to overturn the law without drawing the citizens' outcry, Caesar would already have married Queen Cleopatra and presented her to Rome as his wife? If Rome would have accepted the queen, Caesar would have divorced Calpurnia without guilt."

Marcellus was frustrated. "He could have married her according to Egyptian law while he was in Alexandria."

"Which would have caused him no end of trouble when he returned. The marriage would never have been recognized by Rome."

"I would prefer to marry Lady Adhaniá by Roman law so she will be legally tied to me. I want the right to protect her and take her out of the situation in which you and Queen Cleopatra have placed her."

"I will not put this before Caesar," Antony stated forcefully.

Marcellus stood and continued pacing. "I have sweated blood for Rome. I have done everything Caesar asked of me—I ask only this one thing in return."

"Nay. Speak of it no more."

"Then I shall follow Adhaniá to Egypt, give up my Roman citizenship and live in her country."

Antony looked startled. "Does she ask this of you?"

"She doesn't know I want to marry her." He drew in a ragged breath. "I don't even know if she wants to marry me. I do know Lord Ramtat is arranging a marriage for her. She is not happy about it, and neither am I."

"If that's the way of it, Caesar would never give his consent. He admires Lord Ramtat and looks on him with favor and respect."

"I will have her."

"Do you love her, or merely desire her? If it is only desire, take her to your bed. It would probably cause a scandal, and her brother would call for your head, but it might serve to put out the fire inside you."

"I intend to marry her."

Antony shook his head. "I know how you feel, but Rome

cannot lose its master architect to Egypt. Caesar will put a stop to any such plans."

"I wonder if you would be so ready to follow Roman laws if *you* loved an Egyptian and *you* were not allowed to marry her? Knowing your temperament, I believe you capable of turning your back on Rome's laws and following the object of your affection to Egypt."

"You see too much." Antony nodded. "There is an Egyptian woman I would risk everything to possess, but she is not mine and never shall be. You know of whom I speak."

"And you know how I feel."

"Of course I understand—I am not without a heart. But the answer is still the same."

"Then I will bid you good day." Marcellus walked away with his red cape flaring out behind him and anger driving his steps.

Thalia had to determine quickly whether to find Tribune Valerius or run after the ox cart. The street-wise girl set her chin, knowing the only way she could help Adhaniá was to follow the kidnappers to their destination. If she lost sight of them, no one would know where to find Adhaniá.

Thalia was good at dodging in and out of shadows to avoid being seen. She trudged along just out of sight of the mounted men who rode beside the cart. Her heart plummeted when she finally realized the men were taking Adhaniá out of Rome.

Wearily she stumbled forward, falling several times on the uneven stone road. Once she even skinned her knee and felt blood trickle down her leg, but nothing would deter her. Adhaniá's life depended on her.

Just when Thalia thought she could not take another step, a farm cart came rattling along behind her. With the cunning that had kept her alive in dangerous situations, she casually waved to the startled man who drove the cart. She waited until the cart had passed, then leaped onto the back, holding her breath. When she was sure the driver had not seen her, Thalia quietly slid behind a barrel of fish, which smelled so bad it was hard to keep from gagging.

But always the girl kept her eyes on the cart in front of her, determined not to lose sight of it.

Thalia was more frightened than she had ever been in her life—not for herself, but for her dear Adhaniá. The Egyptian dancer had shown Thalia a life without hunger and rescued her from sleeping in damp caves. She owed Adhaniá her life, and she would gladly give it to see her safe.

The moment Marcellus returned home, he was met by an anxious Heikki. "Lady Adhaniá is missing!"

"What do you mean, missing?" Marcellus's face was expressionless, showing none of the turmoil he felt inside. "You are supposed to be guarding her."

"Layla, her servant, told me Adhaniá slipped out to the Forum to meet with your mother. I went directly there and searched everywhere for her, but she was nowhere to be seen. I questioned shopkeepers and was told by a flower vendor that he saw two women being roughly handled by several guards. She knew nothing else, or if she did, she was too frightened to say."

Marcellus's brow furrowed. "Adhaniá met with my mother?"

Heikki nodded. "According to Layla, your mother has contacted Adhaniá a couple of times."

Fear, deep and dark, slammed against Marcellus, and his eyes burned with anger. "Come with me—I will pay a visit to my mother and her husband."

* * *

It was dark inside the cart. Occasionally Adhaniá caught a glimpse of a flickering torch through the warped wooden slats. The space was cramped, and it was hard to breathe. The wheels bumped over rutted roads, and because her hands were tied behind her, Adhaniá was having a difficult time staying upright. She tried to brace her back against the side of the cart, but that merely jarred her body.

She wondered where they were taking her.

Worse still, what would happen to her after she arrived?

She listened carefully, hoping to catch the guards' conversations, but she could hear nothing above the sound of rushing water. She was certain they had left Rome behind long ago and were somewhere near the Tiber River.

Adhaniá refused to lose hope. Marcellus's mother had told her the truth—there was a plot to assassinate Caesar, and Quadatus had to keep both women from telling anyone what they knew.

A sob escaped her throat when she realized they had turned onto a dirt road. The violent rocking and swaying of the cart made bile rise in her throat. She began working at the rope that bound her wrists, but it was securely knotted. Tenaciously, she continued to twist her hands and yank on the rope. After a while, she was rewarded when she felt the rope give a bit, and she could actually move her wrists. It was enough for now. If the men saw she had escaped her bonds, they would only retie them tighter.

Just when she thought they would go on forever, they stopped, and one of the guards pulled her out of the cart.

She was unsteady on her feet, and it was dark. Straining her eyes, Adhaniá saw the outline of a small structure, probably a house. With one man carrying a torch to light their way, two remained on guard at the front of the house, and two others led her inside and up rickety stairs. From what she could see, the house had been unoccupied for some time.

Ominous shadows flickered against the walls, and Adhaniá shivered when she saw spiderwebs clinging to the corners.

None too gently, they forced her into a room.

"What is this place?" she demanded, twisting away from the man who held her too tightly and too close to his body.

"You're in no position to ask anything," the surly guard with the scar down his face told her. "When the master's finished with you, I hope he lets me have a go at you, pretty one."

His smile was more a leer, and she twisted away, dodging his groping hands and hitting him in the face with her elbow. "I would rather die than have your hands on me."

His face reddened with rage. With his fist doubled, he struck her so hard she went flying across the floor. Adhaniá felt blood on her mouth, but with her hands tied behind her, she could do nothing but let it trickle down her face.

"We aren't supposed to touch her," the rail-thin man with an unhealthy pallor reminded the other guard. "You know Senator Quadatus's orders."

The man ran his hand down the scar on the side of his face. "You'll see me again, dancer."

When the guards departed, they took the torch with them, leaving Adhaniá in total darkness. Her face hurt where the man had struck her, and she felt her lip swelling. At last her eyes became accustomed to the faint moonlight filtering through the small window. The walls of the room were cracked and peeling, and the floor was layered with dust. Adhaniá cringed when a mouse skidded across the room, disappearing among a heap of filthy rags in the corner.

With an effort, she managed to get to her feet, but she tottered with weariness and pain. Her throat was so dry, her tongue stuck to the roof of her mouth, but she dared not ask those men for a drink of water.

Adhaniá worked frantically with the ropes. She had to escape—and soon. All she could think about was Caesar unsuspectingly going to the Senate, where assassins would be waiting for him.

Tears filled her eyes when the rope finally loosened and fell to the floor. Rubbing her chafed wrists, she moved quickly to the window. She was grateful it did not look upon the front of the house, where the guards were posted. She scrutinized the tall tree that would be her avenue of escape. It was some distance away, and she wasn't sure if she could reach it.

And even if she did escape, in which direction would she travel?

Glancing into the distance, she saw the glow of lights.

Rome.

Now that she knew the direction, she had only to escape without the guards hearing her. She was determined to make her way to the city before Caesar left for the Senate.

Standing on the narrow road, Thalia had hidden behind a thicket and watched the man pull Adhaniá from the cart and force her into the house. Her instinct was to rush forward to rescue Adhaniá, but what could one small girl do against five men with swords?

Now she faded back toward the road. The best way to help Adhaniá was to find a cart heading toward Rome. Tribune Valerius would know how to rescue her.

Tired and weary, the child ran back down the road, watching for a cart.

Clouds threaded the evening sky and covered the pale moon; it looked as if it might rain before long. Adhaniá would have no better chance to escape than now. Quietly, she perched on the window ledge, reaching out to the closest branch.

It was too far.

She would have to jump. But if she missed the branch, she

would fall to the ground, probably breaking bones. Her heart raced at the urgency of her mission, and she tried to clear her mind to concentrate on her athletic abilities. She made a forceful leap forward, and her fingers barely closed around the closest branch—it was small and swayed with her weight, and the rough bark cut into the palms of her hands. With renewed strength, she swung her legs forward and pulled herself safely onto a larger branch.

Her jailers would probably be looking in on her before long, and when they discovered she was missing, they would begin a search. She had to be well away before that happened.

She scraped her arm sliding down, but bit her lip until the pain passed. Cautiously, she worked her way to a lower branch.

Gasping for breath, she dropped to the ground and slammed her body against the side of the house. She was fleet of foot, but she would be in the open until she reached the nearby woods. Moonlight shimmered across the tops of swaying pine trees as she took a cautious step forward.

Just ahead was a narrow road leading away from the house—she must avoid that route and keep to the woods as long as possible.

She needed a horse.

Glancing toward the rundown stables, her heart sank—two of the men were lighting torches and yelling to the others. They had already discovered she was missing and had begun a search. They must have thought she had gone for a horse because they were concentrating their search in that direction.

Adhaniá gathered her strength as a small cloud covered the moon, and she ran across the exposed area, weaving her way behind bushes and sometimes flattening her body on the ground.

A strong wind struck with a suddenness that took her

breath away. Gathering clouds quickly covered the sky and spread a darkness so deep, Adhaniá could barely see her hand in front of her face.

But that only worked to her advantage.

In the distance thunder rolled and lightning shimmered and forked across the sky, giving off enough light for her to locate a path leading toward the river.

Darting to the nearest tree, she made it to the first hill, where she could clearly see the lights of Rome.

But the city was a long way off, and she feared she would not get there in time to save Caesar.

CHAPTER
TWENTY-NINE ✗

Marcellus gathered twelve of his soldiers and ransacked Quadatus's house, searching for Adhaniá. Neither Quadatus nor Marcellus's mother could be found, and there was no sign that Adhaniá had ever been there. A sobbing Durra told Marcellus that his mother had not returned after her meeting with the Egyptian dancer.

Fear tore through Marcellus's mind. He did not trust his mother or Quadatus, and Adhaniá was at their mercy. "Where do you think my mother is?"

"I don't know, Tribune Valerius," she said solemnly. "I wish I did."

Grim-faced, Marcellus hurried from Quadatus's house. Once outside, he spoke to his soldiers. "Spread out through the city. Begin at the Forum and ask questions of everyone." He mounted his horse and turned to Heikki. "You will accompany me."

The two men rode back toward Marcellus's villa with the hope that Adhaniá had returned. As they rode through the gates, Marcellus saw a crumpled figure on the ground near the front door. Thinking it might be Adhaniá, he dismounted and knelt down.

"Thalia," he said, lifting the child in his arms and stalking toward the house. She was shaking with fatigue and cold. "What has happened?"

"The mistress," she said weakly. "They have taken her."

"Do you know where?"

"Yes, master. I followed them out of Rome. I can show you the way."

The child was trembling, and it had begun to rain. "Just tell me where it is. You are too ill to go. I will leave you in Layla's care."

She wriggled out of his arms and placed her hands on her hips. "I will not lie idle while the mistress is in danger. It will save time if you let me lead you."

"Quickly, then, change into dry clothing and bring a cloak. We have little time."

Moments later they were ready to leave. "She will ride with you," Marcellus told Heikki, handing the girl up to him. "Keep her as dry as you can."

With fresh horses, they rode through the streets of Rome and out into the countryside. Swiftly Marcellus followed Thalia's directions, and he wondered how the frail child could have accomplished the daunting task of making it to the country and finding her way back to Rome.

When they reached the farm, it was raining hard. Marcellus was off his horse almost before the animal stopped. He ran through the darkened house with sword drawn, calling Adhaniá's name.

But there was no answer.

Heikki managed to find a torch and light it. A search of the house revealed nothing. But when Marcellus stepped into the upstairs room, the faint scent of jasmine lingered in the air.

Aching, he closed his eyes. "She has been here," he told Heikki.

"I know. I smell the jasmine, as you do."

Bending down, Marcellus discovered the frayed rope. "They probably tied her up with this. The fact that it is here could mean she worked the rope loose."

Heikki nodded near the window. "And the blood on the floor?"

"I can only imagine they hurt her in some way." The child had just come upstairs, looking so exhausted Marcellus lifted her in his arms. "Sleep, little one. You have done well for your mistress."

She gave him a sleepy smile and closed her eyes.

In desperation, Marcellus moved to the window, where he noticed a tree with several broken branches and scattered foliage on the ground, indicating someone might have attempted to climb down it. He knew how ingenious Adhaniá could be when she put her mind to it. He turned to Heikki. "Do you think it possible she could have escaped?"

Heikki stared into the night. "I fear she was not successful. She was far from help, and I calculate by their tracks that there were at least five men. There could have been more because the abandoned ox cart probably transported her here." He glanced up at Marcellus. "If I were in Egypt, I would know what to do—but here, I am lost. You will have to tell what must be done."

Marcellus knew no one could track better than a Bedouin. "I fear my mother led Adhaniá into this trap. We will go separate ways and try to find some sign of her."

They went outside, and although it was raining, Heikki was able to read the signs. "Five riders left from here," he pointed, "probably for Rome. But I don't think Adhaniá was with them. None of the horses seems to have been carrying double."

Marcellus placed the sleeping child into Heikki's arms. "Take her home. I will meet you there." With quick strides Marcellus mounted his horse. "You go by the road, and I will take the path near the river. If neither of us have found Adhaniá on the way, I will go to Caesar for help. He will know what to do."

Heikki nodded. "Adhaniá is clever; she will not give up. She will fight them all the way."

"I know. That's what worries me. We both saw the blood, and we both know it was hers."

Finding a trail near the river, Adhaniá decided to follow it for a time, although she would eventually have to turn toward the main road to Rome. She was athletic and had great stamina, but she was pushing herself almost to the end of her strength. Once she was forced to stop and bend over so she could catch her breath. Her jaw was throbbing and her cut lip hurt, but she tried not to think about the pain in her arm, where the stab wound had started bleeding again. Her sandals had not been made for running, and after a while one of the straps broke. Not wanting anything to slow her pace, she quickly tore a strip from her gown and tied it around her sandal, then broke into a run.

She had lost all sense of time and distance, but she was certain she'd been running for over an hour. At one point, she heard horses nearing her position, and she dove to the side of the road, tumbling down an embankment. Waiting until the riders passed, she peeked through a thornbush and recognized her captors searching for her. She did not dare move until she watched them ride away.

Adhaniá thought of Caesar, a man of power—Rome needed him. She thought of Queen Cleopatra and how much she loved the man. Then there was little Caesarion, who would never know his father if he was assassinated.

Those thoughts gave wings to her feet and renewed her strength and courage. Ignoring her pain, she kept forging ahead, even though her body ached from the need to rest.

Crossing a stream, she bent down and cupped her hands, drinking thirstily. The cool water soothed her parched throat. The rain had stopped, making it easier to see where she was going.

She thought it might be time to turn toward the main road. It was harder going, making her way through the trees with thornbushes snagging her gown and tearing at her flesh. Suddenly, she stopped in her tracks, her heart almost jumping out of her body: Just ahead she saw the glow of a campfire. Holding her breath and flattening her body against a tree, she called on all her courage and inched closer. It could be Quadatus's guards, or it might be a stranger. Either way, she needed a horse, and she would take it from whoever had built that fire.

Adhaniá gazed quickly to the east and saw a slight glow—it wasn't long before sunup, and the passing of time made her desperate.

Moving forward quietly, she went from tree to tree until she was in sight of the campfire. Gazing about, she saw only one horse—but between her and that horse was the sleeping figure of a man, and from the size of him, he was a giant.

Taking a steadying breath, she moved closer still, balancing her weight on the toes of her sandals. She kept a wary eye on the sleeping man; his even breathing told her he was in a deep sleep. She was almost within reach of the horse when the animal reared its head and gave a loud neigh—at the same moment, she stepped on a twig, making a cracking sound.

She watched the man stir and awaken, and she stopped dead still. He reached toward the sword that lay beside him—but she was faster—swooping down, she grabbed it, turning the tip toward him.

For a big man, he was surprisingly quick on his feet. He unsheathed his dagger, looking at her in shock.

"So you thought to rob me while I slept," he said, lunging at her. "Am I a fool that a scrawny girl can catch me unaware?"

He was even taller than she'd thought—his black hair was long and tangled about a pleasant face—he was even smiling. She judged him to be a young man, but not a Roman. Spanish, she thought. Muscles bulged beneath his jerkin, straining across broad shoulders. Adhaniá was no novice at swordsmanship, but instinct told her this man made his living by the blade. Her only advantage would be to strike first, and to strike quickly.

With a swift lunge, she thrust the sword forward, and the sound of metal against metal clashed through the air while moonlight flashed on the blades. With a quick jab, she stripped the dagger from his hand and sent it flying.

He smiled as the point of his own sword was held to his throat. "I'd wager there is not one female in a thousand who could have unarmed me with such precision. You took me by surprise, pretty lady."

There was a certain gallantry about him, and she was sorry to be taking his horse.

But she must.

"I am not a thief, and I did not come to rob you." She shook her head. "But I must borrow your horse for a time. 'Tis a matter of life or death that I reach Rome."

The man's brown eyes sparked with humor. "I am in no position to argue the point." His laughter rang out clear. "I won't be telling my friends I was bested by a women who is as cunning with a blade as she is beautiful."

She mounted his horse in a smooth motion and stared down at him. "What is your name?"

He swept her a bow. "Raphael is my name, little beauty."

"Where can I find you to return your horse to you?"

He looked startled for a moment. "I had not expected a thief to return stolen goods."

"I told you I am not a thief. If I could accomplish my mission in any other way, I would do so."

He stared at her as she spun the horse around. "Everyone knows where to find me. Just ask around Trajan Forum for Raphael," he told her. "But how am I to get to Rome if you have my horse?"

"I have left your food and water with you," she said. "Make yourself comfortable, and I shall send someone back for you, although it may take some time."

He grinned and flourished her another bow. "It would seem I am at your mercy. But may I have my sword back? It belonged to my father."

She nodded, tossing the weapon so it landed on the point, the hilt bobbing back and forth. Without another word, she rode off at a swift gallop. The moon moved lower in the sky, and she feared even now she would be too late to save Caesar.

When Heikki reached Marcellus's villa, Layla ran out to him. "Have you word of Lady Adhaniá?"

"Not as yet." He handed the child down to her. "She needs dry clothing and a warm bed. It was luck that brought her into Adhaniá's life," he said gruffly. "Tend her well."

Layla nodded. "She was brave to risk her life for the mistress."

Heikki had found his gaze following Layla more and more of late. He could recognize her laughter in a room filled with people. She was delicate, her eyes soft with kindness. His body came alive when she brushed past him, and he knew his feelings for her had deepened.

He took the child from her. "I will carry her."

As he walked beside Layla, he almost stumbled because he was watching her instead of where he was going. Something was blooming and growing inside his heart. How could he love her when he loved Adhaniá? In this world so different from Egypt, he had found a woman he wanted to spend the rest of his life with. Adhaniá was brighter than the sun—this woman had the steady softness of the moon.

His father had been right—he had let Adhaniá go from his heart, and this small woman had taken her place there.

CHAPTER THIRTY ✗

Adhaniá bent low over the horse, attempting to make the animal run at a faster pace. The poor beast was struggling to respond to her commands, but he was past his prime and finally slowed to a trot. No amount of urging on Adhaniá's part could make him go any faster.

To make matters worse, a heavy mist now hung over the land, shrouding everything in shadows. Adhaniá kept her gaze on the road, fearing she might lose her way. Overwhelmed by frustration, she felt tears gathering in her eyes.

At what time would Caesar go to the Senate?

Probably in the morning hours.

If Ramtat were there, he would tell her not to give up. But she was so weary, and everything was against her—the fog, the horse that could do little more than trot and had now slowed to a walk.

A sudden noise caught her attention. At first it was hard to identify because the fog muted every sound. Too late the fog cleared a bit, and she saw several horsemen bearing down on her. Adhaniá decided it would be wise to get off the road, but it was too late—five riders blocked her path, and her horse had come to a dead halt.

Adhaniá recognized Senator Quadatus's guards. Sliding off the horse, she decided to try losing herself in the fog. But the men circled her, bumping her with their mounts. And she saw the man she dreaded the most, his scar more prominent than before because his lascivious smile pulled his lip into a cruel snarl.

She was surrounded, and there was nowhere she could run. If only she'd kept the sword instead of giving it back to Raphael, she would have a way to defend herself.

The leader of the guards bumped his horse into her, backing her between his horse and one of the others.

"You'll pay for making a fool of me," he said, thrusting his heavy boot into her stomach and sending her careening onto the rough road. She landed hard but managed to drag herself to her feet.

Like a phantom warrior he came out of the mist, sword slashing, bodies falling before him. With four guards down, Marcellus turned to the scar-faced man.

"Move out of the way, Adhaniá," he warned.

Marcellus's voice was deadly calm, his eyes flashing like fire when he turned to the last man—the one who had been tormenting Adhaniá. "It is your turn now. Make ready to die!"

"Tribune Valerius, surely you would not raise sword to me," the man pleaded, looking at the bloody carnage that had been his companions. He had no doubt that he was about to meet his death, for how could a mere guard such as himself cross swords with a tribune of Rome and expect to come out alive? "I was but following orders."

"Arm yourself. I have no time for cowards."

Adhaniá watched Marcellus's sword strike with such force, it knocked the man to the ground. Dismounting,

Marcellus stood over the guard, his sword poised above his heart. "If you have any last words, say them now."

"Please, honored Tribune—don't kill me for carrying out my master's orders. I'm but a poor man with a family."

"You die because you put your hands on something that belongs to me."

"Your mother? I did not hurt her—I merely took her back to Senator Quadatus as I was ordered."

"Not my mother." He nodded toward Adhaniá. "Her."

"But . . . but—"

"Wait," Adhaniá cried, running forward. "First make him tell you where they took your mother."

Marcellus shook his head. "You heard him; she is with her husband."

Knowing she had no time to debate the matter, she placed her hand over his. "Ask about your mother."

He nodded. "You heard the lady—she wants to know where you took your mistress."

"Why should I tell you?" The man licked his trembling lips. "You'll kill me anyway."

"Aye," Marcellus agreed, "but you can die quickly, or you can die slow."

The guard nodded in acceptance. "My master has her sequestered at the Inn of Trajan."

Marcellus glanced at Adhaniá. "Satisfied?"

She nodded and turned away.

Marcellus thrust his sword straight into the man's heart, and watched him twitch only once before his eyes took on the blankness of death.

Then Marcellus dropped his sword and drew Adhaniá into his arms, holding her against his heart. "I thought I had lost you."

She pressed her face against his rough armor. "I am not so easy to lose."

He tilted up her face, seeing the bruised jaw and the cut lip, and her gown stained with blood. "Did they hurt you?"

Her gaze met his. "No more than my dignity. But do not think of that. We have to reach Caesar as soon as possible!" She pulled away from him and caught the reins of one of the dead guards' horses. "Your mother warned me that Quadatus and other senators are planning to assassinate Caesar when he enters the Senate today!"

Marcellus looked at her in disbelief. "That cannot be. Antony will be with him. Do you recall other names that were mentioned?"

She reached back in her mind, trying to recall the names his mother had mentioned. "Quadatus, of course. Cassius, a man named Brutus. She said there were others but did not mention their names."

"Not Brutus. Caesar trusts him. Brutus has always been Caesar's friend."

"What does it matter what their names are? Let us assume Caesar will be met with assassins today. We must warn him. If the information proves to be false, what harm will be done? I trust your mother, whether you do or not."

She flung herself onto the horse. "We must warn Caesar!"

It was difficult for Marcellus to believe anyone would attempt an assassination in the Senate with so many witnesses. Still, Cassius was bold, and Marcellus could not discount the possibility.

"Let's go directly to the Senate, where I can stand beside Antony against the others, if they be traitors."

Ides of Martius
15th Martius

Caesar climbed the steps of the building that temporarily housed the Senate, his mind already on the military campaign he would launch against Parthia. Everything was in readiness, and he would be leaving in two days' time.

Antony, who walked at his side, was suddenly stopped and drawn into a conversation with Senator Gaius Trebonius. Caesar's thoughts turned to Cleopatra. She had been worried about his safety today—something about a warning and a comet or some such nonsense. All women, even queens, could work themselves into a frenzy over imagined dangers.

As he was about to enter the building, Senator Tillius Cimber approached, kneeling down to offer him a parchment, which Caesar refused with the shake of his head.

Tillius then grabbed Caesar's toga, and Caesar glanced down at the man, thinking he was acting strangely. At that moment, Ciusa loomed from out of nowhere, dagger in hand, and attempted to drive it into Caesar's throat, but Caesar managed to deflect the blade.

Something is dreadfully amiss.

Could Cleopatra have been right?

He struggled to escape as other assassins closed in on him from all sides. Cassius's dagger was the first to strike with accuracy, and it dug into Caesar's face, bringing a cry of agony from the great man.

Brutus was the next to strike—his dagger slicing into Caesar's thigh, sending him to his knees.

Twenty-three wounds were inflicted on the dictator. It all happened so quickly, those who would have come to Caesar's aid were in shock. Already he was a dying man. Blood spattered the conspirators and pooled on the marble floor.

In his dying moments, Caesar grasped his toga and pulled it over his face, denying his enemies the chance to watch him die.

The greatest general Rome had ever known, dictator of most of the world, breathed his last.

CHAPTER
THIRTY-ONE 𝄋

Adhaniá and Marcellus raced the sun, but by the time they reached Rome it had already burned the fog away.

Marcellus knew it would be but a short time before Caesar would enter the Senate. They did not slow their pace as they raced through the marketplace, and crowds of people scattered to miss their horses' flying hooves.

When they reached the Senate building, Marcellus leaped from his horse at a run. "Remain with the horses," he cried over his shoulder. He ran through the crowd that gathered each morning to greet the senators with praise or complaints.

But something was different today—he could feel it. The crowd was silent, as if in shock. With renewed effort, he elbowed his way past them.

His gut wrenched.

He was too late!

The closer he got to his goal, the more desperate the onlookers' reactions were. There was crying and lamenting, women falling to their knees and shaking their fists in the air.

Drawing his sword, he shoved people out of his way, hurrying inside the building. Marcellus found Antony on his knees with Caesar's bloody body in his arms.

Antony raised his gaze to Marcellus, tears dulling his eyes. "He is dead," he said softly, as if he was afraid to speak of it aloud.

Marcellus dropped his sword and went down on his knees beside Antony, unmindful that the great Caesar's blood soaked his tunic. "They succeeded," he said, dropping his head in sorrow. Grief tore at him, and it was almost more than he could bear.

"There will be a reckoning for this," Antony said with feeling, his throat clogged with tears. "I will not stop until I find every one of the traitors and put them to death."

Marcellus stood, not knowing what chaos would result from this day's work—Rome could erupt into civil war at any moment. "Yes, those responsible must be brought to death," he agreed, still stunned. "But for now the people are in a panic, and the news will soon spread throughout the city, then all across the land. The citizens of Rome need to see you—they need to know there is someone to lead them through these dark days."

Others had gathered, murmuring in disbelief. Many senators were naming the traitors and pressing Antony to seek justice for Caesar.

Marcellus turned to a tribune who was crying openly, and knowing Antony needed time to compose himself, he gave the orders. "Find General Rufio and inform him what has happened. Have him muster Caesar's Sixth Legion and bring them here to Antony at once. Return as soon as possible. General Antony will have orders for you at that time."

There were two other officers who were staring at Caesar's dead body as if they were dazed—as if the most powerful man in the world was not supposed to succumb to death at the hands of mere mortals. Marcellus retrieved the sword he'd dropped earlier and angrily slammed it into the scabbard. "Pull yourselves together, tribunes—Rome has need of you."

Many ducked their heads, but one met Marcellus's angry stare. "Senator Quadatus sent word that Caesar needed us at once, and that we were to go to his house. When we arrived, there was no one there but servants. We should have been here to protect Caesar."

"We will speak of this later. Make Caesar's body ready with a coin in the mouth, and build a funeral pyre so all Rome can witness what those madmen did to him."

Antony nodded. "I must present myself to the mob, when all I want to do is hide my face in shame because I was not at Caesar's side when he needed me most."

Marcellus looked grim. "You cannot blame yourself—you did all you could to prevent this from happening. Those traitors planned this well. It was no accident that you were pulled away from Caesar's side this day. Had you been with him, you, too, would have died."

Antony nodded. "I may have failed him in life, but I shall not fail him in death."

Marcellus watched his friend's shoulders straighten as he stared at his blood-stained hands. "All Rome will weep this night, but tomorrow we hunt down traitors!"

Antony still appeared dazed, and stumbled when he tried to take a step. "Have someone purify this place." He paused. "Nay, I have reconsidered. Let no one touch the blood of Caesar, but allow all who want to enter witness where the tragedy took place."

Apollodorus entered the chamber where his queen reclined on a couch, a handmaiden waving a feathered fan to cool her in the afternoon heat.

When Cleopatra saw his face, she knew something had

happened. She knew Caesar was dead even before Apollodorus could speak of it.

She sat up regally, swung her gold-clad feet off the couch and stood. "Leave me, everyone but you, Apollodorus," she said, in a voice that was strong and seemingly unaffected. After the others had backed out of the chamber, she turned to him.

"Tell me everything."

She held herself upright, but her lips trembled as he told of Caesar's assassination—at least what he knew of it. Apollodorus had rushed to his queen's side before learning all the details. He had known Cleopatra since her childhood, and in all that time, he'd never seen her weep.

But she cried now—she sobbed, and she trembled, and she went to her knees.

When she reached out to him, Apollodorus understood she wanted him to help her stand.

With tear-bright eyes, she looked at him. "Make ready to leave, and quickly. Now that Caesar is dead, I fear for the life of his son."

Apollodorus bowed and backed to the door. "I have already sent a man to have the barge made ready."

Adhaniá had dismounted and gathered the reins of both horses, moving away from the crowd of mourning citizens. Both men and women were crying unashamedly. She hung her head, knowing they had not reached Caesar in time. She thought of Queen Cleopatra, and her body shook with helpless tears. She had been too late to help the queen—she had failed her.

All was lost.

She knew Marcellus would have much to do and wondered if she should return to his house or go directly to Queen

Cleopatra. Then she knew what she had to do—Marcellus's mother needed help, and she was going to go to her.

In that moment, she saw a group of soldiers shoving their way through the crowd, and then she saw Marcellus striding toward her. The citizens moved aside to make way for him, many reaching out, asking if it was really true that Caesar was dead.

He did not answer but headed straight for Adhaniá. He took the reins of his horse from her. "Everything happened so quickly. There is much I need to do. Can you make it back to my villa on your own?"

She shook her head. "Nay. You know now your mother spoke the truth. She is in danger, and I shall not desert her."

He looked as if the weight of the world was on his shoulders. "Adhaniá, Caesar was murdered. There will likely be riots breaking out in the city—and even more than that, it is almost a certainty there will be civil war. Our society hangs by a thread. I have no time to go looking for my mother, who is probably with her husband, laughing at us all."

"You are wrong! I fear Quadatus will do her harm for warning me of the impending assassination. Caesar is already dead, and there is nothing we can do to help him now. But I will not abandon your mother to Quadatus's cruelty."

He hung his head in weariness. "I don't seem to be thinking clearly. But let us go to her if it will put your mind at ease."

Although it was market day, the Forum was deserted. Shops were closed, and even the vendors had not displayed their wares. It seemed the people of Rome had taken to their houses and were hiding behind locked doors in fear of their lives.

Marcellus dismounted and helped Adhaniá from her

horse. He looked so weary, and his eyes were so sad, she wanted to comfort him.

He abruptly turned away to enter the inn. "It might be safer if you remain here."

"I certainly shall not," she stated firmly, running to catch up with him. "Your mother may need me."

They encountered no innkeeper. Marcellus headed for the stairs, and Adhaniá followed closely. "I'll open every door to find her if I must," she said.

But there was no need—Quadatus had heard their footsteps and opened the door of his room a crack to see who it was. When he saw his stepson, he slammed the door shut and shot the bolt.

Marcellus threw his weight against the door, and it splintered; with another thrust, the door burst open.

Marcellus confronted his stepfather, who was cringing in a corner. "How . . . did you find me?" Quadatus asked, his voice quivering, for he knew he stared into the eyes of death.

"I just followed the stench of a cowardly traitor. Your plan worked, Quadatus. But you will die the same day as a great man ten times your worth."

Quadatus's face reddened, and the muscles in his neck throbbed. "Of what are you speaking?"

Marcellus unsheathed his sword. "Do not play games with me. Rather, spend your last moments repenting for a squandered life."

"I would never be involved in a plot to kill Caesar. How could you even think it?"

"Just because you are a fool and a coward, do not mistake me for one." Marcellus moved closer to Quadatus, and the man went to his knees, shielding his face with his arms.

Quadatus waited for the sword to strike, and when it did not, he glanced at his stepson. "You kill an innocent man if you strike me dead. I have not left this inn all day."

Adhaniá was standing behind Marcellus, and she heard a muffled sound coming from the next room. Rushing forward, she found Sarania gagged and tied to the bed. She removed the gag, distressed by the woman's weakened condition. Her eyes were ringed with dark circles, and there were bruises on her face and arms.

Sarania licked her lips. "Little dancer, I have been so worried about you. Is that my Marcellus's voice I hear?" she asked hopefully.

"Dear lady, it is your son. Save your voice and your strength. You are safe now." Deftly, Adhaniá untied the ropes and helped Sarania to stand.

She swayed on her feet and clung to Adhaniá. "Help me get to my son."

"How dare you suggest—" Quadatus blustered as Adhaniá reentered the room.

"I do dare, Quadatus. I know you were not at the Senate today—you are not that brave. Perhaps your death will send proof to your surrogates that they will be next."

"Those senators are not my surrogates."

Marcellus stepped closer. "I will hear no more words from you."

"Wait!" Sarania leaned heavily on Adhaniá.

Marcellus paused with his sword raised, taking in his mother's appearance with a sweeping gaze. "Would you have me spare him?"

She stumbled forward. "I would have him tell the truth of your father's death." She raised a pleading gaze to her son. "I beg this one thing of you."

Quadatus rose to his feet. "You have no say here, woman. Get back to the other room."

"She has every right to be here." Marcellus's sword was leveled on Quadatus's heart. "Ask what you will, Mother."

She stood, swaying before her husband. "First, Marcellus, I would have you know I did not marry this man of my own free will. He killed your father, and he threatened to take your life if I did not become his wife."

Marcellus looked as if he had been delivered a mortal blow. "You married him to save me? Did you not know you could have told me the truth, and I would have protected you?"

Sarania shook her head. "Not after what you witnessed between us in the garden that day." Tears dampened her eyes. "I did not give myself to this man that day, Marcellus— he forced himself on me."

Marcellus cried out and swung his sword, but Sarania stepped between it and her husband, not even flinching when the blade stopped just short of her head. "Give him your word, Marcellus, that you will not harm him if he speaks the truth."

Marcellus scowled. "No!"

"Give your word, my son."

Marcellus wanted nothing more than to plunge his sword into the man's black heart. Why did his mother want him spared? Looking at her, as if seeing her for the first time in years, he wanted to take her frail body in his arms and beg her forgiveness for his heartless neglect. He wanted to ask her pardon because he had suspected her of plotting with Quadatus to slay his father. He looked over at Adhaniá, who nodded at him through her tears. To give his mother what she asked might in some way atone for all the years he had hated her. "I give my word," he said through gritted teeth.

"You see, husband, my son will not harm you." She stumbled forward, and when Marcellus reached out to catch her, she slid her arms around him as if to embrace him, but instead slowly lifted the dagger from his scabbard. Marcellus looked at her questioningly, but she shook her head and turned to face Quadatus. "Tell my son why you killed his father—you know Marcellus is a man of his word and will not strike you down."

Quadatus had thought he was a dead man, but for reasons he didn't understand, Sarania was standing between him and death. Knowing he was safe from reprisal, he unleashed the full force of his hatred on Marcellus. "Your father had something I wanted," he spat.

"My mother," Marcellus said with disgust.

"I swore I would have her as my wife, but she would not have me. I did what I had to," he said, as if his wants made his methods acceptable, at least in his own mind. "It was a cold bed she offered me, but in my way, I have loved her above all else."

Sarania still stood between Quadatus and her son, the dagger hidden in the folds of her gown. "Did you slay my husband?"

"Not personally, though I was there. It took three of my men to overcome his resistance."

"I am so sorry," Sarania mouthed to her son when she saw the rage burning in his eyes.

Quadatus saw the rage in Marcellus's eyes as well. "You gave your word," he reminded his stepson. "Am I free to leave?"

Sarania took a step closer to the man who had killed her beloved husband, then tormented her for so many years. "You say you love me, yet you threatened my son if I did not marry you. You kept me prisoner for years. I despise you now, as I did the first day I saw you." She took another step toward Quadatus, and before Marcellus or Adhaniá realized what she was about to do, Sarania raised the dagger and plunged it into his heart.

"This," she cried, "is for the husband I still love, and for the son you denied me."

Quadatus's eyes widened in disbelief, and he fell hard

against the floor, flailing his legs and reaching out to her. Then the light went out of his eyes, and he stilled in death.

Sarania stared at her bloody hands and said softly, "Now you cannot hurt my son."

She stepped back and collapsed in Marcellus's arms.

CHAPTER
THIRTY-TWO ⚕

Torchlight fell across the Forum, throwing ghostlike shadows against brick walls. Marcellus stood stoically beside General Rufio, commander of the Sixth Legion, so they could both show their support for Marc Antony.

Antony had finished addressing a weeping mob, and silence ensued as Caesar's funeral pyre was lit. Antony's shoulders slumped with the heavy weight of his responsibilities. He had the daunting task of pulling together a wounded nation and reuniting opposing parties to help heal the rifts.

Marcellus looked at Rufio. "The sun has set on a day that has changed Roman history forever."

"Aye," Rufio agreed. "Blood has been spilled, and now the assassins are on the run."

"But we shall catch them," Marc Antony said, stepping back, looking exhausted. There was a long silence as the pyre burned. Finally Antony said, "I have sent a message to Caesar's nephew, Octavian, strongly suggesting the little weasel come to Rome."

Marcellus took a last glance at the fire, which was now

merely flickering embers and ashes. "If there is nothing else you need of me, I will go home," he said.

Antony clapped his arm. "You have been my support in these days since Caesar's murder, and neither of us has slept much. Find what little repose you may. I will need to see you in the morning."

Marcellus nodded as he descended the steep steps and mounted his horse. He needed to see Adhaniá, to hold her in his arms so he could forget, if only for a moment, the tragedy of Caesar's death. He had asked her to take his mother to his villa so she could rest and heal. That was where he'd find them both.

Guilt rode beside him as he entered the arched gateway of his home. He had much to say to his mother. He had misunderstood the situation, and she had suffered for it. It would be a lot to ask of his mother, but he needed her forgiveness.

A young boy ran forward to take his horse, and he entered his house, rubbing the back of his neck, thinking he could even fall asleep on the hard floor if he could just lie down.

Planus greeted him. "You look tired, master. Would you like to bathe?"

Marcellus let out a long breath. "Not just yet. Find out if Adhaniá has gone to bed. If she hasn't, ask if she will see me."

"But, master," Planus said worriedly, "she . . . Lady Adhaniá has gone."

Marcellus snapped around to face his servant. "Gone! Gone where?"

"The queen's man, Apollodorus, came for her yesterday afternoon. She was to sail with Queen Cleopatra this morning."

Marcellus felt as if his heart had turned to stone. He turned away, braced his hand on the wall and lowered his head. Of course. He should have expected her to return to

Egypt, but not so soon. He felt as if a part of him had been ripped away.

Straightening, he spoke in a weary voice. "Is my mother here?"

"Yes, master. Lady Adhaniá settled your mother in her own bedchamber. When the rioting was going on in the streets, Lady Adhaniá sat beside her all night so she wouldn't be upset."

"Tell her I have returned and will see her tomorrow."

"Yes, master."

Marcellus went to his chamber, tossed his helm on the couch and removed his own breastplate, dropping it on the floor. He lowered himself onto the bed and stared at the wall, feeling so much he could not grasp it all.

Laying back, he stared at the ceiling. She had left him. She had gone where he could not reach her. His heart cried out for her—his body craved hers.

Turning on his side, he closed his eyes on the nightmare he was living and slept.

Adhaniá watched the waves crash against Queen Cleopatra's barge, knowing each stroke of the oar was taking her farther from Rome and Marcellus. She had not wanted to leave, but a command from the queen must be obeyed.

Even if Adhaniá had defied the order, there was nothing for her in Rome—no reason to stay. One day Marcellus would marry a beautiful woman of his own people, and he would father children, and he would be happy. But Adhaniá knew she would never find happiness for herself. She would always yearn for a love she could not have.

Thalia came up beside her and stared at the churning water. "Never could I have imagined such an adventure. I have always wanted to see Egypt, but I never thought I would take a voyage on Queen Cleopatra's own barge."

Adhaniá smiled down at the child. The day Apollodorus had arrived at Marcellus's villa with a message that the queen wanted her immediately, Adhaniá had known they would be leaving Rome. Thalia had gathered her few belongings and piled them in a heap on the bed. With hands on hips and chin angled stubbornly, she had announced that Adhaniá was not leaving without her. The little imp was a comfort to her. She always said, or did, something amusing.

Adhaniá thought of Queen Cleopatra in seclusion, too upset to see anyone but her handmaidens. She and the queen had both lost men they loved.

To pass the time Adhaniá helped little Caesarion's nurse with his care. The child was sweet and unspoiled, which was surprising, considering he was granted his slightest wish.

She thought of Ramtat's son, Julian, and hoped he had not forgotten her. It would be good to see him again.

Sometimes in the late evening the queen would come on deck and stare back in the direction of Rome, and at those times, Adhaniá imagined her thoughts were of Caesar. Even a queen with the world at her feet could suffer a tragic loss, and Adhaniá hurt for her.

Then Adhaniá's thoughts would turn to her own grief.

What was Marcellus doing at that moment?

He had said their night together had been perfect—did he still feel that way?

Marcellus was up and dressed before dawn. When he was preparing to leave, his mother came to him. Her smile was hesitant.

"Mother," he said, seating her in a chair, "you have more color in your face today. I hope you are well."

"I truly am. Your Adhaniá is quite extraordinary. Were you aware that she is versed in herbal healing?"

"She had mentioned it."

"Apparently it is an age-old Egyptian science. I drank the herbs she mixed with honey and had the first peaceful night's sleep I have had in years. She left herbs with me which I am to take each day—she said they would restore my strength. Do you not think she is rather young to be so wise?" She shook her head. "I thought she was a mere dancer—I had no notion she was a highborn lady of Egypt. I misjudged her, but she behaved like the lady she is. I have much to ask her to forgive."

"Mother, now that you mention forgiveness, it is a wonder you will even speak to me. I ask your forgiveness for all you have suffered. I am your son—I should have taken care of you. Instead, I believed the worst, and that must have wounded you deeply."

She placed her hand on his. "Do not take this burden on your shoulders. There was no way you could have known the truth."

He rubbed his forehead, still feeling exhausted. "I promise you that I will make it up to you now."

"My son, a mother's love has no conditions and places no blame."

He lowered his head, touched by her words, and he knew he had to speak of other matters. "There is so much to do. I have a meeting with Antony. The assassins will have to be hunted down and brought to justice. I hear Cassius is raising an army, and likely Brutus is doing the same."

Sarania looked into her son's eyes and saw heavy sadness. "I have a scroll Lady Adhaniá left for you." She reached into her overdress, withdrew it and placed it in his hand. "Read it when you are alone."

He stood up. "Unfortunately, I have no time now. I must not be late for my meeting with Antony."

"I see clearly that you love her."

"I—" Marcellus started to deny it, then shook his head. "It is a hopeless love."

"If it is real love, the kind I had with your father, you will find a way, my son. Love is so precious, and you never know when it will be taken away from you." She took a deep breath. "Did she ever tell you what I asked of her?"

"Do you mean about the meeting by the fountain?"

"No. The night I sent Durra to beg her to keep you home. I knew Quadatus had arranged for your assassination."

Marcellus lowered his head as understanding slammed into him. "So that was why she insisted on dancing for me. I thought it strange at the time. When I insisted she leave, she . . ." He threw his head back and stared at the decorative cupola. "Is there no end to the harm I have done to those I love?"

"I can guess what you are feeling. But do not punish yourself for what has passed. I have learned to let go of those things I cannot change—perhaps you should do the same."

Marcellus could no longer wait to read the words Adhaniá had written. He was unaware that his mother had quietly risen and left him alone. His hand trembled as he unrolled the scroll:

> *Tribune Valerius—or should I call you Marcellus, for that is the way I think of you—we have reached the end of our association. Though I have been recalled to Egypt, I will always remember you with warmth and hope you think of me in the same way. If ever you come to Egypt, it would gladden my heart to see you. I beg you will grant me a boon: In my name, Heikki went to Queen Cleopatra and asked to be given one of her fine horses, and she granted that wish. You will find the animal in your stable. If you would have the stallion delivered to a Spaniard by the name of Raphael, I will be forever in your debt. Ask around Trajan Forum and someone will tell you where he can be located. And if you will be so kind as to extend my most sincere apology to him,*

I will thank you in advance. I pray that the gods hold and keep you safe in the dangerous endeavor you will surely undertake in the pursuit of Caesar's enemies.

Marcellus stared at the scroll and reread it.

Who is this Spaniard Raphael, and what did Adhaniá do to owe an apology to the man?

Antony looked up from the scroll he had been studying when Marcellus entered the room. "You are late."

Marcellus was weary and dropped down into a chair. "I'm early."

"How does this sound to you?" Antony began to read: "Your Esteemed Majesty, Queen Cleopatra, our parting was brief and hectic, and I had no time to assure you that Rome still stands as your ally. Know that our friendship for you transcends Caesar's death."

He glanced up at Marcellus. "Do you think I put it right? I can never say what I really mean with her."

Marcellus was studying the bright pattern on the rug, wondering why Antony was thinking about Queen Cleopatra when there were troops to muster and traitors to bring to justice. "I believe she will be comforted by your assurances."

"Precisely what I think." He tapped the scroll on the palm of his hand. "Make ready for a voyage to Egypt."

"What?"

Antony blew out an agitated breath. "If you are to be my liaison between Rome and Egypt, you must become a general. I cannot send a mere tribune to speak to the queen."

"Me?"

"Has something gone wrong with your hearing?" Antony looked Marcellus in the eye. "In those darkest moments after Caesar's death, it was you at my side, clearheaded and issuing orders to calm the citizens. You were Caesar's master architect—you will be my diplomat. Your mission is to go to Egypt and assure Queen Cleopatra of our goodwill."

"You are making me a general?"

"I have that power now." A teasing light shone in his dark eyes. "Of course, if you don't want the honor—"

"But you must have need of me here."

"Nay. I need you in Egypt." He handed Marcellus several scrolls for the queen and added another to the stack. "This one states that I have issued you a dispensation so you can marry your little dancer, though I am sure I will have to answer to the Senate when they find out what I have done. Rome will not stand in your way if you still want to marry Lord Ramtat's sister—but Lord Ramtat might."

Marcellus took a halting step, stunned into silence.

"Go. My fastest ship is being made ready to sail next week, General Valerius. Do whatever one does to get an appropriate uniform to wear in the presence of a queen."

Marcellus placed his arm over his chest in a salute. "I am grateful for the honor, but my duty—"

"Your duty is to obey me in all things. If you don't leave, I may well decide to ship you off to Cyprus."

Antony smiled as he watched the newly appointed general hurry out the door. Lord Ramtat would certainly be a force to reckon with. Marcellus would not have an easy time of it when he reached Egypt.

It was later in the day when Marcellus located the Spaniard. He watched curiously as the man exclaimed over the horse.

"I have never seen such a fine animal—it is magnificent!" He glanced up at Marcellus suspiciously. "It isn't stolen, is it?"

"I can assure you it is not."

"No one would give away such a horse without wanting something in return. What does that little beauty want of me? I can tell you, although I make my living by the sword,

I do not kill without a good cause. So if this horse is in payment for such a deed, I must decline."

Marcellus laid his hand on the Badarian stallion, probably worth more than the Spaniard would make in his lifetime. "I was hoping you could tell me the reason Lady Adhaniá presents you with such a gift."

The Spaniard threw back his head and gave a great laugh. "So she's a lady, is she? She didn't act like one when she took my horse from me at swordpoint. Never have I seen such a magnificent woman! She disarmed me before I knew what had happened. Then the little beauty apologized and said she would return my horse. Instead she sends me a horse worth a king's ransom."

Marcellus grinned, his mind going back to the day Adhaniá had competed for the Golden Arrow. "You should feel no shame in being bested by her—you are not the first man she has outfought."

"She told me she was taking my horse on a matter of life and death. I could see her face was bruised, and that she had been in a fight with someone. I have often thought of her and wondered why she was so desperate that night. Can you enlighten me?"

Marcellus mounted his horse and looked down at Raphael. "She was in a race to save Caesar's life. As you know by now, she lost that race. Do not ever expect to see her again. She has returned to Egypt, whence she came. The horse she has given you belonged to Queen Cleopatra."

The Spaniard's eyes widened, and he nodded. "She will be forever in my dreams."

Marcellus controlled his prancing horse with the heel of his booted foot. "As she is in mine."

CHAPTER
THIRTY-THREE ✣

Egypt

Alexandria almost seemed foreign to Adhaniá after her stay in Rome. She walked through the rooms of the villa where she had grown up, feeling strangely detached. She remembered the feel of Marcellus's body, the touch of his mouth on hers, their bodies and minds entwined in passion. He was far away from her, and they would never see each other again.

She would always have the memories.

But were memories enough to live on for the rest of her life?

She pushed all thoughts of Marcellus to the back of her mind—it was less painful that way. Sometime that day Ramtat would arrive with his family. She could hardly wait to see them, especially little Julian and the new baby.

Layla approached her. "Lady Larania has asked that you attend her, mistress."

Adhaniá went directly to her mother's chambers. As soon as she entered, a small boy threw himself at her and clutched her about the knees.

"Adhaniá, you came back!"

Laughingly, she lifted her nephew in her arms while he grinned at her. "You have grown, and you can talk."

He cocked his head. "I can ride a horse," he said, bright-eyed.

"But not as well as your aunt could at your age," a deep male voice said from behind her. Adhaniá spun around to see her brother standing there. He took the child from her and studied her for a moment. "You have changed. There is something different about you."

She went into his comforting arms. "I am older and wiser now."

"Welcome home." He held her for a long moment, and then he released her so Danaë could hug her tightly.

"You were missed, little sister. I add my welcome to your brother's." Danaë examined Adhaniá closely. "There is some-thing different about you," she said, seeing what her husband had missed. "There is a sadness—" She shook her head, not finishing her thoughts. "You have not seen your namesake. She is very like you in every way."

Adhaniá laughed. "Then you had better guard her well, or you will be sending *her* to the queen's household for dis-cipline."

Ramtat scooped up his daughter and placed her in his sis-ter's eager arms. The child cuddled close, laying her dark head on Adhaniá's shoulder and stealing her heart.

"She is wonderful." Adhaniá noticed Thalia lingering in the doorway, smiling at the happy family reunion. "Come and see the baby," she urged.

With eyes wide, Thalia stared at the infant. "She is so small." She touched a tiny hand. "And so soft." She beamed up at Adhaniá. "I have never seen anything so beautiful."

Handing her niece to Danaë, Adhaniá brought Thalia for-ward. "Ramtat, Danaë, I would like you to meet someone special. I will tell you later how she saved my life. I hope you will all receive her into the family because Thalia is very dear to me."

The family gathered around the young girl, smiling and welcoming her. Little Julian insisted Thalia accompany him to the nursery so he could show her his toys. The homecoming was everything Adhaniá could have wished for. But in her heart she would never come all the way home.

She caught Danaë watching her with a curious expression. Later, when she was able to talk about Marcellus without crying, she would tell her sister-in-law much of what had happened to her in Rome, but not now—perhaps not for a long time to come.

Lord Ramtat had honored Heikki for his loyal duty to his sister by making him one of her personal guards. He had a new uniform, and his step was lighter than it had been in a long while. As he went off duty and crossed the garden, the object of his affection, Layla, moved down the path in front of him. He had come to understand that he had never truly loved Adhaniá as a woman—not the way he loved Layla.

He paused to speak to her. "Are you happy to be home?"

She coyly glanced at him from beneath her lashes. "I am happy to be here in this house with this wonderful family. It is a joy to serve Lady Adhaniá."

"And what about me?" he boldly asked. "Could you be happy with me if we were permitted to marry?"

She drew in her breath and ducked her head, as if she were unable to look into his eyes. "I do not know if such a thing would be possible."

He took her hand and felt it tremble. "I believe if I asked it of her, Lady Adhaniá would allow me to take you as my wife. I have loved you for some time now."

He watched her eyes glisten with tears. "I would be very happy if I could be your wife."

Two weeks earlier, when Marcellus had delivered Antony's message to Queen Cleopatra, she had received him graciously. Then this morning, she had summoned him, asking his opinion on a scroll she was sending to Antony.

He had been waiting impatiently for word to reach him of Lord Ramtat's whereabouts. Only today a messenger had arrived with word that Lord Ramtat had returned to his villa in Alexandria.

Marcellus dismounted and moved to the door. It was whisked open, and a servant bowed to the general. When he inquired, he learned Adhaniá was not at home, so he asked to see Lord Ramtat. He was led to a library where many scrolls were stacked neatly on shelves. Several couches were placed about the chamber, and it was apparent the family spent much time there reading.

Ramtat greeted him with a smile and welcomed him warmly. After both men were seated and a servant had poured wine, Marcellus glanced at his host.

Marcellus had only seen Ramtat in his Bedouin robe, and his host appeared quite different wearing a blue tunic and a golden bracelet around his forearm. Marcellus felt gut-wrenching fear that this lordly man would never allow his sister to marry outside her people. After he had explained about Caesar's death, he saw Lord Ramtat was sorely affected.

"Caesar was like a father to me. We have been in mourning since receiving word of his assassination."

At last, Marcellus placed his cup of wine on a low table, ready to speak of the matter that had brought him to the villa. "Has Lady Adhaniá spoken to you about what happened to her in Rome?"

Ramtat frowned. "My sister has spoken little of her time

there, leaving me to think she is keeping something from me. Queen Cleopatra told me about placing her in your custody, and we had heated words over that incident. I tell you this: I am furious about my sister being put in danger."

Marcellus's jaw hardened. "It seems to me you have no one to blame but yourself. You sent her to Rome, placing her under the care of your queen. I can assure you, if I had a sister, she would never be put in such a situation."

Ramtat rose slowly, his eyes blazing. "Roman, you dare criticize my methods concerning my own sister!"

Marcellus rose so that they were standing eye-to-eye. "I do dare because I was there, and I know what she is keeping from you."

"What do you mean?" Ramtat demanded.

"I have come to ask permission to make your sister my wife."

"You dare much to make such a request of me! My sister will never marry a Roman. I am suspicious of your motives, and I will tell you why: Do you think me ignorant of the laws of Rome? I am well aware that it is forbidden for you to marry anyone who is not a citizen of Rome. Do you seek to dishonor her?"

Danaë heard raised voices and quickly came to investigate. The two men were glaring at each other, looking as if they were ready to fight. She had heard enough to know what the trouble was about, so she moved determinedly to her husband's side, placing herself between them.

"What is this about?" she demanded.

"Lady Danaë, forgive me," Marcellus said, bowing to her. "I have a way of being blunt, and I may have misspoken. If that is the case, I ask pardon from both of you."

"You misspoke, right enough." Ramtat glanced at his wife. "This Roman wants to marry my sister."

"I know," she said calmly.

"You know?"

"I heard both of you. Anyone within these walls would have heard you. Can we not discuss this calmly?"

"There is nothing to discuss," Ramtat stated. "I have spoken, and I will not relent."

"Can we all be seated?" she asked. "The children have been overactive today, and I am a bit weary." She wasn't, but she had to defuse the situation.

Both men immediately became attentive to her feelings and dropped down on two different couches while she once more placed herself between them. "Now let us talk calmly." She turned to Marcellus, speaking softly. "It is good to see you again. I understand you are now not only a general but the Master Architect of Rome as well."

"I had not heard that," her husband said. "How did you know?"

"My sister."

"Ah, Cleopatra."

"My husband and I both offer you our congratulations."

"Of course," Ramtat agreed sourly.

"To continue," Danaë said, slowly turning the conversation, "I understand you came to Alexandria as the voice of Marc Antony."

"In part," Marcellus said. "I also came to ask Lord Ramtat if I can take Adhaniá as my wife."

Ramtat's jaw tightened, and he asked churlishly, "What would make you think I would agree to such a match?"

Marcellus held Danaë's gaze because he was discovering she was his only hope of winning her husband to his side. "I have loved Adhaniá almost from our first meeting. I admire her bravery, her loyalty. There are so many reasons I love her, I cannot voice them all. But I can tell you, I have not known a happy moment since she left Rome."

Marcellus turned his attention to Ramtat. "If Adhaniá was my wife, I would strive to make her happy and to keep her safe."

Ramtat looked somewhat mollified. "Have you spoken to my sister of this matter?"

"I had no right to speak to her until Antony gave me permission to marry her. Be assured the marriage would be recognized as legal in Rome. Had Antony not given me permission, I would have left Rome forever to be with Adhaniá here in Egypt."

"You think to take my sister to Rome?"

"I have purchased a villa outside Alexandria. If Adhaniá becomes my wife, we will spend time in both cities. I know how much she cherishes Egypt, and her family. I would not want to take her away from those she loves."

Danaë moved closer to Ramtat and placed her hand on his. "Remember how painful it was when we loved each other so desperately and thought we could never be together?"

"I remember. That is why I resent any night I must spend away from you."

"Perhaps General Valerius feels the same way about Adhaniá. Have you not noticed how unhappy she is since she returned home—she smiles, but she does not laugh as she once did. Could it be that she loves this man and fears they can never be together?"

Ramtat frowned, wondering if his wife could be right. "I will not have my sister marry anyone unless he is her choice."

"I know she loves me—I can't be wrong about that," Marcellus said with assurance.

Ramtat stared at Marcellus long and hard. If he weren't a Roman, he'd be exactly the husband Ramtat would have chosen for his sister. Ramtat glanced at his wife, and he could tell by her expression that she thought he should give his consent for the two of them to marry.

Ramtat arched his eyebrow at his wife and then nodded, relenting. "This Roman does not know you as well as I do or he would realize, as I do, how you manipulated the situation."

Marcellus had most certainly noticed how cleverly Lady Danaë had led them both. "Your wife would make a fearsome general."

Ramtat laughed down at Danaë. "You have no idea."

Marcellus rose. "Do I have your permission to speak to Adhaniá?" He didn't know he was holding his breath until Ramtat spoke.

"My sister is not at home at the moment. You are welcome to wait until she returns."

As Adhaniá and Thalia returned home, the arms of the servant who walked behind them were loaded with purchases.

"Is it really true, Adhaniá? Is your mother truly adopting me? Am I going to be your sister and her daughter?"

"I can assure you it is true. My mother adores you, as do we all."

Thalia could hardly contain her joy. "The most fortunate day of my life was when I filched that loaf of bread. I love your mother and your whole family."

"Then welcome to the family, Thalia. I have always wanted a little sister."

Suddenly Thalia looked frightened. "There is something I have never told you. As long as I can remember, men have been hunting me. I don't know who they are or where they come from because I have always been able to elude them. But they frighten me. If they find out I am in Egypt, they may come for me here."

Adhaniá looked troubled. "Could it have something to do with your past?"

The child shrugged. "I know not. I have a vague memory of living with an old woman somewhere—it was not Rome. I could tell she was keeping me hidden, but I never knew why. When she died, I went to Rome so I could survive. I know no more than that."

"Then put the past behind you. Your future begins here in Egypt."

The two of them entered the library, where Danaë and Ramtat were seated on the couch in deep conversation. They pulled apart, and Ramtat stared at Adhaniá. Danaë was right: there were shadows beneath his sister's eyes, and although she smiled in greeting, there was no sparkle in her expression.

"You have a guest," Ramtat said, watching his sister closely. "From Rome." He watched her face go from disbelief to hope, then devastation. "He's waiting for you in the garden."

Her hand went to her heart, and she took a quick step, then paused. "Tell me quickly. Is it bad tidings—Marcellus has not been . . . he is not . . . ?"

Ramtat glanced at his wife, and they both knew she loved the Roman. "Why do you not ask him—your guest is General Valerius himself."

Happiness burst through Adhaniá, and she ran toward the garden.

"I believe that was proof even you can believe, my husband," Danaë said, smiling.

"Oh," Thalia said, sitting down and looking from Ramtat to his wife. "You speak of Marcellus and Adhaniá. If you had asked me, I would have told you they love each other."

Ramtat took the little sprite's hand and frowned. "Tell me, my new little sister, what else do you know?"

CHAPTER THIRTY-FOUR ✦

Adhaniá spotted Marcellus standing near the pond. He must have heard her because he turned, watching her approach with an unreadable expression on his face.

He looked splendid wearing a silver breastplate molded to the lines of his muscled chest. She knew what it felt like to lay her head on that chest, and it made her ache to remember how close they had been for one night. When he moved, the layer of silver-tipped leather strips caught the setting sun.

He held out his hand, and she slipped hers into it. "Forgive the formal way I am dressed—I had an audience with Queen Cleopatra."

Was that all he had to say to her, after being parted for so long? Her hand trembled in the warmth of his, and she felt a blush climb up her face. "I had no notion you were in Alexandria. How long have you been here?"

He still held her hand. "Two weeks."

She pulled her hand away from his in aching disappointment. "As long as that?" It hurt that he had not come to see her before now.

"I had pressing matters that occupied my time."

"Oh?"

"I was buying property."

She searched his eyes. "Here in Alexandria?"

"Just outside the city. I think you will like the villa."

He sat down on the marble bench and then stood, rubbing his hands together nervously, not understanding why there was such awkwardness between them. "Your brother has given me permission to ask you to be my wife."

She had not expected this, and she did not know how to react. If he loved her, he would have rushed to her side the moment he arrived in Alexandria. "I must refuse you."

He was stunned. "May I ask why?"

She shrugged, thinking she knew the reason he was proposing to her.

Obligation.

"I'm sure your mother told you I stayed the night with you to save your life, and now you feel you have to marry me."

He shook his head at her lack of understanding "If I were merely grateful that you saved my life, I would have sent you a gift." He stepped closer. "My feelings for you have been so marked, I cannot think you haven't noticed."

She nodded. "I remember well the night we were together, and I know you desired me when I danced for you." She shrugged. "So did the other Romans when I danced for them. As well you know, it is a Badari dancer's custom to entice the men she entertains."

He smiled. "You did more than entice me that night."

"I remember that as well. It is not a Badari custom for a dancer to lie with the man she dances for."

"Yet you did."

"Aye, I did."

"Since we are speaking of Badari customs, you are indebted to me," he said with a smile. "Surely you recall what you told me that night in my chamber."

"I said many things that night—some were the truth, others were not."

He touched her cheek with tenderness. "Did you or did you not tell me that since you saved my life you were responsible for me?"

"I merely explained to you an old Badari custom—one that is rarely honored these days."

He pulled her toward him, and she stiffened. "I am holding you to that custom. Will you not be responsible for my care and happiness for the rest of our lives?"

"Do you say this to me out of obligation?"

"Adhaniá, I say this because I need you," he murmured. "Do you not recognize a man who is desperately in love?"

"Why did you not come to see me sooner?"

He took her hand and pulled her to him, clasping her to his heart. "Shh," he whispered thickly. "If you only knew how difficult it was to stay away from you, you would not rebuke me. I wanted every detail to be in place before I came to you."

She did not understand. "What details?"

"I did not want to come to you until I had a home for us here in Alexandria. I wanted everything perfect for you when we start our life together."

Her doubts faded when she looked into his eyes and saw a wellspring of tenderness there. "You love me?"

His voice was deep and husky when he said, "My beloved, my heart, you have walked with me in my dreams every night since we parted. I have come to you because I could not envision a life without you. Don't send me away and condemn me to a life of loneliness." He tilted her face up to his, and doubt crept into his tone. "Unless you do not feel the same way about me."

She was quiet for a moment, trying to grapple with the happiness that lit her heart like sunlight reflecting on water. "I have loved you almost from the moment I saw you," she admitted, as if the words were forced through her lips. "I want to be with you for the rest of my life." She touched his face, his hair, took his hand. "It was difficult to leave Rome, believing I would never see you again."

He touched her face and laid his cheek against hers. "When I returned home and found you gone, there was no light in my world, no hope for the future." He touched his lips to hers briefly. "Will you be my wife?"

She pulled back as happy laughter spilled from her lips. "I will honor my obligation and be responsible for you and your happiness."

He clasped her to him. "Soon, I pray it will be soon." His lips touched her ear, and he whispered, "I want you in my bed so we can recapture the night you gave yourself to me."

She felt her knees go weak and pressed her body against his. "I will speak to my brother and tell him we want to be married right away."

Adhaniá could not believe her happiness. She held his face between her hands and smiled mischievously. "I will make certain he understands that we do not want to wait until he can gather the whole Badari tribe."

CHAPTER
THIRTY-FIVE ✗

A pronouncement came from Queen Cleopatra, honoring both Marcellus and Adhaniá for their bravery and devotion. She blessed their upcoming marriage, and her wedding gift to them was twelve Badarian horses.

The wedding took place two months after Marcellus proposed, and in another month they would make the voyage to Rome. They planned to include Lady Sarania in their life in that city.

Adhaniá loved the sprawling villa Marcellus had given her as a wedding present. Her mother had helped her staff the villa with servants both Egyptian and Roman. Heikki and Layla had been given permission to marry, but Layla would remain Adhaniá's servant and Heikki would be her personal guard.

The party Ramtat had given the newlyweds went on for hours. Marcellus was embraced by his new family. He liked Adhaniá's mother upon first meeting her. He could see she had knitted her family together with love and devotion to one another.

At last Ramtat finally found his sister alone and took her

aside. "I have something for you that I had meant to give to you sooner, but it never seemed to be the right time."

She looked puzzled as he handed her a long ebony box. Across the top, her name was written in gold.

"What can it be?"

He smiled. "You must open it to find out."

She nodded and slid the lid up, gasping at what she saw inside. Tears filled her eyes, and she leaned her head against Ramtat's shoulder. "A golden arrow."

He clasped her to him. "Your name has been entered on the roll of worthy warriors."

"Thank you, dearest brother," she said, smiling through her tears and clasping her precious prize to her.

"Go . . . find your husband," he said in a thick voice. "I give you into his keeping."

Later Danaë came to the newly married couple and whispered that their transportation was waiting to take them to their new home.

The bedchamber was magnificently furnished, the bed covered with a blue silken coverlet. She smiled when she saw the blue lotus blossoms that had been painted on the ceiling.

Adhaniá heard Marcellus's footsteps approaching the door, and her heart beat faster. Amazed that she felt no modesty now that she was Marcellus's wife, she wore only a sheer blue undergown that tied at the neck.

Marcellus paused in the doorway, his gaze sweeping slowly down her body. The light from the dying sun made her gown all the more transparent, while a warm breeze from the open window rippled the gauzy fabric, exposing her naked body underneath. "If I live to be an old man and lose the sight of my eyes, I will always remember the way you look at this moment."

"Do I please you?"

He smiled at the feminine question that was so unlike Adhaniá. Then he sobered. "My dearest wife, you please me greatly." He wore only a white tunic, and he stopped to untie his sandals before moving to her.

Taking her hand, he pulled her forward, groaning as his mouth touched hers. Hungry lips found hers, and starving bodies strained against each other, unable to get close enough to satisfy either of them.

He pulled back, tracing his finger across her slender neck. "You belong to me, Adhaniá."

"I do," she agreed, watching him slip out of his tunic and stand before her wearing only his loincloth.

Her gaze moved across his muscled shoulders to his flat stomach. "I cannot imagine anything more pleasing to my eyes," she said, boldly stepping toward him.

Marcellus slowly untied her gown and pushed it off her shoulders. "I am an architect, but I could never have created anything as perfect as you," he said, lifting her in his arms.

Impatiently, he carried her to the bed and hovered above her, staring into her golden eyes. "My dearest wife, you heal my heart and make me whole again. You legally accepted me as a husband, now will you receive me as a man?"

She smiled, licked her lips and said, "How can I refuse such an offer?"

He threw back his head and laughed. "You are going to disrupt my world. I know your propensity for finding trouble."

She slid her body against his and whispered against his chest, "But you will be there to rescue me, brandishing your sword and hacking away at my enemies, like you did that day on the road to Rome."

Marcellus removed his loincloth and eased himself between her legs. "But one thing I want you to understand," he said thickly, nibbling on her lips. "You are never to dance for anyone but me."

Her eyes closed as he slid inside her, and she thought she was going to die of need. "I dance only for my husband," she said, arching her spine and taking him inside her.

Marcellus's mouth plundered Adhaniá's, stirring her blood. Glancing past her veil of dark lashes, he saw a passion reflected there that matched his own. Hotly, sensuously, he made love to her. "Adhaniá," he whispered, driving deeply into her warmth, "my heart is yours."

She held him to her as he took her body. "And you have mine," she answered with a groan.

When their bodies had been sated, her head lay against the crook of his arm. "I felt something for you that night in the Bedouin encampment," she admitted.

"As soon as that? When I saw you dance, I knew something inside me had changed, but I didn't know what it was until later."

His hand moved across her breasts, and he bent to touch his mouth to each nipple, feeling them swell. His hand moved over her stomach. "I want my baby to be nurtured here." She shivered when his lips touched her stomach.

"I cannot wait until you plant your seed in me so I can give birth to little Romans."

He cocked his head and gave her a bemused glance. "Shall we try again on the chance I did not impregnate you the first time?"

Adhaniá held her Roman to her, knowing she had found her place in life—her destiny and her happiness lay with her husband.

Their journey together had been a perilous one. But somehow, even amid the blood of revolt and in a time of chaos, hope had blossomed and triumphed—and two people from very different cultures had been united in love.

DIANA GROE
SILK DREAMS

Forced into a harem in Constantinople's strange land of flashing swords and swirling silks, spicy aromas and hot breezes that feel like a lover's breath, Valdis is utterly lost. Her family cast her away for seeing portents of the future, and now her visions are turning even more ominous: they foretell the death of the one man who could help her escape, an exiled Viking who braves the wrath of a kingdom to awaken her passion one sinful pleasure at a time. To save him, Valdis must play a high-stakes game of power and seduction that will either get her killed or finally allow her and her love to live their *Silk Dreams*.

ISBN 10: 0-8439-5869-3
ISBN 13: 978-0-8439-5869-0 $6.99 US/$8.99 CAN

To order a book or to request a catalog call:
1-800-481-9191
This book is also available at your local bookstore, or you can check out our Web site **www.dorchesterpub.com** where you can look up your favorite authors, read excerpts, or glance at our discussion forum to see what people have to say about your favorite books.

CONNIE MASON

The Black Widow

That was what the desperate prisoners incarcerated in Devil's Chateau called her. Whatever she did with them, one thing was certain: Her unfortunate victims were never seen again. But when she whisked Reed Harwood out of the cell where he'd been left to die for spying against the French, he discovered the lady was not all she seemed.

Fleur Fontaine was the most exquisitely sensual woman he'd ever met, yet there was an innocence about her that belied her sordid reputation. Only a dead man would fail to respond. Reed was not dead yet, but was he willing to pay…

The Price of Pleasure

ISBN 10: 0-8439-5745-X
ISBN 13: 978-0-8439-5745-7

JOYCE HENDERSON

Kalen Barrett could birth foals, heal wounded horses, and do the work of two ranch hands, so she was hired on the spot to work at the Savage ranch. But the instant attraction she felt to sinfully handsome Taylor Savage terrified her. Each time she glimpsed the promise of passionate fulfillment in Taylor's heated eyes, she came a little closer to losing control—but he always held back the words she longed to hear. If he would only give her his heart, she would follow him body and soul...

TO THE EDGE OF THE STARS

ISBN 10: 0-8439-5996-7
ISBN 13: 978-0-8439-5996-3

DAWN MACTAVISH

Lark at first hoped it was a simple nightmare: If she closed
her eyes, she would be back in the mahogany bed of her
spacious boudoir at Eddington Hall, and all would be well.
Her father, the earl of Roxburgh, would not be dead by his
own hand, and she would not be in Marshalsea Debtor's
Prison.

Such was not to be. Ere the Marshalsea could do its worst,
the earl of Grayshire intervened. But while his touch was
electric and his gaze piercing, for what purpose had he
bought her freedom? No, this was not a dream. As Lark
would soon learn, her dreams had never ended so well.

The Privateer

AVAILABLE JANUARY 2008!

ISBN 13: 978-0-8439-5981-9

What happens when a beautiful lady gambler faces off against a professional card shark with more aces up his sleeve than the Missouri River has snags? A steamboat trades hands, the loser forfeits his clothes, and all hell breaks loose on the levee. But events only get wilder as the two rivals, now reluctant partners, travel upriver. Delilah Raymond soon learns that Clint Daniels is more than he appears. As the polished con man reverts to an earlier identity—Lightning Hand, the lethal Sioux warrior—the ghosts of his past threaten to tear apart their tempestuous union. Will the River Nymph take him too far for redemption, or could Delilah be his ace in the hole?

AVAILABLE FEBRUARY 2008!

ISBN 13: 978-0-8439-6011-2

To order a book or to request a catalog call:
1-800-481-9191
This book is also available at your local bookstore, or you can check out our Web site **www.dorchesterpub.com** where you can look up your favorite authors, read excerpts, or glance at our discussion forum to see what people have to say about your favorite books.